Making CHANGES

USA TODAY BESTSELLING AUTHOR

LILA ROSE

To those who have doubted and thought less of themselves.
Be strong, be sure, and listen to your heart.
You are amazing!

I hope you find your happily ever after. Xx

Chapter ONE

WHILE I SAT in the restaurant waiting for my husband, I couldn't help but glance around at the couples eating together and wonder if they were truly happy. From the way they shared smiles and sweet looks, they certainly seemed content. My shoulders slumped. I wanted to projectile vomit all over them because it had me pondering, yet again, on where had I gone wrong? How had I become the doormat in my relationship?

I had instantly fallen for Robert in my final year at college. I had been in the library sitting in the corner at a desk on my own. A group of idiots across from me were calling me fat and ugly, among other things.

I'd ignored it to start off with, thinking they were only trying to be cool with each other. But after some time, I'd had enough.

Lifting my gaze, I'd glared across at them and asked, "Do you want to suck my little toe?"

Silence followed. One scoffed and said, "Why in the fuck would we want to?"

Shrugging, I placed my pen down and said, "Well, I just thought unless you want to suck each other off, which would be about the size of my little toe, it's the only action you guys will get from the opposite sex because you're nothing but fucking pricks."

"You need to—" The guy didn't get to finish because Robert showed up out of nowhere and took them down another notch or two. Once they'd left, he'd sat with me and asked if I was okay. My heart melted right there and then.

Back then, I was accustomed to being invisible, the girl who wore thick glasses, loose clothing, no makeup, and I didn't care about any of it. If people tried to crap in my cheerios, I told them where to go.

Six years later, I figured out somewhere along the way, I had lost myself, and it pissed me off.

Over time, he'd shaped me into a different woman. One who wore stupid frilly dresses like his grandma used to wear—which got me thinking he may have had a thing for geriatrics—to please him, who did as she was told—eye roll—and who thought herself useless. It was hard not to believe those things after hearing them every day.

Was I strong enough to change?

To be who I wanted to be?

I wasn't sure.

Though as time went on, I was closer and closer to breaking free. To standing on my own two feet and learning once again to appreciate the person I used to be before Robert.

However, the move to do so, to leave him, was terrifying.

Why was love, lust, or even *like* such a miserable aspect of life? It may not be the case for most people, yet for me it was. I should have known my love life was going to suck donkey's balls right from the start.

In my teens I had crushes, but those crushes tore my heart out of my chest, spat on it, and threw it to the ground. Not that I cared. They probably couldn't handle all my sass. Though their brush-offs could have been why I fell for Robert immediately and did as he advised so willingly. Then again, he was a different person to start with. Caring and sweet, he'd taken me places. Wined and dined, only he never sixty-nined me. Which was a disappointment as I'd heard how amazing it was.

I jumped when the chair beside me was pulled out. Robert smiled down at me before he sat, but his eyes were hard and filled with contempt. "Randal will be here soon." His new business associate, or at least that was what Robert hoped. My husband had told me to meet him at the restaurant for a Friday lunch meeting because he wanted to show Randal he was a family man. Apparently that meant he was a man who could be trusted with money and was a man to trust with any legal affairs Randal may ever have. "I asked you to dress nicely, Makenzie." He glared at my dark blue summer dress. I cut off my snort. I thought I had dressed nicely. Once he had even said he liked it. As I went to comment, the dick continued, "You do know people have designed undergarments that help suck some of the fat in? Maybe you should invest in a few."

A blush heated my cheeks. I flicked my eyes down to my hands in my lap and clenched my jaw. It was something I seemed to be doing a lot lately, which annoyed me, made me feel weaker when I never used to be. What I would have preferred to do was throw my water in his face, kick him in the shin, and stab him in the eye with my fork, then sit back to watch him bleed, before storming from the place.

Still, I was grateful I had my imagination; it was only my backbone I had lost.

As my mind caused him harm, the weak me sat there and said nothing. So what if I had put on a few pounds? Did he have to be an ass and point it out? And hell, I was happy with the way I looked.

"Too late to do something about it now. Suck it in," he hissed and then turned in his seat and boomed, "Randal, good to see you."

"Fuckhead." I froze. The word was coughed out through a manly voice behind me, startling me. I itched to turn around, to see where and who it came from, but didn't, and if Robert had heard it, he gave no indication. Instead, he turned back to face me with a bright, fake smile on his face.

"Randal Muller, this is my wife, Makenzie." Robert gestured with his hand in my direction. Looking up, my eyes landed on a god. He was absolutely breathtaking. With his wide frame, I could have sworn he once would have been on the football team back in the day. He was tall, slim, but firm. His eyes were light, like the ocean on a clear, calm day. He ran a hand through his blond hair before smiling down at me.

"Great to meet you, Makenzie. Robert has told me many wonderful things about you."

I just bet he has. I winced and knew he had caught it, if his raised brows were anything to go on. I smiled politely, fiddled with my fork, and said, "Robert certainly has a way with words." *That could cut me to the bone.*

Robert's hand slid across the table and grabbed mine. Anyone would think it was an affectionate touch. It wasn't. His hold tightened on mine. I bit my bottom lip and smiled so I didn't cringe from the pain.

Robert wasn't one to hurt a person. He hated pain in fact, and later he would be very apologetic, saying it was my fault and in the end, he would be so convincing I would somehow believe him. Never once had he beaten me, hit me, or hurt me more than a hard squeeze or pinch.

Instead, he used words to cut me down.

Robert chuckled and said, "Only with you, sweetheart."

Turning my gaze to him, I made sure my eyes held adoration as I replied, "Of course, pumpkin." I had a translation for each pet name I'd used for Robert. Pumpkin was prick.

As soon as Randal sat down, Robert got down to business. At least he tried. Randal cleared his throat, picked up his menu, and suggested, "I'm sure Makenzie doesn't want to hear all about work. Why don't we order?"

Robert laughed. "Of course." My husband turned to me. "Sweetheart, do you want your usual, a salad?"

I pulled my hands from the table and clenched them so tightly my fingernails bit into my palms. What I wanted was a nice, big, juicy steak. "Sounds great." I smiled, refraining from throat punching him.

It seemed the silent me was more violent than what I actually was.

"Tell me, Makenzie, do you work?" Randal asked.

Sitting straighter, I replied, "I don't at the moment, but I would love to get back out into the workforce. I have a degree in business—"

Robert chuckled and ran his hand down my arm. "Sweetheart, don't be silly, you don't need to work."

"Oh, I know I don't need to, but—"

"Honey, that's enough. We'll talk about it later. Randal doesn't want to hear about it."

He asked, you ass.

"Of course." Clearing my throat, I moved my gaze back to Randal and asked. "Do you like to play golf, Mr. Muller?" It was a question Robert had said I could ask. Stick to topics Robert was passionate about so he could talk about himself.

Honestly, he may as well have gotten on his knees under the table and given Randal a blow job.

"Randal, please, and I do actually. Do you?"

"No, I—"

"Makenzie isn't really into sports"—he leaned into Randal—"if you couldn't tell." After a quick laugh, he then talked about golf. My gaze darted between the two men, fascinated by their interaction. Robert was oblivious to Randal's quick sneer and his bored expression. My stomach dipped in nervous excitement. It wasn't just me who was thinking my husband was a dick.

Robert was always, *always* like that. Yes, a dick, but oblivious to those around him, pretty idiotic when trying to woo a client. He was always Robert this, Robert that. Robert, Robert, Robert.

God, why couldn't I find it in myself to stand up and stalk from the restaurant?

My head dipped down, no longer feeling the thrill of not being the only one to recognize my husband for what he truly was. My chin almost touched my chest as my eyes stared at my lap. And even though my body had stilled, my mind kept going, kept flashing past comments made by Robert.

You're so pathetic, Makenzie.

You're too fat.

I can't breathe when you're on top of me during sex. You need to lose weight.

You went out like that? Jesus, I hope no one saw you, Makenzie.

Why can't you be more like Danny's wife? She's good at everything.

I have to picture someone else while I'm having sex with you. How do you think that makes me feel?

You always look like a slob these days.

I saw Heather today. She's so smart, got her head screwed on that one, and she looked hot.

We have nothing in common.

You don't want to have sex with me. It's like I'm living with a roommate instead of a wife.

Sure we have sex, but we need to be friends also and do things with each other. Only it was things he wanted to do, never what I wanted.

Honestly, no matter what I did, how I changed, I was never going to be the one who would satisfy Robert in any way.

In his eyes, I was never going to be good enough. I *was* useless, ugly, fat, stupid, and unworthy.

God, I was sick of feeling that way. I needed to get out before his words seeped into my blood, like they had already in my mind. I knew once they caught the hint that there was a gaping passage straight to my heart and body via my blood, I knew it would be over.

I'd lose myself completely.

"Makenzie?" Robert's irritated voice broke through. "What are you doing?"

Blinking, I realized I was standing. I glanced at Randal and then the waiter. When had he arrived?

I had an epiphany, damn it, and I was going to roll with it. Even if my body felt like revolting as it trembled, and my mind screamed at me to sit back down because I wouldn't find anyone better.

Licking my suddenly dry lips, I said, "Sorry, but I'm not feeling well."

"Oh," Robert cried. He stood next to me and took my hand. When I pulled free, he raised his brows in question. Though, he went on, "Sweetheart, why didn't you say something? Maybe you should head home?"

Studying him, I noticed his clenched jaw and narrowed eyes. He thought I was being a fool for interrupting his talk about himself. A snort left me. I covered my mouth and nose with my hand.

Six years.

Four years of marriage.

Two *somewhat* happy years and then two years of hell.

I had been so stupid. So, *so* stupid. Robert had hated my job, my dad, my sister, my friends, and even my car. Now I had none of them. Silly me had given it all up because a handsome man had paid attention to the geek in college. Regret threatened to overwhelm me and drag me to my knees. I regretted everything I ever did for him.

But no more.

"Yes, I think you may be right." *While I'm there, I'll be packing and leaving, starting fresh.* The thought of it actually brought a smile to my face. My hands still shook, but something inside of me bloomed. Looking to Randal, I offered, "It was a pleasure meeting you, Randal. Sorry to have to leave." *And don't let Robert bite down on your nob too much.*

Randal stood from the table and held out his hand. I quickly shook it. He smiled. "The pleasure was all mine. Hopefully we'll see each other again."

"Yes." I nodded with a small smile. Then I made a slurping sound because my mind was still back on Robert sucking him off. The poor guy. I wanted to reach over and pat Randal on the back, wishing him luck. Still, I refrained and thought I should pat myself on the back because I did tend to do and say silly crap all the time. Robert hated it. I'd learned to accept my uniqueness.

Robert's jaw clenched. "I'll see you at home, sweetheart."

No, actually you won't. I wanted to throw my head back and cackle like a madwoman. Robert leaned in as if he were going to kiss my cheek, until he pulled back and chuckled. "I better not. Can't afford to get sick."

Picking up my purse, I quickly excused myself. As I took the steps away from Robert, my hands shook even more. Was I really going to do it? Yes, I had to. I was tired of being walked over, tired of being the one in the wrong, because apparently, it always turned out to be my fault in the end.

Just like my leaving.

I knew Robert would lay on the guilt trip, pleading for me to understand what we had was perfect and not to leave. He'd insist I would just have to change a few things and everything would be back to the way things were when we had first got together.

Yet the things he would ask to change would be more of myself, and I wasn't willing to let go of myself anymore.

Unless… maybe it was me? All in my head?

Shit. No, it wasn't.

Shaking my head as I stepped out front into a warm afternoon, I had to believe I was making the right choice. It wasn't me imagining things.

Placing my bag strap over my shoulder, I searched through it while the valet waited for my ticket.

"Excuse me?"

As soon as my fingers landed on it, I lifted my head and held it out to the valet, only he wasn't looking at me, but over my shoulder. Following his gaze, I jumped when I found a handsome man standing there.

"Sorry?" I asked, looking left and then right, just to check he was, in fact, talking to me. Had I done something on my way out? I clenched my free hand to make sure I wasn't holding anything, in case I had stolen a fork in my haste. I wasn't. The ticket slipped from my fingers. I glanced back at the valet to see him give me a nod, and then he left me alone with the stranger.

"Hi," the smooth voice said behind me, and again my body jolted when I felt his hand at my elbow. When I turned, I stepped back out of his reach. His hands came up and a soft smile tipped his lips up a little. "Sorry, didn't mean to scare you."

Robert didn't like me talking to men. I flicked my eyes over his shoulder and then back.

Huh, screw Robert, he wasn't there.

"It's okay. I'm, ah, I'm gay," he blurted, and I watched his cheeks heat before his palm thumped his forehead.

A laugh escaped me from his outburst. My palm came up to cover my mouth. I found myself thinking how it was a pity the man before me liked penis.

He removed his hand and smiled down at me. God, he was tall. My head came up to his chest. He wore a designer suit and, as I glanced down, he had on shiny shoes. I supposed most gay men dressed really well, or was that something someone made up? I wasn't sure, but the man before me certainly seemed to take pride in his looks. Even his dark brown hair was gelled to perfection.

"Did I do something?" I asked.

"No. Not at all. In fact, I couldn't help but overhear—"

My eyes widened, and I interrupted, "Were you the one to call my husband a fuckhead?"

His brows dipped, guilt flashing across his features, and then he ran a hand over the back of his neck. "He was being a fuckhead at the time. But that's not why I stopped you. I heard you may be looking for work."

My head jerked back in shock. "And you followed me to offer me a job?" I guessed.

"Well, yes. Sort of. Actually, it's my brother who's looking for an assistant."

Leaning in, I whispered, "Why would you ask me?"

Did he pity me?

"The truth, my brother goes through a lot of assistants and when I heard you had a business degree, I thought you may have more brains than the rest and end up lasting longer."

Straightening, I studied him. He looked as if he were telling the truth, his expression serious, his posture tall. No deceiving hunched shoulders in sight. Still, I couldn't quite believe he would come after me for an assistant job; admittedly, I wasn't really good at reading people.

"I'm not sure," I said, and shifted back a step when I saw my Corvette coming around the corner.

"Wait. Just take my card. Think about it, and if you change your mind, call me." He pulled a card out of his jacket pocket and thrust it out toward me.

Looking from the card to him and back again, I slowly reached up and took it, placing it in my bag.

"Thank you." I shrugged, because maybe thanking him wasn't the right thing to say. "Um, I better get going."

"Right." He smiled. "You are sick after all."

A laugh escaped me. "Yes, I am," I said before getting into my car and driving off, without another look at…. God, I didn't even ask his name.

Shaking my head, I put the chance meeting with the handsome gay guy out of my mind; I had other pressing matters to attend.

The restaurant wasn't far from where we lived. So soon enough, I was driving into our long driveway and up to the two-story, four-bedroom brick home. When I parked, I didn't move. My belly churned. Maybe I was coming down with something, and what I was about to do was actually an act of feeling ill.

Stop it, Makenzie.

It was time to grow some lady balls, big ones that dangled down to my knees.

Grabbing my bag, I flung the door open and climbed out of the car. My heart raced the closer I got to the front door of our house.

A house I had lived in with my husband for four years.

Yet, I found myself thinking there wasn't really anything in the house I would miss. Shouldn't I be crying with what I was about to do? Shouldn't I be devastated at the thought of my marriage ending?

Clarity was a funny, fickle bitch.

My phone buzzed as I walked into our room, my eyes landing on the bed. No good memories were held in that bed. Only hurtful words.

My shoulders slumped. I took my phone from my bag and looked at it. A smile pulled my lips up when I saw a message from my father.

I should have listened to my dad from the start. He always said that the most important thing in life was to be honest, and he'd stood by it when he'd told me Robert was a dick and he wished I wouldn't marry him.

Even after I'd cut my dad and my sister from my life and moved away from my family home, I still received a monthly text from my dad.

It was funny how it had come that day of all days.

Unlocking my phone, I pressed on messenger to open it. It always read the same: **What 'bout now?** He was asking if I had finally come to my senses and left Robert. In the past, I had deleted it out of respect for Robert. He was too foolish to know my father loathed him.

That day, I kept it and with a laugh, I replied, **Yes.**

I squeaked when my phone rang in my hand. *Dad*. Smiling, I answered, "Hi, Dad." Tears suddenly filled my eyes and my bottom lip quivered, so I bit down on it. It had been years since I had spoken to my father. *Years*. Hurt bombarded my senses from the pain I'd put all of us through.

"Puddin', tell me I didn't see things? Tell me I'm not conjuring up my own answer?"

I snorted and then hiccupped a sob back. He'd always called me his puddin' and my sister Taylor, who was Lori to me, was his jellybean.

I missed him. I missed my sister. Before Robert, they were my world. I'd let them go, let them down.

"I-I'm sorry," I whimpered.

"No. Don't you say you're sorry."

"I *am* sorry. I should have listened to you."

"Did that little dick hurt you?" he clipped roughly.

"No, Dad." I smiled.

"So? You didn't answer my question. Was I seeing things, Puddin'?"

"No." I smiled.

"Jesus Christ." He sighed. "You need help? I'll get in the car right now and come get you. Jellybean would love to see you. I'll even take her out of class to come with me."

Laughing, I said, "No, Dad. Really, I need to do this on my own. But soon, I would love to see you both." Tears welled. "Really soon."

My dad's voice softened. "Nothing will keep us away. Where are you?"

"At the house. I'm about to pack and go to a hotel."

"You good for money?"

My bottom lip trembled. After what I put him through, he was still willing to help me out. "Yes, for now… and, I may have a job soon."

"Good." I could hear the smile in his voice. He was happy, and I was finally the cause of it. "My puddin's getting back on her own feet, and soon she'll be giving me hell and winning at cards once again."

"You bet your sweet bippy on it." I laughed. "Love you, Dad."

Silence on the other end, and then my breath caught with his next words.

"Always love you, Makenzie. No matter where you are, how long it's been, who you're with, you'll always have my love." His own voice was thick with emotion.

I sniffed and wiped my eyes. "Give Lori my love."

"Will do and we'll see you soon."

"Yes. Bye, Dad."

"Bye for now, but not forever."

Quickly, I hung up as another hiccup sob tore out of me. He'd always said that at the end of every phone call or even when I was living at home and was leaving the house.

I had missed it.

Taking a deep breath, I went to the closet and grabbed my suitcase.

It was time to start my life, and no matter what, I would never be beaten down again.

I was strong, I was brave, and I *was* doing the right thing

Chapter TWO

Pacing beside the bed in the hotel room that evening, I glanced down at the card laying on the bedspread for the millionth time. On the card was his name and number, and that was all. It didn't give me any information about what his job was or if he even worked for his brother as well.

Dylan Jackson.

It was a nice name.

Growling in frustration, I picked up my cell for the millionth time and pressed in his digits. I knew I had to call Dylan before I heard from Robert, because then at least, I could tell Robert I had a job lined up. I could tell him exactly what the situation was. Even if it terrified me.

Was I chickenshit for leaving the way I did and not facing him? Yes. Did I care? No, well, not right then.

Having a job offer fall in my lap was something I couldn't pass up. Unless my employer was a mob boss, hit man, or even a gigolo, then I would let the chance at my first job in many years slip by. I did have some standards.

Though I could perhaps work for a gigolo. I could pretend his appointments were for women with suffering needs. I knew all about those. He was doing his manly duty to help ease their suffering. He was—

"Dylan Jackson."

"Is your brother a gigolo?" I blurted. My eyes widened as my hand slapped over my mouth. Hell, I should have cleared my mind before calling.

"Sorry?" Dylan asked with humor in his voice.

"Oh, my God, I'm so sorry. This is Makenzie. You met me today at the restaurant and offered me a job?"

He chuckled. "The offer still stands, and you calling me tells me you're interested. Also, don't worry, my brother isn't a gigolo."

Sighing, I offered, "I'm sorry again. Your card didn't say anything, so I thought if you worked for your brother, and then I thought what type of business he runs. Sometimes my mind overthinks things, and I blurt it right out."

Still, with a voice where he sounded like he wanted to laugh, he said, "It's fine. Would you like me to tell you about the job and what it would entail?"

"Yes, please."

"You would be helping him keep his women, who work the streets, safe and you'll also be making their appointments with their clients for them. You just have to approach the cars first."

My body froze. Dylan had to be messing with me.

I sat on the bed and said, "Dylan, I think I'll hang up now. I don't want to chance it where a client may think I'm a hooker as well." I didn't end the call though. I waited for his laugh, and it came loud and long.

"Makenzie, I think I like you."

Smiling, I knew I liked Dylan. "The feeling could be mutual if you don't mess with me anymore."

"I'll try my best not to. Really though, you'll be handling calls, running errands, helping to organize his clients. Don't worry, your business degree will come in handy. Also, you'll have to wipe his butt."

I snorted out a laugh. "You're terrible, Dylan Jackson. What does your brother actually do, and do you work for him?"

He snorted. "You really don't know who I am?"

"Should I?"

"Kenzie, I can call you that, yeah?"

"Yes." I grinned. My old friends and sister called me that always. Not Robert though. He didn't like to shorten names.

"Great. Now tell me, you ever heard of D. Jackson?"

"Um," I said while I thought, "no."

"Oh, man. I'm a singer, honey. At least I used to be. I haven't done shit for a while now because I was sick of being in the spotlight."

"Really?" I asked.

"Yeah." He laughed. "Promise I'm not messing with you. Started out when I was sixteen. My brother pulled me out of the shit when I was twenty-one, and I've been out of the game for eight years now."

"Wow."

He chuckled. "Yeah, wow. Never thought I'd meet a woman who didn't know me."

"Do women still, ah, try something even though you're gay?"

"Ah—"

"Sorry, I shouldn't have asked that."

"No, all good. No one really knows I, uh, prefer men. Anyway, let's get back to your job. My brother is a music producer. He's pretty big. You heard of Grayson Jackson?"

"No, I haven't."

"Honey, have you been living under a rock? How old are you?"

Snorting, I said, "I guess you could say that, and I'm twenty-eight."

"Okay. A year before I finished up, Grayson became my producer. He was thirty at the time. He took over everything when our parents died five years ago."

"I'm sorry."

"We're not. They weren't very nice people."

"Again, I'm sorry."

He chuckled. "You're cute. I suppose I better tell you more about the job."

I leaned back against the headboard. "Yes, please."

"There is a chance to live on his property because he'll keep you so busy all you'll have time for is sleep…. Shit, but you're married, and your husband doesn't seem like the man who'd like you staying away for hours on end."

I liked that Dylan swore. Robert had always hated people who cursed, yet I thought it a way to express yourself more. Dylan also seemed like a person I could trust. After all, he did tell me his story.

"I've left my husband," I whispered into the phone, gripping it tighter to me. It felt strange saying it aloud, and to a person I hardly knew. Regret suddenly flipped my stomach, wishing I could take my words back. I shouldn't have said anything. Robert had always told me no one should know our personal business; that it was better left between the two of us.

"Are you okay?" His voice was low, holding concern.

"I think I will be," I said and left it at that.

"I guess our chance meeting today was fate. I was supposed to offer you that job."

I laughed. "I guess you're right." Only time would tell if my life improved and I regained my sass back.

"Now, will you be moving into my brother's place?"

"What?" I whispered.

"I said there's a chance to live there because he will be working you hard. Kenzie, there's plenty of room. There'll be times when you probably won't even see him, but it will be better to assist him being close. Stick with him for a year at least, and I'm sure he'll give you a stellar report for when you move on."

Moving in with another man hadn't been on my cards, but then Dylan said there was an ample amount of space, so I found myself liking the idea. At least then I wouldn't have the hassle of finding a place and forking out a lot of my money on rent. Hell, it all seemed perfect.

"I think that would be okay."

"Grayson can be a bit… cold, but I'm sure you'll be fine with him. Just don't let him walk all over you."

Like you did your husband, I felt was left off the end of his sentence.

"When should I start? Wait, doesn't he need to interview me first?"

"Leave that up to me, and you can start Monday. In fact, I'll have a car come by to pick you up. Where do you live?"

"I'm staying at the Chardour Hotel on Prim Street. But I don't need a car. I can drive myself. Thank you though."

"Okay." His voice was soft. "I'll see you at 8:00 a.m."

"That early?" I whined.

Dylan laughed. "Yes, Grayson loves to start early, but usually you wouldn't need to start until nine. I thought you'd like to make an impression on your first day."

"I think I'm kind of scared to meet your brother."

"Don't be. Well, not too much."

"You're not helping."

His laugh was deep. "Sorry, I can't help it. I like talking to you, Kenzie."

"And I you, Dylan. I feel we're going to be good friends." The observation warmed my heart since it had been so long since I'd had a friend.

"Hmm, so do I, which will piss Grayson off even more."

"Dylan," I snapped. It seemed he liked to get my nerves rattled speaking about his brother that way.

Once his chuckle died, he said, "Sorry, it's really brotherly love. Okay, I'll text you the address and meet you out front on Monday."

"Sounds great. I guess you do work with your brother if you're going to be there?" I asked.

"No. But I don't live far from there, so I do like to stop in and annoy him. We're both bullheaded."

"Great, so my boss is stubborn as well." Damn, I probably shouldn't have said that since Dylan's brother was going to be my boss. "Sorry, I shouldn't say that sort of thing. Sometimes things fly out and I can't seem to stop them."

"It's refreshing. I like it, and I'm sure you've got what it takes to stick around. You'll be fine Monday."

Did he think that because I could accidently shout something I shouldn't to his brother, which no doubt Dylan would get a kick out of it, or did he actually think I'd be fine? Either way, I still replied, "Thank you, Dylan. For this and everything."

"My pleasure," he replied before ending the call. I placed my phone back into its cradle and stood from the bed. I went to the balcony windows and looked out.

The day *was* meant to be mine.

It truly seemed as though an awful chapter in my life had ended with another exciting one just about to begin.

A wide smile crept onto my face. I clasped my hands together in front of me, only to throw them up in the air while I let out a shriek of happiness. I skipped from one foot to the next and did a silly jig.

As my heart raced, I came to a stop and again looked out into the fading sun.

Suddenly a frown replaced my smile.

Guilt burned my insides. I was happy, yet Robert would soon be arriving home to the note I left him saying I couldn't do it any longer. I needed to find myself, the person I used to be again. He'd be hurt, and I'd be the cause of his pain. I'd left a Dear John letter for God's sake

After six years, I was willing to give it all away. I could only hope I was making the right choice.

God, you can't do the simplest things, Makenzie.

What do you call this? I can't eat it. It's full of fat, and you shouldn't eat it either.

I like curves, darling, but don't you think yours are getting a little too big?

You look pretty, but maybe put a little more makeup on.

Maybe you should cut your hair like Trish's.

Yes. I was making the right choice, damn it. Because I was smart, I was good, and I wasn't worthless.

Walking back to the bed, I moved to the table beside it and took a bite of the cheesecake I'd ordered earlier, and I also took a swig of the scotch.

I was my own woman again, and I could eat and drink what *I* wanted to without anyone questioning it. A sense of calm settled over me. I could do it. I could find myself again.

That was until my phone rang. Quickly I picked it up off the bed and looked at the caller ID. Robert. Suddenly the cheesecake and scotch in my stomach seemed like the wrong idea.

No. I wouldn't back down.

I could do this. I could talk to him.

Shakily, I answered, "Hello?"

"I thought you loved me," were Robert's first words.

"I did." *I think.* Sighing, I shook my head at the lie because I was worried about *his* feelings. I didn't love my husband. It only occurred to me a few days earlier when I questioned my love for him and realized it was gone.

"Can't you see how this has hurt me? My wife decides it's time to find herself when I never thought she'd lost herself."

"Too many times I've been hurt—"

"How? I'm not some drunk who spends all his time at a bar and then comes home to beat you. I've given you everything, and this is what you choose to do."

"All you see in me are bad things, things you think need fixing. I've changed so much for you, and it will never be enough."

"Why haven't you said anything earlier?"

Tears welled, and I let out a frustrated breath. "I've tried."

"No, you haven't, or else I would have fixed things, and you would be home where you belong right now." He sounded annoyed, like all of it was an unnecessary bother. It hurt, but it also pissed me off.

Shoulders sagging, I dropped to my knees to the floor and leaned my upper body onto the bed. "I *have* tried, Robert. You don't like to listen," I told him.

"*You* probably didn't try hard enough. You know how busy I've been with work. How stressed I can get, and all I want to do is come home to eat a nice healthy meal and rest. But when I get home the house is usually messy, yet I don't say anything."

I clenched my teeth together. It was the same old rant, yet the house, to me, was always clean. God fucking forbid there was a dust bunny under the stupid heavy couch I couldn't pick up.

"Then you've cooked something that we really shouldn't eat most nights, and still I don't say anything."

I snorted. The ass did say something, and even if it was the healthiest meal, it wasn't good enough. Robert ignored me and went on.

"I've asked you to entice me more in the bedroom, and you don't listen to that either. You forget to do the banking and again, do I say anything about it? No." He sighed. "Maybe a break is good about now. I have to head out of town for two weeks anyway. I'll put some money into your account to stay wherever you're staying, and when I get back, we'll talk then. At home, where you belong."

I never got to reply. He ended the call, which was always Robert's way. He wanted the last word and liked the conversation to go his way. I didn't get to tell him about the job, about how I didn't want his money. I knew he called for a time away because he thought I wouldn't be able to cope without him.

He was being an asshat. I *had* tried on many occasions to talk to him, to tell him how I felt. He never listened, and even if he had, he would turn it all around to make everything my fault.

Not this time.

Guilt would not play a part in my decision. I was doing the right thing for my sake. Absently, I wiped away the tears that had fallen, drew in a deep breath, and stood from the floor.

Nothing would change if I went back there. Robert would still be the same, and I'd still be thinking day in and day out that all the problems we had were my fault.

If *I* just changed.

If *I* cleaned better.

If *I* did everything he wanted just to make him happy, then *we* would be happy.

Marriage shouldn't be like that.

It was a partnership, two people working out their problems together. Not one blaming the other or one causing the other to think *she* was to blame for everything that went wrong.

When Robert realized I was serious about the fact I was leaving him—no, that I *had* left him—then it would be time to pull my shoulders back, tug up my pants, and throw my big girl balls over my shoulder and stay strong.

Backing down was no longer an option.

Sitting on the bed, I ate another few bites of the cheesecake, took a large gulp of scotch, and then I ran myself a nice hot bath. With bubbles and all.

It wasn't until later, when I lay in bed and my mind ran a mile a minute, that I let myself cry. I allowed myself to feel like a failure because no matter what I did, I couldn't get my marriage to work. I tried everything, changed who I was, yet nothing worked.

Six years was a long time to walk away from.

Still, it was time to end six years of self-doubting and hating.

So even through the tears, the heartache, I knew I would never go back. I couldn't. It was time to find the person I was again.

Chapter THREE

I WAS A bundle of nerves. My hands shook on the steering wheel while my stomach did the mamba. I was seriously worried the dancing would continue right out of my butt. Not only was it my first job in four years, but Mr. Jackson sounded like a mean boss, so I had a feeling there was a high chance I was going to screw up on the first day and get fired. After all, I did have a knack for blurting out the wrong things from time to time.

I guessed only time would tell.

For my first free weekend, I spent it pampering myself and cherishing the thought of how proud I was of myself. It was a big step leaving a marriage, especially one that left my emotions bruised and battered. But it would be worth it.

I also tried to ignore the nights where I'd spent the time a blubbering mess, drinking straight from the wine bottle while eating my way through the menu and watching romantic comedies.

It was a new day. A fresh start.

And all I could do was hope I still had a job by the end of the day. I had also packed my bags and checked out of the hotel to move into Mr. Jackson's house.

If Robert knew, he would be beside himself.

"Doesn't matter what Robert thinks anymore, Makenzie. I am my own woman. I can do what I like. I can even perv at a man without feeling guilty and… why God? Why would you make that fine man gay?" I asked to the sky as I came to a stop in front of the underground gates where Dylan stood smiling as he waited for me. He wore another perfect suit on his perfect physique with his perfect hair styled. He pushed his sunglasses to his head and approached the car. Once he had the passenger door opened, he climbed in and said, "Morning, honey. You ready for your first day?"

God. He even smelled like heaven.

"Y-yes. I think. Maybe. Can I say no and not have you think any less of me?"

He threw his head back and roared with laughter. "You're too cute." He smiled over at me. "Anyway, I thought I had better meet you out here because you don't have a remote for the underground parking."

"So, this building is just his business, right?"

Dylan shook his head as he pressed a button on a handheld device. The gates opened with a clicking sound. "His business is actually on the bottom levels. His apartment is the top level, where there are six bedrooms, three on each side of the building. Three living areas, four bathrooms and a kitchen behind the main living area. Then just under his apartment floor is the gym and swimming pool. Under that are guest rooms, and then the rest is all business, business, business."

He gestured with his chin to look toward the building. I looked out and then up and up again. The place was huge, and soon I would be working *and* living in it.

It had to be one of the tallest and widest buildings I had ever seen. To each side held other businesses, only they were nothing in height or width.

"Wait," I whispered, leaning forward to look up once again. "Do I have to clean any of it?" Because honestly, if I were some sort of house cleaner, I would reverse on out of there. I'd struggled to clean Robert's and my home.

Dylan snorted. "No. He has housekeepers who do that. Now, are you actually going to drive in?"

I bit my bottom lip and nodded, then shook my head. "I'm not sure if I should. The place looks very intimidating."

"Kenzie, I believe you'll be just fine here, and anyway, I've got your butt." He threw his hand out toward the place. "Sally forth, good lady."

"Don't you mean back?" I asked.

"Huh?"

"You'll have my back, not butt."

He chuckled. "That's what I meant."

Sighing, I nodded, tucked my black hair behind my ear, and gently eased my foot off the brake.

"Why are you driving like a granny?" Dylan asked.

"I'm scared the place will revolt and figure out I'm a clumsy, weird woman who doesn't belong here and kick me out." Beside the fact underground parking kind of freaked me out. Though, I wasn't letting Dylan know that. I had a feeling if I did, he would need to test out just how frightened I was.

"You're too funny. Hurry up, I need to tell… sorry, I, ah, told Gray to be expecting his new assistant this morning, and the way you're driving, we may not get there by dinner."

Rolling my eyes, I pressed harder and went faster down into a dark, dingy area. A light flickered to my left. I thinned my lips and bit them between my teeth.

"So, um, where should I park?" I asked. Only Dylan didn't answer. I turned to him and screamed when I found his face only inches from mine. He shifted back and burst out laughing. His hand went over his stomach as his laughter kept going.

Smacking his arm, I snapped, "You should not scare a person who could easily have driven us into a pole or something."

"I couldn't resist," he panted. "Oh, God. You just made my morning." He pointed his hand to the right. "Park over there. You'll see a reserved sign for Assistant."

Grumbling under my breath, I moved the car to the right and down the row until I came to the free spot, which indeed did have a sign saying Assistant. Pulling in, I undid my seat belt and slowly turned to Dylan, only to flush when I saw he was gazing up and down my body. "Did you just check me out?"

He smiled. "I could have."

"But, why?" I asked, aghast. "You're gay," I pointed out.

He blinked slowly. "Right, ah… I was just making sure you're wearing the right clothes to impress my brother."

Tilting my head to the side, I wasn't sure I believed him. Still, I asked, "Am I?"

He shrugged. "Honestly, I'm not sure anything will impress him."

Crossing my arms over my chest, I leaned into my seat and pouted. "If you keep scaring me, I won't even get out of the car."

Shaking his head, he smiled, then winked. "Let's do this." He got out of the car and came around my side, opening my door. "If I promise not to scare you for the rest of the day, will you get out?"

Tapping my chin with my finger, I pretended to think about it. "Maybe."

He sighed, only he was smirking when he did so. "Come on, cute stuff." Reaching in, he grabbed my arm and tugged. Climbing out, I straightened my pencil skirt and white blouse and then placed my handbag on my shoulder. "I'll send someone down for your bags," Dylan said as he took my keys and then hand before we started for the elevator. Thankfully, it was close to my parking spot.

"But I may need my keys for a quick escape," I mentioned.

He snorted. "I'll get someone to drop them off to you when they're done."

"Maybe they shouldn't grab my bags in case I don't even last the day."

He pressed the button to the elevator and turned to me.

"Enough self-doubt." He didn't understand how hard it was for me to stop. I had been with a man for six years who offered daily taunts freely, which caused most of my self-doubt. "You *will* still be here by the end of the day, and you *will* not take any of Grayson's crap. I think that's been one of the biggest issues he has. Either his assistants want to sleep with him, date him, marry him for his money, or they run screaming when he applies a little pressure with a loud voice." The elevator dinged and we stepped in. We both turned to face the doors, and Dylan pressed the fortieth floor while I clenched his hand tighter in mine. He cleared his throat. "Stand up for yourself, and he'll respect that."

"Are you sure?"

"Yes." He nodded and then smirked. "By the way, you may not want to go into the underground parking lot alone. It's haunted."

"Dylan." I clipped my warning.

"Joking. Last one for the day. Honestly, the whole building is the safest in this area. It's manned twenty-four hours a day with security and cameras. Nothing to worry about down there."

Drawing in a deep breath through my nose, I nodded and then unlatched my trembling hand from his to wipe it on my skirt.

"Scared?" Dylan asked.

"No. Yes. Well, more nervous actually. First job in a long time, remember."

The elevator suddenly stopped. I looked at the screen, and it said Ground Floor. The doors swished open, and behind them I saw a gorgeous woman. Her long, straight blonde hair was over one shoulder and just about came down to her hip. She wore a short black dress that hung off one shoulder and stunning black heels.

As soon as her eyes saw Dylan, she rolled them and stepped in, turning her back to us. I glanced up at Dylan to see him glaring daggers at her back. He looked down to me and shook his head. The rest of the ride up was quiet and awkward. I couldn't help but fidget as my stomach rolled and rolled on the inside. The closer we got to our destination, the worse I felt. I shifted from one foot to another, clasped my hands in front of me, only to change my mind and move them around to my back. I adjusted my bag on my shoulder and shrugged a few times. I twisted and turned, then bit my bottom lip.

Finally we arrived, and as soon as the doors opened, I heard Dylan's sigh of relief as well. Once the woman before us stepped off, Dylan took my arm and led me slowly behind her. He leaned in and whispered, "I have never seen anyone so restless before. Try to stand still in front of my brother."

"I will." I nodded. "So, who was the stunning woman?"

He scoffed. "An up and coming model, at least trying to be, and the most recent flavor of the month for my brother." He crinkled his nose up at her back. While he led me forward, I took a chance to look around the area I would be working. The place was packed with people at desks or running around doing whatever they had to do. I wondered what the other floors were like, and why Mr. Jackson needed such a large building for his producing business. Soon enough I would find out.

When Dylan came to a stop so did I because his hand was still holding my arm. He looked down at me. "You wait here for a second. I'll tear Gray away from harpy lady."

When I nodded, he walked the few steps to the closed office door and entered without knocking, closing it behind him. Seconds later, voices rose behind that door, and I winced. Suddenly, the door was swung open. I jumped, and my hand went over my heart.

Dylan stepped out first with a frown on his face. He came to my side, and then I looked back to the door to see the woman step out. She shifted to the side of it with a smirk on her red lips. My body stilled when the last person stepped out. My boss.

He was tall, taller than his brother; he was also wider. His large shoulders had to turn sideways to make it all the way out. Then his body tapered off to thinner hips. Just from a first glance, I knew he worked out a lot. I brought my eyes up because I didn't want anyone to think I was checking him out when I wasn't, not really. I had to know what I was up against and the giant man already intimidated me.

His dark-brown hair, dark eyes, and chiseled cheekbones, complete with a five o'clock shadow matched his whole broody look. When I saw his hard, narrowed gaze on me, I stiffened, yet I then found myself straightening, jutting my chin out and up.

"Grayson, this is Makenzie Mayfair. Your new assistant."

"At least he picked an ugly and fat one," the harpy beside Mr. Jackson whispered. Of course it was loud enough for all of us to hear.

My boss narrowed his gaze even more down at his woman, and Dylan coughed out, "Bitch," behind his fist.

Ignoring her, and instead of giving her the finger like I wished to do, I held out my hand to my boss and said, "Nice to meet you, Mr. Jackson. If you could tell me what you want me to start with, I'll get on it."

Slowly, he looked down to my hand and then up again. "Answer the phones for now, take messages. I'll deal with you later." His voice was deep, rough, and would have driven any woman crazy with need from it.

But I was immune.

I was immune to his looks, his face, and his attitude. Everything. I had one thing to do, and that was my job. I'd ignore anything else that could occur. Dylan was right; his brother was cold and intimidating, or had I been the one to say that?

I didn't know. I didn't care. The job would look great on my resume so I would stick it out for a year tops.

After he spoke, he spun back around without the courtesy of shaking my hand and entered his office with the harpy, closing the door behind them. I swung my gaze to Dylan and gave him wide eyes.

He smirked. "Yeah, I kind of forgot to tell him I found a new assistant and sometimes he can be an ass."

"Dylan," I whispered harshly through clenched teeth. His brother certainly was a rude ass to not shake my hand. God, I didn't have frigging cooties or anything.

He scratched his chin and looked away from me. Obviously he was about to fib. "I was sure I did tell him. Anyway, you're here now, and he didn't tell you to get lost. So sit on down at that desk and impress the douche."

I glared at him for a few more moments before harrumphing, punching him in the arm, which he rubbed after, and then I walked around the desk to sit down.

"Well, I'm off—"

"No!" I yelled and started to stand. Dylan was at my side ushering me back into my seat. "You will not leave me until I know what I'm doing."

"Grayson will show you. For now, do as he's asked. I'm sure you can't fuck up answering phones."

"Well, no."

"Great. I'll be back to have lunch with you. Good luck." He kissed my cheek and bolted for the elevator.

Groaning, I palmed my face and ran my hand over it. What in the hell was I doing? Why did I leave Robert again? Why was I set on starting fresh?

All of it was new and freaking me out.

I didn't know if I could do it. My stomach was a bundle of nerves and knowing my luck, I'd probably break wind and then the scary boss man would come out, ask what that smell was—because it would smell with the way my stomach was running amok—and then I would have to explain I had a problem with my butt.

No. Stop it, Makenzie.

I could do it. I could calm down, relax, and I could hold in my gas, even if I ended up looking like a prune face. I would not fart on my first day.

Oh, God. Why am I thinking about farting? My stomach gurgled. Leaning down, I picked up my handbag and placed it on the desk, while I felt around for some Tums. I glanced around the office and noticed I was receiving a few quizzical looks back. Placing a smile on my face, I offered a nod. Some nodded in return while most rolled their eyes and went back to what they were doing.

Setting a Tums in my mouth, I put my bag back on the floor and then sat back in the chair before I rolled it closer to the desk. It was already seemingly tidy. Still, I straightened a few things and turned on the computer.

I was starting to feel a little less frazzled… until the phone rang. My body jolted. I fumbled for the handset and then once I placed it against my ear, I totally forgot what I was supposed to say. I gripped the phone tightly. My eyes widened, and I was sure I panted a couple of times into the phone. Crap, what was the company called?

Eventually, I tried, "Mr. Jackson's office?"

"Give me, Grayson," a man's voice demanded.

"May I ask who's calling?"

The man sighed. "I'm guessing you're new, so I'll let it pass this time. Next, I won't. Place my voice to memory, lady. Name's Vice."

Another rude ass.

"One moment please." Oh crap, how did I transfer over or link to Mr. Jackson's phone so I could tell him obnoxious Vice was on the phone? Panic started to form in my chest. I quickly placed the handset down and stood, taking the couple of steps to my boss's door and knocked.

"Enter," was barked.

Opening the door slowly, I spotted Mr. Jackson sitting behind the desk with Harpy sitting close to him on his desk. "Ah, a Mr. Vice is on the phone."

His eyes narrowed. "Transfer it in."

"I would if I knew what button to press." I cringed when his jaw clenched and a tick started on the side of his forehead. Harpy started giggling. Mr. Jackson abruptly stood and stalked around his desk. I moved out of the way just in time as he waltzed past me.

"Get over here," he clipped. I quickly scuttled over and stood beside him. "Press this to place the call on hold. Press this to connect to my phone and then press this again to tell them you're putting them through. Then hang the fuck up. You got it?"

Not really, but if he quickly left I would try to write it down so I'd remember.

"Yes." I nodded.

"Right, do it then." He shifted back and stood there with his arms crossed over his chest.

Looking at the phone and then to him, then back again once more to the phone and my boss, I asked, "Shouldn't you be in your office to take the call then?"

He glared, grumbled something under his breath, spun, and stalked back into his office. I picked up the phone and pressed the button to place Vice on hold and then the button to connect to Mr. Jackson's office. I waited and then, "Jackson Media, Arts Department. This is Angelia, how may I direct your call?"

"Ah, sorry, I pressed the wrong button."

A tickle of a giggle sounded on the other end. "Where are you, babe? I can help."

"I'm supposed to connect to Mr. Jackson's phone. I'm his assistant, and Vice is waiting on the line for him."

She sighed. "You better not keep that douche waiting long. He may be Mr. Jackson's friend, but he's an important one. Do you see the button second in at the top?"

"Yes." I snapped up a pen to take notes.

"You'll connect to Mr. Jackson's office and then press the one under it to get back to Vice and then the one at the top left to connect the call to boss man's office."

"Thank you, I think you just saved my butt."

Another tinkle of laugh sounded. "My pleasure. See you at lunch, babe," she said and then hung up.

I did as she asked and waited. "Yes?" was growled into the phone.

"Connecting you to Vice now."

"Took too long. I've already spoken to him," he snapped into the phone and then hung up.

It was my turn to grumble under my breath as I placed the phone back into its cradle.

Patience. I had a feeling I was going to need a lot of it to deal with Mr. Jackson. Thankfully, I knew how from being around Robert for six years.

God. Just thinking Robert's name had my shoulders slumping. I couldn't understand where I had gone wrong. How I'd pushed back my usually outspoken manner when it came to him.

I had to find myself.

I had to gain back my confidence and learn to not roll over, bearing my stomach so no one could inflict a fatal wound.

I was going to be who I was before Robert.

I was.

Chapter
FOUR

AFTER AN HOUR, harpy walked out of Mr. Jackson's office. She glanced at me with a smirk on her face, then flicked her hair over her shoulder before continuing on to the elevator. Nearly every head turned to watch her go. Male and female. In the time she'd been in there, I had taken four other phone calls and hadn't screwed up any of them. I was proud of myself.

I was in the middle of looking at the files on the computer and trying to get the gist of what I would be dealing with when Mr. Jackson called from right beside me, "Meeting. Now."

I nearly jumped out of my skin. I hadn't even heard him approach. "Okay, I'll let people know you'll be out of the office for…?" I trailed off, waiting for him to tell me how long the meeting would take.

"You're coming to take notes."

"Right." I nodded, grabbing the notebook I found in my drawer, and a pen. As I stood, I glanced to my boss to see his eyes on my notebook. He shook his head and started walking to the right. I quietly followed behind, near jogging to keep up with him. As we walked, people called out a greeting to the boss; he ignored them all. I tried to wave and smile at them to lessen the blow. They then ignored me.

Rolling my eyes, I shook my head and then slammed into someone's back. Looking up, I watched as Mr. Jackson turned his head slowly and glowered down at me before opening the door and entering. The large meeting room held a conference table, which was already full of people sitting around it. My grumpy boss sat at the end of it, and I took the chair leaning against the wall behind him.

"William, what's the update on Evelyn's cover?"

"It's just about ready for a proof. I'll be sending it up for your eyes this afternoon."

Boss nodded and moved his hard gaze to the left. Not that I could see his eyes, but the way people tensed, I knew his eyes had to be.

"Owen, how's Zoe handling the new song?"

"She complained at the start, but once I said you hand-picked it for her, she's been doing fine. Actually, she wants to erase some of her tracks and continue with songs like that one."

A nod. "I'll have my assistant e-mail some to you when I get back."

I wasn't exactly sure what I was supposed to be doing, but as the meeting went on, I wrote everything down. The only problem I had was when Mr. Jackson didn't call a few people by their names. I didn't want to seem like a fool in front of everyone and ask him who they were. Instead, I went with my own idea and hoped it wouldn't bite me on the ass later.

As soon as Angelia, who I waved at once Mr. Jackson had called on her, finished talking about some cover art for a musician by the name of James Carter, Mr. Jackson stood, nodded, and then walked from the room. I jumped up, dropped my pen and notepad and was about to follow when Angelia approached.

"You'd better get back to him, but babe, I so want to know how your first day is going. Lunch at twelve, yeah?"

Smiling, I said, "Sounds good."

"Awesome, cafeteria, second floor."

"See you there," I said and then actually jogged back to my desk. I had just placed my notebook down when I heard behind me, "In here now."

Closing my eyes for a second, I drew in a deep calming breath, blew it out, and grabbed my notes before entering his ginormous office. The views were amazing. I wouldn't have minded a chance to take them in, but the scowl on his face told me he wanted the information I had and then me gone.

"Okay," I started and sat in the chair opposite his over-large desk. Was he trying to overcompensate for something? Mr. Jackson cleared his throat. Oh, snap, had I said that aloud? I hoped not. Just in case, I sat straighter and rattled off everything I took down. Well, everything except for the ones who had no name.

Finished, I glanced up at him and bit my bottom lip. Then watched as his hand pressed something on his desk, looking at it when he shifted his hand away to lean back in his chair, I saw it was a voice recorder.

"I was sure there was more."

"Oh, I got it all."

"Then spit it out so we can both eat."

Eat? Was he going to eat me? Oh, God, now I was blushing and wishing Robert had at least satisfied me in bed, but he hadn't. Of course it had been all my fault, but not once had that man made me come. *Great, now I'm thinking about coming.*

Clearing my throat and taking my mind out of the gutter, I tucked my hair behind my ear and read him the rest of my notes.

"Bald guy with a monobrow said he was going to call you this afternoon as soon as he found the file he was sent for an up-and-coming artist. The woman with, ah, her shirt gaping open and short black hair, informed you that the contract of Alexander was ending in a month and wants to know if you want to renew it. The man who had a coffee stain on his white silk shirt said Michael still hasn't got back to him on the timeline of when Avery will be finished with her album." There, I'd done it. Slowly, I raised my gaze to my boss. My head jerked back when I thought I saw a lip twitch, but they seemed to thin out instead.

"Before you go to lunch, why don't you actually google this company and learn who you're talking about." He leaned forward, his elbows on the desk. "Have you ever heard of Jackson Media?"

"Well, no. Still, I am capable of doing the job right. I may be out of practice, but I'm a fast learner, and I will know everyone's name before the next meeting." I prayed.

"You'll be returning all e-mails and calls to them with my answers by the end of the day, Mrs. Mayfair, so I suggest you learn them quickly."

Exiting the office, I quickly sat and started doing my homework.

I had some time before I was to go to lunch unless… was I supposed to have lunch at a different time than the others? Who would be there to man the phone? Was I supposed to let an answering machine take the calls?

Frustrated with not knowing, and finding myself with only one option to obtain the answer, I picked up the phone and pressed the direct line into Mr. Jackson's office.

"Yes?" His voice sounded as though it echoed. I didn't bother saying anything though; it could have been just a problem with my line.

"I wasn't sure when my lunch break would be… and if—"

He snorted. "Thinking about lunch already?"

Was that a dig at my weight? The douche.

Through clenched teeth, I bit out, "No." I took a breath and said, "Angelia had said she would meet me in the cafeteria, and I didn't know who would be here to answer the phones or what the protocol was since I haven't had anyone tell me."

There, take that, you prick on a good-looking stick.

"Helena from recording will be up to man the phones while you're at lunch, and next time Mrs. Mayfair, I don't need to know your menial information. Get to the point right from the start." With that, he hung up.

Rat bastard.

As I stabbed at the button on my mouse starting my research of the company and its people, I mumbled to myself, "Of course, Mr. Jackson. Anything you say, Mr. Jackson. Right to the point, Mr. Jackson." I let out a frustrated growl.

"If you wish to grumble, Mrs. Mayfair, please close my door after you leave."

My eyes widened. Tensing, I slowly spun my chair to face his office. No wonder there had been an echo on the phone. I heard his voice from within since his door was goddamn open.

Standing, I went to his door with my cheeks flushing. I grabbed the knob and closed the door. Only, before I got it all the way, Mr. Jackson called my name.

"Yes?"

"If you actually do everything I say, you may become the longest-running assistant." He arched a brow at me.

I closed my eyes. After a calming breath, I opened them and offered, "Sorry, I—"

He cut me off. "That will be all."

Nodding, I shut the door, went back to my seat, and slumped down in it.

One year.

I only had to last one year, and if I could put up with Robert, I could certainly do it with Mr. Jackson as well. Didn't mean I couldn't hurt Dylan for his brother's actions. He was, after all, the one who got me this job in the first place.

As soon as Helena showed, who was yet another beautiful, scowling woman—something I was seeing a pattern of—I picked up my bag, thanked her, and made a run for it before Mr. Jackson could step out of his office. While I stood at the elevator watching it rise from floor to floor, my cell rang. I took it out of my purse. Dylan's name popped up on the screen.

"Hi, I'm just about to hop into the elevator. Are you here?" I asked.

"Sorry, honey. I can't make it, but I'll be around when work finishes to take you upstairs."

"But—"

"See you then," he called before he hung up.

I had been looking forward to seeing Dylan for lunch, so I could give him a few choice words. It would just have to wait and knowing my luck, I'd be extra angry when it was quitting time.

A few looks and noses turned up in my direction on the ride down to the second floor. I wouldn't let them get to me though. I no longer cared what people thought of me. I had thick skin, so who cared if they thought I didn't suit the company. I had to learn to love myself the way I was. Or at least try to.

Angelia was waiting just outside the doors when they opened. She was stunning and was also one of the few who had curves like me. When she spotted me, she grinned, skipped over, and linked her arm in mine. I wasn't used to people being so openly friendly after one small phone call. I found it strange yet sweet she was willing to befriend me.

"I could eat a horse, I'm that hungry."

"She probably already has," came from behind us.

I tensed. Angelia rolled her eyes at me, looked over her shoulder and hissed, "Shit, Kim, don't be all jealous of my awesome body just because you're thinner than a rake. Men get disappointed when they haven't got anything to hold onto, you know that, right?" She then dragged me toward the cafeteria. "Don't mind the bitches around here and let me tell you"—she raised her voice—"there are many. You just have to give them shit back."

My smile was tight. I wished I could, but I had been biting my tongue for years. I had become a silent fighter. My brain was great with fighting back and giving smart quips and dress downs. It may take some time for me to wrap my head around the fact I didn't have to be silent any longer. I could be who I was back in the day, and that person would have also put that woman in her place.

Warmth settled over me, and I found myself smiling.

Leaving Robert had already led me on a new, happier path. So even though guilt ate at my insides and worry touched my heart for hurting Robert, I knew I was doing the right thing for myself.

We took our lunches to a table in the far corner of the cafeteria and sat. No sooner had we started eating when the chairs around us filled up.

"Babe,"—I blinked, realizing Angelia was referring to me since she didn't know my name since I hadn't said it on the phone earlier. "This is Abby, Dara, Ryan, and Hudson." She gestured to the people around the table.

"Nice to meet you, babe." Hudson smirked.

"Makenzie, actually." I smiled.

"I guess you're new today. Angelia always takes the newbies under her wing. Until they turn into the others," Dara said.

"Others?" I asked.

"Snotty bitches."

Wow, and there I thought people outgrew high school drama when they graduated.

"Don't worry." Abby smiled at me. "It's not that bad here. You soon learn who to stay away from. Anyway, I work in the arts department with Angelia, so does Ryan." I looked to Ryan, who munched on his food and offered me a salute. "Dara and Hudson work in the sounds area."

"Where do you work?" Dara asked.

"I'm Mr. Jackson's assistant."

Ryan sucked back a breath and started coughing on his food. Hudson groaned and smacked his back, then slapped a fifty to the table. Dara was next, then Abbey, and after Ryan had calmed down, he also placed a fifty on the table. I saw Angelia roll her eyes, pick up the money, and pocket it. Then she told me, "They like making bets to see how long Mr. Jackson's assistants will last. I don't play their game, but I keep the money safe until the bet ends."

"I have a week, sorry, babe," Hudson said and winced.

"I have two," Abby told me around a bite of her chicken and salad wrap.

"Two days for me." Ryan grinned. "Nothing against you of course, but Mr. Jackson is a hardass to work so close with."

Dara snorted. I looked there. She leaned back and studied me. "I have a feeling she's different. I'm changing my three weeks to four months." They then started yelling and stating new dates. Apparently, Dara had always won, so they had a feeling she would be close to the date I would leave or get fired. I shrugged it off. I couldn't blame them really, since Dylan told me his brother had been through so many. I could only hope I'd be different than the rest.

Angelia leaned across the table, and asked, "How was your morning?"

I shrugged. "Good, well, okay. I'm sure it will get better."

"If you have any problems with the computer or anything, just call down to me."

"Thank you."

"You single?" Hudson asked suddenly.

My cheeks pinked. "Y-yes, actually, no, ah, it's complicated." I sighed and noticed everyone was waiting for an answer. "All I'm willing to say is that I left my husband on Friday."

Hudson whistled and opened his mouth to presumably ask more, but Angelia smacked him in the back of the head. "No questions." She turned to me and added, "Just putting this out there, all men suck. If you want to turn the other way and start looking at women"—she pointed to herself—"I get first dibs at your new sexual experience."

A quick flash of me licking a fish popped into my head. It was my turn to choke and cough on my food.

"Um… I'll think about it."

She threw her head back and laughed. "Joking. Not about me being gay, but I think we'd be better off as friends than lovers."

"I have a feeling she'll always be a penis lover, Ang," Ryan piped up and grinned, throwing a wink my way. "I'm good for a rebound."

My head jerked back. Had I been too long out of the dating game? I didn't know it was normal for men to state their intentions straightaway.

"Not all men are like these two," Abby said as she threw a carrot at Ryan. "They're just sex crazed."

Dara snorted, then laughed. "You should have seen your face though."

Grinning, I shook my head and went back to my food. I had a feeling I was going to enjoy lunch each day with my new colleagues. Even if they had bet on when I would leave.

Chapter FIVE

THE AFTERNOON HELD no bad incidents, thank God. It was around four when Mr. Jackson called me back into the office. He gave me his responses I needed to disseminate to everyone from the morning meeting, and with a final dismissal of, "That will be all," I got up and left. I was glad I took my time earlier to memorize everyone who was at the meeting, so it wasn't hard to either call or e-mail the necessary people. All were curt with me, but that didn't bother me. I knew I didn't smell. I'd even sniffed my armpits one time. So, I put their reactions down to them being douches, people I didn't have time for. When five thirty arrived, I was relieved I had survived my first day back working. Just as I was about to shut off the computer, my boss came out of his office and said briskly, "See you tomorrow."

I didn't bother replying because he was already on the move again to the elevator. I finished logging off the computer, tidied my desk, and leaned over to grab my bag, which was when I heard, "Brother, how was your new assistant?" Peeking over the desk, I saw Dylan getting off the elevator as Mr. Jackson moved through the doors to get on it. I didn't hear my boss's answer, but Dylan suddenly threw back his head and laughed. As the elevator doors closed, Mr. Jackson's scowling face turned to me, and his eyes narrowed even more. I sat up and couldn't stop my eyes from rolling at him. Surely he was far enough away he couldn't have seen it, though just as the elevator doors were closing, I witnessed his brows dip lower.

Oh well, I was off the clock anyway so he couldn't fire me for an eye roll, and certainly he wouldn't have in the first place. Then again, it was Mr. Jackson, and I didn't know him enough to be 100 percent certain. All I did know was that he was one grumpy, good-looking man.

"Hey, cute stuff." Dylan smiled as he walked my way. The coworkers who were also packing up looked from Dylan to me. Great, they'd be thinking I got the job because I was sleeping with my boss's brother.

Let them gossip. I didn't give two hoots what they thought. All of them seemed rude except Angelia and her group.

"Hi." I grinned, standing.

"How was the first day?" He leaned in to kiss my cheek. I blushed. It wasn't every day I had a stunning male touch his lips to my skin. Dang him being gay.

"Tiring. I'm just about ready to crash."

"Let's get out of here then, and I'll show you upstairs." He hooked his arm in mine and moved us toward the elevator. "Grayson said you did well, even if some things were unorthodox. I can't believe you described Lexi as a woman with black hair and her boobs hanging out."

I gasped. "I didn't say that. I said her top was half undone."

He snorted. "Same thing, honey."

The elevator didn't take long to arrive. As we got in, I said, "Not the same thing, I was nicer about it."

He shook his head, smirking, then got out a key, and put it in the lock I hadn't even noticed on the panel. When he turned it, he pressed the forty-second floor. Stepping back, Dylan leaned against the wall. He saw me looking and said, "You'll get a key and a spare off Grayson. It's the only way anyone can get to the upper floors. Unless someone who's already in the apartment lets a person up. And if you're the better-looking brother like me." He winked, and then asked, "Did you make any friends at least?"

Smiling, I told him, "I did in fact. Angelia in the art department. She also introduced me to her friends. Ang offered that if I were to turn gay, she would be willing to be my first love. Only Ryan said I was a penis woman, so he offered to be my rebound."

"What the fuck? Who's this dick Ryan? I'll beat the shit out of him."

Laughing, I placed a hand on Dylan's arm, and said, "Relax. Abby informed me Ryan was like that to all women because he's sex crazed, like Hudson who asked if I was single. It's not like I'd take any man up on any offer."

There was a ding, and then the doors opened. I gasped at what I saw. Dylan took my hand and led me off the elevator.

The apartment was stunning and the biggest I had ever seen. Dylan stood me just outside the elevator so I could take in what was before me, which seemed to be a large living area. Everything in it appeared designer and was perfectly placed. I wasn't sure the room even got used.

"This is the formal living room. You have one to yourself, and Grayson has his own in his quarters. But this one is mostly used for small functions Gray holds."

Nodding, my eyes drifted back to it. It certainly was large enough to hold even a big function of at least one hundred people or more. The room was round with couches and chairs on the plush carpet in the center. To the outside of the room, the floorboards were stained dark. Next to the wall of windows at the back of the room was a piano and near each corner of the room sat two doors, which I guessed led to Mr. Jackson's rooms and—gulp—mine. A TV sat over a fireplace to the left of the room and to the right was a bar with another door behind it.

"Robert and I have a nice home, but this… this is amazing."

"You had, Kenzie."

Looking to him, I asked, "Sorry?"

"Robert and you *had* a nice home. It's his now, right?"

Flushing, I nodded. "Yes, you're right."

Dylan placed an arm around my shoulders and pulled me into him. "Sorry to bring the dick up. But… look, I'm glad you left him that day after what I heard. No man should talk to a woman like the way he did. Especially his wife."

"I know," I whispered.

"Something in your eyes that day told me you'd been putting up with a lot. You've made the giant leap by leaving him, but it's the right leap. I'll make sure you see it."

"Thank you, Dylan. I-it's been hard."

"That's because you're too kind and sweet, and being that way, you'll always worry about your decision and how Robert is feeling." He knocked his hip against mine. "Hang with me more. I'll teach you how to have a backbone."

My lips tipped up in each corner, but since discussing Robert, I suddenly wasn't feeling excited about the place or my actions any longer. Regret coiled inside of me. I really did feel bad for leaving Robert. Maybe I could have changed more to be who he wanted, even without love.

God, I was now living in the house of my boss, a man I hardly knew. It was a risk, a big risk, and it scared me. Dylan was right though. I was too nice, sweet, and I didn't have a backbone, but really he didn't know me. Well, no, that wasn't true. I had been myself around him, even though we'd only spoken for a tiny amount of time. Regardless, I'd been the real me, like the person I had been before Robert. My hand fluttered to my chest at the new realization.

I had been myself.

Speaking my mind without worry of what could come of my words.

Without fear it could bite me on the butt.

That wasn't quite right. There was always fear present, yet since leaving on Friday, I'd found myself doing and saying what I wanted.

With Dylan, I was me.

Leaning into him, I tipped my head back and smiled. "Thank you."

"For what?"

He wouldn't understand. I shook my head and said, "Just for everything. I haven't had a friend, a real friend in so long. I'm glad you overheard Robert that day and came after me. If you hadn't…" I shrugged. "I think I would be back to who and where I was with Robert."

He gave me a squeeze. "Then I'm glad I did also."

A door to the left opened. I tensed when I saw Harpy step through dressed in an amazing long, white form-fitting dress. Her eyes landed right on us and narrowed. Then Mr. Jackson stepped out and…. Damn him for looking so good in a tux.

His eyes widened just a fraction when he saw us, though as he placed a hand on Harpy's back and led her our way, his expression went back to his usual scowl.

"Dylan," he clipped. "Mrs. Mayfair. What are you both doing up here?"

I whipped my head around to glare up at Dylan.

"Calm down," he mumbled to me. "Gray, you always have your assistants stay here to be at your beck and call."

"Yes, but I assumed that Mrs. Mayfair wouldn't be in the situation to do that." We both watched his eyes flick to my hand.

Lifting it, I then understood his meaning. I was still wearing my wedding ring.

Heat hit my cheeks. I glanced from my rings to Dylan, then Harpy, who leaned against her man seeming bored, and then to my boss. His brow raised—he wanted an answer.

God. What did I say?

It was simple enough. I left my husband, but it wasn't something I wanted Harpy to hear right then.

Mr. Jackson's eyes moved from mine, to his brother's, and then to the arm Dylan still had around my shoulders. I quickly sidestepped away. Then again, I shouldn't have to. Dylan was gay… unless his brother didn't know.

No. I would stand my ground. I had to. Moving back to Dylan's side, I lifted my chin and told Mr. Jackson, "I'm no longer with my husband, and I can promise the situation won't cause any grief to you or your business."

He studied me. Harpy at his side snorted and then mumbled, "Hubby probably got rid of her."

Lifting my hand, I rubbed under my nose with my middle finger. Dylan chuckled beside me. Unfortunately, Harpy didn't see because she was studying her fingernails.

Mr. Jackson blinked slowly, something happened to his lips for a second, and then he ushered Harpy closer our way. He cleared his throat and said, "See that it doesn't, and Dylan, I'm sure you're more than willing to show Mrs. Mayfair around."

"Already on it, brother." Dylan smirked and shuffled us to the side so they could pass to the elevator. "Come on, Kenzie. I'll show you to your room where all the magic will happen."

"Dylan," Mr. Jackson bit out.

"Yes?" Dylan turned us to face them as they entered the elevator.

"I'll be calling you later."

Dylan laughed. "Right oh, brother." As the doors closed, Dylan saluted them and then, to my shock, gave them the middle finger. Harpy glared. Mr. Jackson's eyes narrowed, only I saw the lip twitch and shake of his head.

Once we were alone, I asked, "Does your brother know you prefer men? He didn't seem too comfortable having you alone with me in here."

Dylan chuckled. "Ah, no, he doesn't know. I do like to give him hell though."

I pushed the confusion aside on why Dylan wouldn't tell his brother and smiled instead. "I can see that. How old are you again? The middle finger, really?"

Dylan beamed. "You can't talk. I saw the nose rub, and I'm sure my brother did also. Still, I can't help my reactions. He brings out the child in me." He reached to take my hand. "Come on, let the tour begin."

SOMETIME AFTER DYLAN left, I sat in my room on the king-size bed with a smile on my face. Honestly, my room was more like a suite because the bedroom connected to its own living room, which was the size of a small stadium. There was also a large walk-in closet and an en suite off to the left of the bed. I couldn't believe Mr. Jackson had his assistant stay in the same apartment as his.

Then again, Dylan did warn me Mr. Jackson's clients were demanding, and sometimes I would be the one to have to deal with whatever they wanted at any hour of the day. Later, I would do more study about the business. I needed to learn what I could. I didn't want to seem as if I were in the dark on everything in the music industry.

I was finding everything was exciting, so much so that even with my stomach tied in knots at the thought of my next phone call with Robert, when I would have to tell him again it was over, I smiled.

Lying back on the bed, I let out a laugh. I had a job. I was making my own money to do with what *I* wanted. I had a nice place to stay, even if I had to put up with Mr. Jackson, but so far, I felt it would be worth it.

Chapter

SIX

IT WAS A few days later where if I could take back the thought "It would be worth it," I would. I'd shove that thought right up Mr. Jackson's ass. The morning after my first day, I was woken early to loud banging on my door. Frantically, I'd thrown back my covers and raced to answer. Once getting the door open, I'd stood there panting, looking up to an annoyed Mr. Jackson, whose eyes had just done a quick sweep of my bedroom attire of pants and tee that read "Zombies need love too" with a narrowed gaze. Then he'd barked, "Kitchen, now. We have to go over some things. Get dressed first," before spinning and walking away.

Slowly, I'd shut the door and turned to the bedside table where the digital clock sat. Five freaking a.m. Dylan had thought I would start at 9:00 a.m., so I'd set my alarm for seven thirty. How freaking naïve I had been.

I'd brought up my hours with Mr. Jackson as I'd sat at the table in the kitchen, which was on his side of the apartment. He'd told me my hours were whenever he needed me

63

and left it at that. Still, that could mean anything. I could be in the shower and he'd need me, or on the toilet or getting a pap smear done, or I could even be masturbating and he'd need me…. God, I hoped it wouldn't be any times like those.

We ended up going through some client session times in the studio—I had to organize their courtesy calls, then make sure they showed up. Then while Mr. Jackson ran through some songs for some clients, I made sure Bibby Owen's—an up-and-coming artist, who I knew nothing about—tour schedule was smooth and all set. The whole time, Mr. Jackson had been short and snippy with his responses. Harpy, much to my relief that she hadn't joined us, either hadn't given it up the previous night or perhaps she'd still been tired. It had been enough having to deal with my boss, who was a regular ray of sunshine. Having Harpy parade around in slutty lingerie— as I was sure that was what she'd be wearing—would have pushed me over the edge. Not even coffee could have saved me.

By the end of that day in the office, I'd been exhausted. Seriously, my eyes felt like they were about to drop out of my head, bounce off my boobs, and fall to the floor, and hell, my feet ached more than a prostitute working her corner. Dylan had already called and told me he wouldn't see me that day, so I'd made my way up to the apartment on my own, with my own special key card for the elevator. I'd left the spare locked in my desk drawer. I would have been excited about the key, but being irritable, I'd dragged my feet. Who would have thought a thirteen-hour day, half sitting at the computer and the other half running from floor to floor doing Mr. Jackson's bidding would have made me feel like a train had run over me? Then again, I hadn't worked a long day in over four years.

However, the next two days were the same: waking to my door being pounded on, working nonstop, and putting up with Mr. Jackson's coldness.

Friday I would have gotten to sleep in until 6:00 a.m., that was if I hadn't already been up and ready sitting on the end of the bed waiting for Mr. Jackson to bang on my door. I had wanted to show him—when I opened the door—I was dressed and ready for the day.

After a half hour passed and he hadn't shown, I decided to take a calming breath and feed my beast of a belly, since it kept growling at me. I made my way out of the bedroom and into the kitchen. I always felt uncomfortable in the kitchen as it was set on Mr. Jackson's side. It was like I was intruding on his land. Though he assured me on my second day the cupboards and refrigerator were stocked, and I was free to help myself. I'd almost snorted when he explained the payment for that, and my rent, would come out of my weekly wage, so not exactly "free" then. But still, it was a great deal and who was I kidding, so luxurious I struggled to leave the damn place.

So tiptoeing into the kitchen, I sighed happily. Not only was the boss not around, but the way the sun shone through the floor-to-ceiling windows across from the kitchen was beautifully peaceful.

Walking to the refrigerator, I grabbed the creamer, and a yogurt to go with the fresh bananas I saw in the fruit bowl on the long counter behind me. Turning, with them in my hands, I screamed at the top of my lungs.

Shaken, I set the items on the counter and then held onto the edge. "You nearly scared me to death." I glared at the man who stood just inside the door to the right of the room.

"I thought you would have heard me. Then again, over your humming I suppose not." Mr. Jackson raised a brow at me and strode over to the coffee machine.

I was humming?

I hadn't realized.

Blushing, I shrugged and asked, "Ah, did you want some breakfast?"

He filled his mug, turned, and leaned his hip against the counter beside the refrigerator. Finally, he said, "No."

"Okay," I drew out. Even with the slight dip in my belly, I went about grabbing a bowl, which took me a while to find, cutting up a banana and then pouring yogurt over it. The whole time Mr. Jackson stood there and watched. There was no way I was going near the coffee machine while he stood in front of it, so I placed the creamer and yogurt back in the fridge.

Picking up my bowl, I went around the kitchen island and sat in the tall chair on the opposite side. I took a mouthful, chewed, swallowed, and then risked a glance at my boss. He remained leaning against the counter, only he was looking down at his phone in his hand. My shoulders sagged in relief. For a moment there, I thought he had watched me the whole time. To avoid the awkwardness in the kitchen, it would be best to work out when his schedule for eating was. Then I would eat before or after him.

It wasn't so bad if we had work spread out over the table and ate, which we'd done those first few early mornings, but since there was nothing but silence between us, I felt strange. I was in his home, his kitchen, eating food from his refrigerator, his cupboards. Didn't he find it weird also? He was still concentrating on his phone, so it seemed my being there didn't bother him, then again, I wasn't sure much did. It kind of sucked how put together the man acted and looked. Even in the earlier hours, he was still handsome.

"What?"

His question made me jump. "Sorry?" I asked.

"You've been staring at me like you have a question, so ask."

Shit. He knew I was looking at him. My cheeks heated. I looked down to my near empty bowl, and then back up, his eyes on me, waiting…. A question. I had to think of a question. "Ah, I was just thinking, um, I mean, isn't this strange for you? Having a stranger staying in your apartment, being in your kitchen?"

He glanced back to his phone before placing it in his back pocket. He straightened. "No." He started for the door that led into the formal living area where the elevator was.

"Aren't you going to brush your teeth?" I blurted. My eyes widened when his body suddenly stopped, and he slowly turned to me. All he had to do was raise a brow for me to cave and ramble some more. "You have your coffee black. Surely it can't be good for your teeth or breath. Isn't it always good to brush them before leaving for the office?"

Why in the world did I say that?

If he hadn't been standing there looking at me like I had lost my mind, I would have thumped my head against the counter.

With my spoon in my hand, I waved it in the air and added, "Sorry, none of my business. Carry on."

"I'm not sure you should be thinking about my mouth, Mrs. Mayfair."

Coughing through the air caught in my throat, I shook my head. "No. So not what you think. I won't. Not anymore. My lips are sealed. All welfare of your oral… ah, hygiene is up to you."

"Thank you, Mrs. Mayfair. I think I can handle my oral care from here on out. I have been doing it since I was a boy."

A boy? *And I honestly think my boss should not say the word oral around me ever again. Maybe I need to start a petition to have it taken from the workplace forever.*

"'Kay," I squeaked. It was then I saw his lips twitch. The man was teasing me. Dang it.

"See you at work, Mrs. Mayfair," he said and turned.

"Um," I started, and he looked over his shoulder. "Can you please call me Makenzie or Kenzie? Either is better than Mrs. Mayfair."

He nodded, and it didn't go unnoticed as he left that he didn't offer the same of himself. So I guessed I was stuck with calling him either Mr. Jackson or just boss. His intenseness shook my nerves. I never knew if he was in a good mood or not. I could not get a read on him at all. However, his teasing told me there was a side to my boss I never knew about. So even after the eventful, hardworking days where he would snap and act aloof, I thought there was a chance working alongside him could work, no matter his attitude.

Could was the main word I'd concentrate on.

After I cleaned the dishes and *brushed* my teeth, I made my way down to my desk. Darby, who worked a few desks over for one of Mr. Jackson's music managers, waved after I sat and met her eyes. She was also quite new and was by far the nicest on the floor, so I'd invited her to have lunch with me and my new colleagues, who were fast becoming friends, the previous day. We all got along well, which helped me get through the long day.

With each passing day, the guilt I felt for leaving Robert was easing. That was until my cell rang that morning and I glanced at the screen to see his name pop up. My stomach dropped while my heart took off in panicked flight. With a shaky hand, I silenced my phone and placed it back on my desk. Work was definitely not the place to have a conversation with my ex. I thought I would have had another week, since it was only Friday. He must have gotten back early.

Throughout the morning, my phone rang at least ten times. Every time I felt the vibrations on the desk, I jumped, and my heart jolted in my chest. My nerves were on edge, and I knew if I didn't deal with the dooming call soon, I would end up a mess by the end of the day, and it could lead me to make stupid mistakes with work. Something I couldn't afford because I didn't want to lose my job.

"Mrs. Mayfair," Mr. Jackson's deep voice said from behind me, making me jump in my seat. I looked over my shoulder at him. At first sight of my face, he arched a brow at whatever he saw. Then his face blanked. "I'm heading to a lunch meeting on the second floor. You may as well have your lunch now also. I've called for Helena."

Strange how he could call Helena by her name and yet, even after that morning, I was still Mrs. Mayfair.

"Thank you, sir," I mumbled and shifted my eyes back to the computer. I sensed him still behind me for a few moments more, and then he strode past. I sighed, my shoulders sagging.

"Kenzie, you going to lunch?" Darby called.

Biting my bottom lip, I nodded, and then said, "Actually, I have to make a call first. Um, can you watch the phone until Helena gets here, and then I'll meet you down there?"

"Sure can." She smiled.

Nodding, I stood and picked up my phone. I knew the only place I would get privacy was in Mr. Jackson's office. Taking a quick look around, I snuck in there without anyone noticing.

My hands shook, my heart pounded, and my belly sank.

Still, before my nerves got the best of me and I ran from the room like a chicken, I pressed Robert's name and placed the phone to my ear.

My hand trembled so badly I had to use my other hand to still it by wrapping it around my wrist.

While it rang, I walked over to the window and looked out, only I wasn't really seeing.

"Makenzie, where in the hell are you?" Robert answered.

"At work," I replied quietly. "Actually, I only have a moment. I just wanted to let you know I'll call you tonight."

I was met with silence on the other end.

"Robert?"

"You're at work?"

"Yes."

"I've been gone a week, and you have a job. Hell, you don't even call your husband to inform him." He sighed. "We'll talk about this when you get home."

"I-I'm not coming home, Robert. I told you this before you left."

"I gave you time, Makenzie. I thought you would have come to your senses, would have seen how much your action and words have hurt me. Your husband. Obviously you haven't, or you just don't care for my feelings at all."

"It's nothing like that, Robert. I do care about your feelings, and I hate that you're hurt by my decision to leave, it upsets me also—"

He snorted. "If it did, you would be home and not at some foolish job."

"I like my job," I whispered.

"Where are you even staying? At some hotel? How are you affording this? With my money? I can easily put a stop to your account, so you come home to take care of me."

My head dropped. I wasn't his nurse. I wasn't his mother. He didn't need to be cared for. Marriage was a partnership, and with Robert, it would never be like that.

"I only stayed at a hotel for the weekend. The job I have comes with a place to stay. You can cancel my card, Robert. I don't need it. I have a job, my own money now, and a roof over my head." Taking a deep breath, I added, "I'm also filing for divorce." I clenched my teeth together and waited for his reply.

"You're filing for divorce. *You?* After everything I've done for you. All the support I've given you. Are you sleeping with your boss, Makenzie? Is this how you got a job so quickly *and* a place to stay? You've become a hussy to get out of our marriage?"

"No! I would never cheat—"

"I guess it's good that I've been stepping out on you for the last year. I'm not even sure what I saw in you in the first place. You were overweight, awkward, and weird, even when we met. You had a strange family, a job that wasn't good enough. I thought I could help you out, guide you to be a better person. I guess I couldn't."

My ears were ringing, my eyes screwed tightly shut, and my breath… I couldn't seem to get enough air. "Y-you cheated on me for a year?"

"Well, I wasn't exactly getting it at home, and if I did, it was terrible."

Pain slashed through me. I shifted from one foot to another and rubbed at my forehead with the back of my hand. My head hurt. My heart ached. "A year?"

"Yes."

Standing straight, I wiped away the few stray tears I had let fall and glared out the window. "It's good I know this now." I nodded to myself. "The decision to leave you is finally an easy one. One I will no longer feel bad for—"

"Makenzie," Robert said quietly, a tone he used before he became sweet. He saw the error of his way, but I was no longer his lap dog.

"No, Robert. Thank you for telling me. I may have been overweight, hell, I still am if the things you say are anything to go by, but I don't care. You can shove your cruel words of how perfect every other woman is compared to me, how awkward I am, how strange my family is… you can take all your words and shove them right up your ass where I hope they'll fester and rot." I laughed without humor. "To think I was dreading this call because I was stupid enough to feel terrible about leaving you. To think I was worried about your pain, *your* feelings. I realize it's always been like this. You've molded me into a person who thought I wouldn't be able to live without you. A woman who deserved to put up with every harsh word you threw at me. No longer, Robert. The divorce papers will be in the mail by the end of next week, you prick."

"Makenzie, sweetheart. I didn't actually mean anything I said. I was hurt. I would never—"

"No. I don't want to hear it." I shook my head. "You'll just end up twisting everything in a way where I'll end up thinking *I* was in the wrong. I won't let you do it any longer. I'm taking back my life. I'm going back to the person I was before I met you, and that person would have told you you're a selfish motherfucking prick, asshole. A dickhead for what you've done to me. Goodbye, Robert." I hung up the phone, growled in the back of my throat, and then threw it to the floor. My chest heaved with every breath I took. I placed my hands on it, then ran one up to cup the back of my neck. "Holy shit," I breathed. "Holy crap," I whispered, and then a giggle escaped me. I covered my mouth with my hand.

Was I finally going mad?

No. I wasn't. Saying those words, finally calling Robert what I had wanted to for so long was… refreshing, thrilling, yet I was crippled with fear.

My hands went to my heated cheeks. "Oh, God." What had I done? What happened if everything I was trying to achieve failed? What happened if Robert was the only man God had created for me, and I just threw the chance all away?

I quickly went to my phone in the corner of the room and picked it up. It wasn't broken. Maybe I should call him back? Apologize for what I said?

"Don't," was ordered roughly behind me.

Screaming, I spun to see Mr. Jackson standing inside the room with the door closed behind him. His eyes were darker than normal, his stance stiff, with his arms crossed over his chest.

My eyes widened. With the phone in my hand, I shoved both hands behind my back and tensed. How long had he been in the room? "Y-your lunch meeting…. You, ah, you're not supposed to be here." To have heard any of that. Frantically, I looked around the room, refusing to meet his hard stare. "I'm sorry for, um, being in here. I'll, ah, just go to lunch." I made my way toward the door, only Mr. Jackson didn't shift.

Sighing, I looked at the floor and asked. "How much did you hear?"

He didn't answer.

"Am I fired?" I asked. "I mean, I know I shouldn't have been in your office without you here, but he kept calling. I needed…." God, my bottom lip trembled. There wasn't a chance I would cry in front of my boss though, no matter how many times Robert's hateful words of his cheating bombarded my mind. "It won't happen again." And even though my eyes were glassy with tears, I looked up with a narrowed stare and met Mr. Jackson's eyes.

"Take the rest of the day off," he ordered and moved away from the door.

"No." I shook my head. If I did, my mind would… I'd obsess over the call. "I would like to get back to work, please."

"Fine." He nodded once. "Send Helena to get you something for lunch."

Did he know I wouldn't be up for lunch with Angelia and everyone?

"Thank you," I whispered and went to the door. I heard him grunt behind me. I opened the door and walked out to stop at my desk where Helena was sitting. She looked up surprised to see me there. "Mr. Jackson asked if I could do some extra work. If you could grab me a sandwich from downstairs, I'll start what I have to."

She rolled her eyes. "If you tell me what's so pressing, I can deal with it so you can—"

"Helena," Mr. Jackson clipped behind me. I glanced there to see he had a folder in his hand. He must have forgotten something before his meeting, which was what led him back to his office. "Only Makenzie can deal with it, so get her lunch, and when you get back, go to lunch yourself."

My heart beat rapidly for a different reason. He'd called me Makenzie. Did that mean I could call him Grayson? Or sweetheart, honey-lumpkin, pookie-pie? My eyes widened.

Why was I suddenly thinking of calling him a pet name? If I could slap myself in that moment, I would have. I just had to put it down to Mr. Jackson being kind enough to help me out.

"Yes, sir." Helena purred, stood, and squeezed between myself and Mr. Jackson. I quickly sat down, placing my phone in a drawer in the desk.

Before I could thank my boss again, he was already off, striding toward the elevator.

Mr. Jackson was a puzzle.

One I wasn't sure I would be able to work out.

Surprisingly, I was fine with that.

Chapter SEVEN

ROBERT HADN'T CALLED again. I was convinced he would and was actually relieved but surprised with how quickly he'd given up. My mind had been all over the place in the last week, going from patting myself on the back for the way I'd handled things, to being petrified I'd screwed it all up. It wasn't until the end of the week before I realized I hadn't made it to my lawyers to get the paperwork started and sent off to my ex.

When Monday arrived, I found I didn't have to go to my lawyer because the company one paid me a visit just as Mr. Jackson left for another lunch meeting. By the time Helena came around for my lunch break, I had all the paperwork signed and Bob, the company's main lawyer, promised he'd have the papers served.

I knew Robert would have received the paperwork, yet he didn't call. It was then I finally reached the conclusion he wasn't going to give me any more grief over our relationship dissolving.

I found myself relieved Robert wasn't going to contact me, and I also felt warmed Mr. Jackson took it upon himself to set something up with the office lawyers.

Actually, for a second there, I honestly could have kissed the man. I had been dreading setting it all up, so Mr. Jackson had made it easier on me and I appreciated it.

After my boss had found me in his office, I had thought things would be awkward between us. They weren't. Well, of course things were never normal; nothing could be when dealing with a man like him.

Still, he never once brought up the situation he'd caught me in, and I was grateful for it.

What also helped was the fact I tried my best to dodge him when in the apartment. I studied his home schedule—when he would eat, work out or veg out, which wasn't often—so for a while, I managed to keep out of his space; mainly the kitchen when he was there.

Most of the time I had dodged him. Some days he would switch it up and come sneaking in the kitchen while I ate breakfast or dinner, scaring the bejesus out of me. I swear he was some sort of ninja who never made a sound. Each time he did it, his lips would twitch when I would accuse him of his ninja acts. In fact, I asked Dylan just that. We'd seen each other every now and then for either lunch or dinner in the first week. He'd invited himself over for dinner that night, so it was my perfect opportunity to investigate his brother's stealth-like skills.

"So, be honest, has your brother trained with a ninja master. I don't know, in the 'Deep Forest' or somewhere?" I admittedly used air quotes and made up the place.

Dylan cracked up laughing, so much he nearly choked on his mouthful of food.

Just as Dylan assured me his brother hadn't had any such training,

Mr. Jackson walked into the kitchen. I wasn't sure why, but my heart jumped an extra beat when I saw him. Or maybe it was just heartburn?

"You're here again," he noted to his brother.

"Can't seem to stay away from this lovely lady." Dylan smiled and winked at me. I rolled my eyes, used to his silly flirting.

My boss shook his head and grabbed a glass. "Makenzie, I need you to be up early in the morning."

"Ooh, Dad wants you to have an early night," Dylan taunted.

I pointedly ignored Dylan or else my thoughts would run wild with calling my boss Daddy while he spanked me…. Jesus, where was my mind going with such scenarios?

Clearing my throat, I said, "Don't worry, Mr. Jackson. I'll be bright-eyed and bushy-tailed in the morning for the conference."

"You're still letting her call you Mr. Jackson, brother?" Dylan laughed. "Kenzie, just call him Grayson. He won't bite your head off for it."

"No, it's fine. Mr. Jackson is my boss, and—"

"You live with him."

I blushed, hating my inability to get control of my embarrassment. "Not really, I mean—"

"Makenzie," Mr. Jackson clipped. I quickly shut up and looked at him. He took a sip of his orange juice and then said, "Call me Grayson."

"But—"

He arched a brow at me. Again, my lips clamped shut. *Grayson.* I ran through my mind. I liked saying his name. I'd never met another Grayson, and I found the name just rolled off my tongue, as if my tongue got a thrill from saying it. Dylan looked from me to his brother and then back to me. He did it a few more times.

"Interesting," he murmured. His comment puzzled me. My brows drew down wondering what he meant by it.

"What?" Grayson bit out with a glare for his brother. I wanted to know what was interesting as well.

Dylan smiled, leaned back in his chair, and shrugged. "Nothing at all."

It was all too strange and cryptic. No doubt some sort of ninja speak, but the moment passed, and before long I said good night to Dylan and headed to bed.

I saw Dylan a lot more the following week. Nearly every day he called, and three times he stopped by the apartments to eat dinner with me. I enjoyed his company, so I didn't mind at all, but I had a feeling his frequent visits were to annoy Grayson in some way. How I didn't have a clue. Their brotherly relationship was strange, but it fit. Anyone could see they were fond of one another.

At first, I felt awkward calling Grayson by his name. I actually refused to do so in the workplace. There he would always be Mr. Jackson, and when I saw him on the apartment floor and we spoke, then I called him Grayson. The first time I did it, as I was coming out of the elevator onto our floor and he was heading in to go to the gym, I'd smiled and said, "Enjoy your workout, Grayson." I wanted to test out his name on my lips instead of in my mind, and I enjoyed how it sounded aloud. Then my head tilted sideways when I saw a look in his eyes I didn't understand. The elevator doors closed without him saying anything in return.

Shutting out the memory, I opened my walk-in closet door, so I could look at myself in the floor-length mirror. I was about to walk out my door to attend a dinner meeting with Grayson. I didn't understand why I had to be there. His usual lunch or dinner meetings were held with just himself and his client, and then he'd come back with his notes on what I had to do. Still, he had asked for my attendance, so when I found out we were going to an elegant restaurant, I dressed in a short-sleeved floor-length, dark green dress. Lace covered the chest area, where it then dipped and tightened into the green satin and then flared out from just above my hips. It was my favorite dress, one I only purchased a month before leaving my ex and one I hadn't had a chance to wear as yet. My black hair was styled in a messy, but fashionable bun, a few curly stray bits dangling down to surround my face. My makeup was light, only because I never really knew how to wear it and I also hated the feeling it left my skin in.

Slipping on my black heels, I nodded to myself in the mirror and walked out of my room. I pulled my shoulders back, feeling confident and excited about the night. As soon as I grew closer to the formal living area, where Grayson said he would meet me, I heard two voices. One male and deep, which told me my boss was there, and the other was female and annoying.

Harpy was in the house.

God, was she going also?

Over the last two weeks, I had seen her here and there. Sometimes meeting with Grayson in his office, other times as I was walking from the kitchen and she was exiting his side of the apartment. Which told me she had just been in his bedroom, with him… not that I cared. That was ridiculous.

I didn't.

I don't.

She just drove me insane with her catty looks and her upturned nose.

Opening the door, I stepped through, and their conversation stopped. I glanced up to see both of them looking at me. Grayson was in a tailored suit, looking handsome, and Harpy was wearing a long, red satin dress. At least I wasn't overdressed, but by the shocked expressions on their faces—well, at least Grayson's only flashed to shock for a second—I was sure I had something wrong with the way I looked. I had an urge to ask them if I needed to change, if I looked okay or too fat in the dress. It did seem a little tighter than normal. I didn't want to embarrass my boss in front of his client. However, I clamped my mouth shut. The old Makenzie would have asked Robert because she would have wanted to please him. The Makenzie who was back to her old, better self, kept her mouth shut because I didn't care if they were judging me for how I looked, and kept on walking.

"We had better be going, right? The reservation was for seven?" I asked, heading toward the elevator.

"Yes," Grayson answered.

I felt them at my back. We all stood in an awkward silence, one where I felt the need to fidget. Instead, I gripped my hands tightly around my clutch purse.

"If she's going, doesn't she need some paper and a pen to take notes?" Harpy, which I had to stop calling her, or I would mess up and say it aloud, said behind me.

Glancing over my shoulder, I smiled, waved my purse in the air, and said, "I have it under control." Since I didn't want to look like a fool taking notes while we all ate, I'd placed a voice recorder in my bag. It would do all the work for me. I supposed I could have just given it to Grayson so he could record it all for me. Then again, I hadn't been out in a long time. I was looking forward to a nice meal, a glass of champagne, and I was also going to try to enjoy the company.

If only Dylan were going.

Silence. All the way down to the main floor. I followed Harpy—damn it—Harper and Grayson out through the lobby wondering why we weren't taking one of Grayson's cars when I saw a limousine parked out the front. An older man, in his sixties at least, stood at the rear door. He gave us a nod and opened the door. Both Harper and Grayson got in without saying a word.

I stopped, smiled at the man, and said, "Thank you."

"My pleasure, miss."

Climbing in, I sat off to one side while Harper and Grayson sat next to each other on the back seat. Harper—yeah, twice in a row I'd gotten her name right—leaned into Grayson and whispered something. He grunted. At least I wasn't the only one he grunted at.

Instead of watching them out the corner of my eyes, I chose to take in the limousine. I hadn't been in one since my wedding day, even then it was smaller than the one I was in. There was a drink station opposite me, and I would have loved to have poured myself a large stiff drink. I refrained. If I got drunk, I never knew what would come out of my mouth.

The drive was torture. I wanted to beat my head against the side window with how quiet and awkward it felt.

When we arrived at the front of the restaurant, I noticed there was a queue waiting. When the driver opened the door, Grayson climbed out first, his hand came in, and Harper took it with a smug smile sent my way.

"Come on," I heard her say. I looked out to see her pull Grayson toward the front door. At least the driver was nice enough to help me out.

"Thanks again."

"Have a nice dinner." He smiled.

Rolling my eyes, I said, "I'll try."

He chuckled.

"Mrs. Mayfair," Grayson clipped my name. My last name always seemed to be clipped during work hours.

Looking over, he was waiting with Harper just at the entrance. Apparently we were cutting the line. Something Robert would have sold his shriveled-up nuts to be able to do. My smile brightened at the thought.

I quickly rushed over after the goodbye to the driver and stopped just behind them. As we entered, I held back my gasp. The place was beautiful. Not as big as I thought it would be. The ceiling was high with a huge chandelier right in the middle. Under it there was a circular area of booths, but only about five. The walls were also lined with large booths, each seeming to have their own private wall set between them. To the far wall, opposite the entrance, was a bar, only in front of it was a tall iron fence with a vine crawling all over it.

I heard a sigh and turned to see Grayson looking down at me. His lips thinned; he seemed frustrated with me.

"Sorry." I smiled. "This place it amazing though."

His lips twitched, something I got a thrill from seeing. Why? I didn't have a clue. He turned, and with a hand to Harper's back, he led her toward a booth to the left of the room. I quickly followed.

"Does she have any class at all?" Harper asked Grayson. Thankfully, he didn't answer, or I just didn't hear it.

Maybe I did lack class for such a place. Only, I didn't give a flying fuck. If having class meant I acted like I had a pole stuck up my ass, as Harper did, I didn't want anything to do with it.

As we moved closer to what I assumed was our booth, I noticed two men were already sitting there. One older, around fifty, the other younger. The men stood, and the older man already had his hand out for Grayson.

Grayson turned his attention to Harper and my way after shaking the man's hand. "This is Harper, and my assistant, Makenzie." No explanation of who Harper was to him, something I thought was strange, and from the quick frown from Harper, she did too. "Ladies, this is Ethan Tucker and his uncle, slash manager, Monty."

"It's a pleasure," Harper purred, going right in for a cheek kiss.

Looking to the floor so no one could see my eye roll, I waited for them to greet her back and then glanced up smiling, and said, "Nice to meet you both." I then thrust out my hand to first Monty, who grinned and replied with a, "How you doin', darlin'?"

"Good, thank you." I moved my hand to Ethan. He took it slowly, and then I jolted when he ran his thumb over the top of my hand. Did his hand want to make out or something?

His eyes bore into mine, his smile more of a flirty smirk. God, the guy could be my baby brother; he looked to be around twenty tops. "Mr. Jackson's assistant, right?"

Flushed, I nodded and gently tugged on my hand. He didn't let go. "Y-yes."

"Good to know." He winked. Maybe Ethan had been sucking back some shots before we arrived.

"Ethe, take a seat and stop flirting," Monty demanded with a laugh. That was flirting? *Huh, okay, wow.* Finally, Ethan dropped my hand. He chuckled and turned into the booth. Monty continued before he slid in after his nephew, "Sorry, 'bout that. He can't seem to help himself when it comes to good-lookin' women."

I bit my bottom lip to stop the giggle wanting to escape. The only reason I found it funny and pleasing was the scowl on Harper's face. She quickly wiped it away and slid in the other side of the booth, so she was next to Ethan, who in turn ignored her.

Grayson moved in to sit beside Harper and that left me with a choice to either sit next to him or Monty. There was enough room in the booth on both sides.

Before they noticed I was standing around looking to both sides, trying to make up my mind like a fool, and worrying about sitting so close to Grayson and having his scent affect me like it did every morning he came into the kitchen, I decided to sit by Monty.

He gave me a warm smile, which I returned. I looked across the table and knew I hadn't made the right decision when I saw Grayson staring back. I should have sat next to him, at least then I wouldn't have to face him through the whole meeting.

My cheeks heated, and I averted my eyes to the table. His scent drove me wild, but his eyes… they were a whole other story. Usually they didn't hold much in them; only certain moments would he let it slip and show a hint of his emotions.

Those times were mainly when his brother was around, and I could see the warmth he held for Dylan in them.

His eyes were intimidating most times, except then.

"Who wants a drink?" Monty asked, waving down a waiter.

My eyes flicked to Grayson, to see him lean back in his seat. "I would like to know why you were so adamant about a meeting with me first, Monty."

Monty smiled. "Come on, Grayson. I'm sure you can have a drink, eat, and relax before we get down to business."

Grayson smiled. "I find it better to get business out of the way first before relaxing."

Monty leaned forward, resting his elbows on the table while he studied Grayson. Harper shifted closer to Ethan to whisper something into his ear. He shook his head and stared at his uncle before his eyes moved to me, and he winked again. A smile slipped onto my lips, and I shook my head at him. Yes, he'd been sipping something before we arrived, I was sure of it, and I'd ignore his clear sober eyes.

"Good evening, my name is Marcus, and I'll be your server tonight. What can I get you to drink first?"

Glancing up, I noticed Marcus eyed first Grayson, Harper, Ethan, Monty, and then me with a pleasant smile on his young face.

"Can you give us about ten and come back?" Monty asked.

"Certainly."

As soon as Marcus left, Monty said, "You've seen the footage of Ethan singing. Sure you saw how good he is and he's already got a decent size fan base."

"Yes?"

"The music producers he's currently with aren't doing shit for him. They put him on the back burner because Ethan didn't want to use some of their songs, and let me tell you, the songs they picked would have turned Ethan's career to shit."

"What makes you think I won't do the same?"

"Heard you're fair. You're good at choosing the right songs for singers. I want—"

"Makenzie." Harper interrupted. The look Grayson gave her was deadly, though she didn't see it as she was too busy sneering at me. "Why don't you go to the bar and fetch us some drinks." She giggled. "I'm sure I can handle your job for you." Her hand came up, and she wiggled her fingers at me.

I bit back my desire to throat punch her and call her out on her shit—hell, did I look like a waiter?—but there was no chance I could afford to cause a scene. Sometimes it was just easy to swallow the bullshit and play nice, as much as it pained me.

Not wanting to look to Grayson or to take more time away from the business talk, I gave her the voice recorder I already had on my lap and stood.

Smiling sweetly in her direction, attempting to be über professional, I asked, "I'll be back shortly. What would everyone like to drink?"

"Just bring us a stout, darlin'," Monty said.

"Champagne." Harper grinned. I turned to walk off when Harper called out, "You didn't take Grayson's order."

I went to answer, but Grayson got there first with his clipped, rough tone. "She already knows what I want. Can we get back to fuckin' business now?"

Suck on those eggs, Harpy.

I didn't look back to see Harper's expression; I only hoped she'd paled. Grayson hated interruptions when business was on the table. Though I did hear Monty give off a chuckle.

I wasn't sure what Harper was playing at with her ordering me to get drinks like some minion beneath her. Not that I cared. The scene she made and the way Grayson looked peeved was enough for me.

Walking behind the vined divider, I saw the bar was busy, so I knew I'd be away from the table a while. I stood back until there was a parting in the group and then squeezed in. The waiters were already taking other orders at either end of the bar.

"Makenzie?"

Startled to hear my name, I turned left. "Mr. Muller?"

He smiled and moved to my side. "I thought I asked you to call me Randal."

Chapter EIGHT

Not in a million years did I think I would ever see Randal Muller again, the man who had been there the day I had an epiphany and left Robert.

He looked good, really good, just like the day I met him. He was wearing a dark suit, a smile, and then his lips moved.

"Huh?" I asked, flushed and then said, "Sorry, um, pardon?"

He chuckled. "I said, I would have never thought to see you here tonight, but I'm glad I have." He quickly glanced around, with his brows pinched. "Is Robert here with you?"

Shaking my head, I licked my dry lips. His eyes went there, and again my cheeks heated. "No, I'm here with my boss. I mean, he's at a dinner meeting, and I'm here to take notes."

He smiled. "You got a job, that's great. Where are you working?"

Just as I was about to tell him, the bartender called, "What can I get you?"

I glanced over the bar and smiled. "Can I get two stouts, one champagne, any kind, a scotch, dry, no ice, and a mineral water please?" Looking to Randal, I asked, "Sorry, did you want anything?"

"No, I'm good."

The bartender went to get the drinks, and I turned back to Randal. "Am I keeping you from a date?"

He smirked, his hand gently taking hold on my elbow. "No, I actually had a business meeting myself." He glanced around quickly and then leaned in closer to say, "I honestly thought Robert didn't want you to get a job."

Biting my bottom lip, I looked to the floor and then to Randal. I let out a sigh and admitted into his ear, "He wouldn't have, but… I left him." I was surprised at how easy it was to tell Randal, but I was sure what helped was the fact he didn't seem to like my ex that day either.

His pulled his head back to meet my stare. "Really?"

"Yes." I nodded.

He hummed under his breath and then leaned in again. Only that time, I stiffened. I wasn't sure why, but for some reason I didn't want him too close, suddenly feeling awkward. He said, "I'm glad you did, Makenzie. I wasn't a fan of the way he was talking to you."

I didn't know what to say, so I shrugged. My heart suddenly felt like it was taking a dive off the highest tower.

"That'll be forty-five sixty," the bartender interrupted.

Once I had added them to the table's tab, I glanced back to Randal, who had shifted back, releasing my arm to see his eyes raking up my body slowly. When he met my gaze, he grinned. Not fazed he'd been caught checking me out. I swallowed nervously, confused as hell why he'd bother checking me out.

"You never did say where you're working now."

"She works for me," came a gruff voice from behind me.

My whole body tensed. I watched Randal's eyes shift from me to Grayson, who stood close, as in *really close,* behind me.

His arm came around, held out toward Randal. "Grayson Jackson, and you are?"

Randal took Grayson's hand and shook, then said, "Randal Muller. I had the pleasure of meeting Makenzie a few weeks ago."

Grayson grunted. "And I have the pleasure of having her as my assistant at Jackson's Media."

"Ah, music man. Right. I'm an architect."

"Right."

What in the heck is going on?

Did Grayson move an inch closer?

I wasn't positive, but the fact his body heat warmed me was a good indication.

"Kenzie," Grayson's low, growly voice said right near my ear. Oh, God. He shortened my name. That was the first time he'd done it. "We've wrapped up the business deal. It's time to order food so we can get home."

My eyes widened.

Did he just insinuate what I thought he had?

"You live together?" Randal asked. His voice, no longer pleasant, held an edge to it.

"We do," Grayson answered.

"Not like that," I rushed out and then laughed nervously. "I mean, yes, we live together, but I'm his assistant. If he has a need for me, I'm there, at his beck and call." Shit, I was making things worse. From the heat in my cheeks, I was sure they were aflame and had spiked the room's temperature by at least fifteen degrees. Grayson grunted behind me only it was different from his usual one; he sounded amused.

"I'm sure." Randal snorted.

"Wait, it's not like that. He had all his past assistants stay at his apartment. I work for him, but I sleep in a different area than him. Besides, he has a girlfriend, Harpy." I gasped. "I mean Harper. Her name is Harper, and she's really beautiful. She's a supermodel. All gorgeous and skinny and… nothing like me." I let off a nervous laugh. "I mean come on, I'm not his type at all and—" *I need to shut up.* "It was nice to see you again, Randal, but I had better get these drinks back." I picked up the tray beside me.

"Makenzie," Randal called, and I looked to him. He was now smiling. "Here." I watched his hand place a card on the tray. "If you want to get a coffee sometime, just call me." It was then he leaned in, ignoring the grumble behind us from my boss, and kissed my cheek. Then he whispered, "You may not be his type, but you are mine." He stepped back, took in my shocked face, chuckled, and walked off.

I couldn't move. I was honestly flabbergasted. Randal Muller had said I was his type. He wanted to get coffee. With me.

My hands shook, making the drinks rattle.

"Goddamn it, let me take it," Grayson clipped, and took the tray from me. I stared blankly up at him; he was studying me. "You didn't expect him to ask you out?"

My head jerked back. "Well, no."

"Even after all the flirting he was doing?"

Tilting my head to the side, I asked, "He was?" I had thought, but I wasn't positive.

His jaw clenched. "Jesus," he bit out with a shake of his head. "Come on." He turned on his heels and stalked back to the table.

"Finally," Harper cried. As soon as I sat down, she asked, "What took you so long? God, you can't even do one simple, quick task, you take—"

"Sorry about that, I got caught with an old friend. Oh good, here comes the waiter, I'm ready to order. Anyone else hungry?"

"Sure am, darlin'. Talkin' business can make anyone hungry." Monty grinned at me. "Looks like you'll be seein' us around a bit. Grayson's decided to give Ethe a chance."

"Oh, that's great." I smiled.

Ethan winked. "I think you being around will make the move to the city worthwhile."

Grayson's grunt was loud enough for us to all hear. "I doubt you'll see her actually."

"We'll see," Ethan replied with a shrug.

What was going on? Both Ethan and Randal seemed to be flirting with me; at least I thought they were. God, never in a million years did I think something like that would happen. I wasn't ugly, but I did have extra weight compared to women like Harper, and I was sure I embarrassed myself every time I spoke. Or…

"Do I have a sign on my forehead saying I haven't had sex in years, please flirt with me?" Not that I minded, the attention was sweet, something I hadn't had in such a long time. So long I didn't know how to take it or act about it or actually believe it.

Suddenly, Monty burst out in a guffawing laugh. Ethan chuckled and said, "Not that I can see."

Grayson choked on his drink, enough that it spurted out of his mouth landing on the table. Next, he was coughing.

Harper was just glaring at me.

My hand went over my mouth. I turned my wide eyes to Monty and whispered, "Did I say that aloud?"

"You sure did, sweetheart."

My whole body flushed. "I am *so* sorry. I was sure I said it in my head. Still, that was no way to speak in front of clients."

"I don't mind, you, uncle?" Ethan said, his mouth in a big smile.

Monty scoffed. "Not at all. Hell, made the night, I reckon."

Shaking my head, I moved my eyes to the table and said, "No, it wasn't right. Please forgive me." I looked up to Monty and Ethan. "Sometimes my mouth has a mind of its own. I'm trying to curb it. My husband hated it when it happened. In fact, he—"

"You're married?" Ethan asked.

"Well, no, we split a few weeks ago—"

He winked. "That's good to know."

Shifting uncomfortably in the seat, I looked out into the restaurant and saw a waiter. Quickly, I waved him over, "Oh look, a waiter. Let's order." *So we can eat, and I can go home to die of humiliation.* I was too scared to look at my boss. What I had said was so inappropriate I was terrified it had cost me my job.

So throughout the rest of dinner, I ate, talked with Monty and Ethan, while Grayson added his bit here and there. Though, when he did, I never glanced his way and Harper seemed to be pouting for some reason in the corner. Complaining of this and that while she did it. Her soup was too cold, her steak too raw, the lighting was too dim.

Thank God for Monty and Ethan. They kept the night fun for me.

We were all standing outside waiting for our cars when Ethan asked, "Makenzie, would you like a lift home?"

"Oh, um, thank you—"

"Won't be necessary, she lives with me."

Sighing, I palmed my forehead. Not this conversation again.

Harper laughed loudly. "She may live in the same apartment, but not exactly with you, silly." She looked to Ethan, and added, "They're on opposites sides of the home." She curled her hand in the crook of Grayson's elbow. "Grayson has always liked his help close so they can deal with the menial things."

Ethan snorted. "Sure, sugar." Looking back to me, he rolled his eyes. I stifled a giggle. "I guess I'll see you at work," he said and then leaned in. That was when I got my second cheek kiss that night.

I took hold of his arm, so he stayed close, and I whispered, "I think you're really handsome and I love that you think I deserve your attention, but you're young enough to be my baby brother."

"Let's go with stepbrother at least. Then the flirting won't feel too taboo." He kissed my cheek again. "You deserve a lot of attention, Makenzie."

"Ethan," Monty called from their truck.

Ethan grinned. "See you soon." He turned, shook Grayson's hand, said something, and then, completely ignoring Harper, he got in the truck and they disappeared.

Let the awkwardness begin.

Thank God our limousine was the next to come forward. Grayson had the door open before the driver even got out of the car. Harper climbed in first and then Grayson turned to me, his brow raised.

"Ah, you can go next."

"Makenzie," was all he said.

"No really, you hop on in."

"Makenzie." My name was growled low.

Rolling my eyes, I went over to the car and climbed in, moving to the left so Grayson could sit next to Harper, which he did, once he was in.

Glancing out the corner of my eyes, I saw Grayson lean forward and press some button. "Bill, could you take us to 25 Rowe Street first, please?"

"Certainly, sir."

"But I thought I was staying at your place tonight," Harper whined.

"After showing up uninvited when you knew I had a business meeting and then the way you acted tonight, I think not."

Oh. My. God!

The tension in the car was the highest I had ever felt. A need to change the subject, or even to do something filled me.

"Sooo, how about them Dodgers? Been playing a good game this season. At least the weather has held out for them."

I swear I saw Grayson's lips twitch. While Harper glared at me and then hissed, "Just shut up."

I bit my lips between my teeth and shifted on the seat to face forward. I was just lucky the car soon came to a stop.

The door opened quickly, so I presumed Grayson had opened it. They both slid out.

The door closed, and it was then I heard harsh words being said near the car. They weren't close enough for me to make out what was being said, but I looked out in time to see Harper shout one last thing before she stomped off into her apartment building.

Quickly, I turned back to face the front and jumped out of my skin when I heard the door being opened. I sensed Grayson climb in, heard the door being pulled shut, and then the car was moving once again.

Was he okay?

Did they break up right there in front of me?

Did he need consoling?

Why was I thinking of consoling him?

He was my boss; I shouldn't even be thinking of consoling him. Of taking him in my arms while he cried. While he buried his head in my chest and sobbed…. *Stop.*

I had to think of something else.

Sing a song of sixpence, a pocket full of rye. Four and twenty blackbirds baked in a pie.

"Really, why would someone make up a nursery rhyme about birds being baked in a pie?"

"Is that what you were humming?" Grayson asked, causing me to squeak and jolt.

Groaning, I asked, "I said that aloud?"

"Yes."

"Sorry, but yes, I was humming it."

"How is it I haven't noticed your fumbling mouth before?"

Turning in the seat so I could see him, I shrugged, my hands fidgeting on my lap. "I guess we haven't really been around each other for long periods of time, and I happen to do it more when I'm nervous, really nervous."

"Why were you nervous back at the restaurant?"

"Ah, Randal and… yeah, Randal." And the fact I felt your body heat so close to mine. God, abort that thought in case you blurt something else. "And, um, Ethan."

He didn't say anything, only studied me.

"I really am sorry, about, um, before…. Could I lose my job for it?"

"No."

My body relaxed back into the seat. "Thank you." I licked my dry lips, found some courage and asked, "Are you okay?"

His brow arched. "Why wouldn't I be?"

I thumbed out the window. "You know, back there with Harper."

"You mean Harpy." He smirked.

Groaning, my hand went over my face. "You were never supposed to hear that. Besides, Dylan was the one who came up with it."

I might as well throw his brother under the bus.

Grayson actually snorted. "That doesn't surprise me."

Silence.

I was never good with silence.

"So, are you?"

"Am I what?"

"Okay?"

"Do you always need to fill the air with talk?"

I pretended to think about it. "Yes." I nodded. He grunted, and then I went on, "You never answered."

Oh wow, he rolled his eyes at me. "That's because I chose not to."

"Well, you could have just said that," I grumbled, crossing my arms over my chest. To the floor, I admitted, "I'm not sure my coming to the dinner meeting tonight was a good thing."

"How's that?"

"Well, I failed at getting drinks in an appropriate time. I blurted out a really rude thing, and I think the more I'm around you, the more you could think I'm a little too crazy for the job."

Glancing to him, I saw he was watching me once again. Finally, he said, "It shouldn't have been your job to get drinks. Yes, you seem to have blurted out an inappropriate matter, yet the clients didn't seem to care at all. In fact, they found it quite amusing and seemed very taken with you. Lastly, you're not crazy, just different… in a good way."

"Well… okay then," I said and tried to will my heart to slow in my chest. Suddenly, I felt like rubbing up against him and purring. I clenched my fists and crossed my legs to keep from moving.

When we arrived at the apartment, I climbed out first and then thanked Bill, the driver, with a hug. He chuckled good-naturedly. I then walked into the building, waving at Mike, the security guy.

Grayson met me at the elevator. As it opened and I stepped in, Grayson called my name.

"Yes?" I asked, leaning against the wall.

He leaned next to me and looked down in my direction. "You said you… blurt stuff out when you're nervous."

"That's right." I nodded.

His eyes shifted back to the doors before he noted, "You seem to do it just about every time I'm around for long periods of time."

I balked. "Ah—"

"Do I make you nervous, Makenzie?"

Should I lie?

Could he smell a lie? Sense it? He seemed very perceptive.

"Yes," I whispered.

"Good."

Why was it good?

My breath was suddenly erratic. My body shivered as goose bumps danced across my skin. Was there a draft in the elevator?

The night was full of surprises.

First Ethan, a younger man who seemed taken with me for some reason. Then Randal, the touches, the looks, and then once he knew I was no longer with Robert, he made his intentions clear.

He thought I was his type. Maybe I should call him. I didn't think I would make such a fool out of myself in front of him, like I did Grayson. Then again….

Looking through my purse, I scrunched up my nose. Where was his card?

"What are you looking for?" Grayson asked as the doors opened to our floor.

Walking out, I said, "Randal's card." Spinning around, I asked, "Do you know if I left it on the tray?"

"You didn't."

"So I placed it in my purse?" I wasn't sure I did.

"No."

"On the table?" I asked.

"No."

"Did I drop it on the floor?"

"No."

Growling under my breath, I threw up my hands and asked, "Do you know where it is?"

"Yes."

I rolled my hands in front of myself, wanting him to continue.

"I threw it in the trash on the way out."

I stiffened. "You did what?"

He then smiled, and I wanted to reach out and grab something because his smile did something to me on the inside.

"Good night, Makenzie." He made his way toward his side of the apartment.

"Now hang on one second, boss." When he turned with a small smile playing on his lips, I asked, "Why did you throw it away?"

"I didn't see him fit for a suitor."

My eyes widened. "You didn't… *what*?" I breathed.

He sighed. "You've just come from a marriage, Makenzie. You need time. Any man would give you that. Unless he's a fucking dickhead like Randal."

My mouth dropped open.

I guess…

He had a point.

I did need time, and Randal, knowing how long ago I was with Robert, should have known that. Then again. "He was only asking to go for coffee."

He scoffed. "A coffee means a lot of things, and with the way he was looking at you, it meant he wanted you in his bed right after that coffee."

My head jerked back. "Really?" I bit my bottom lip and blushed.

"Go to bed, Makenzie. If the guy is really interested in you, for more than just fucking, then he'll find another way to reach out to you."

Nodding, I said, "Um. Thank you, for looking out for me."

He grunted and then continued on to his own space.

Chapter Nine

God, I loved weekends. Not only did I get to sleep in, but I also got to do anything I wished. When I was with Robert, we did everything he wanted. He hated the movies, so we never went, and I didn't like going on my own. It made me feel like a loser for some reason, so I missed out on many great shows.

That day, Dylan was taking me to the movies and then for a late dinner at some dive of a bar, who had the best food apparently. I was looking forward to it.

Stretching, I flung back the blankets and climbed out of bed. Another good thing about weekends was I usually had the kitchen to myself. Grayson was either already working, because he never stopped, or out doing whatever a billionaire did on weekends. Thankfully, my work didn't run into weekends, yet. He'd told me he wouldn't need an assistant Saturday and Sunday. However, there could be times I was called in, but so far, I hadn't.

Besides, he also had weekend staff. The business was never closed; he had too many important clients to look after.

Donning my robe, I made my way out of my quarters and went in search of some coffee and a bagel. As I poured myself a mug, I couldn't help but think about the previous night. Sleep had been sparse because I couldn't comprehend Randal and Ethan's actions. I was sure there were many other women vying for their attention, yet they seemed to have latched their advances onto me for some reason.

I took a sip of my coffee and placed a bagel into the toaster.

Then there was Grayson. My boss. Who was sweet enough to look out for me. Though I had no idea why he'd been looking out for me. Honestly, I never thought I would think of Grayson as sweet, yet there I was. Maybe he thought I was too good at my job and a new relationship could cause problems with my work.

I didn't know.

However, I was grateful for his actions.

Before I got to prep the coffee machine, I picked up my phone and pressed the button for music. As soon as one of my favorite songs came on, "Girl Crush" by Little Big Town, I started humming away.

Soon enough, the words registered and a thought of Grayson popped into my head. It was a wicked thought. A thought I shouldn't have had about the man who signed my paycheck.

Still, I let the words from the song fall from my lips.

After some time, a throat cleared loudly behind me. A scream built from deep within my belly and then erupted out of my mouth. I spun to see Grayson standing on the other side of the kitchen counter gazing at me with a raised brow.

That damn brow of his, I wanted to shave the condescending item off.

And then, right there, his lips twitched.

Glaring, I pressed Pause and pointed at him, snapping, "You have to stop doing that or one day, I'll either pee myself or have a heart attack, and it will be all your fault."

"You have a good voice, and that is one song I wished I or my songwriters had written."

I looked everywhere but at him. "Thanks. It's really a good song."

"Have you ever thought of singing—"

A laugh escaped me. "No. No way never. My nerves would eat me alive. I'm a closet singer, and that's how I want it to stay."

He actually smirked, nodded, and said, "Fair enough." When his eyes flicked to my chest, I looked there and blushed. My robe had come open, and I was flashing the swell of my breast. I quickly closed it and tied it tightly around me, turning back to the counter to grab my bagel. I shifted his way, to where the butter and cream cheese were.

Clearing my throat, I mentioned, "You're not usually around on the weekends."

"I can have downtime, Makenzie."

I snorted. Raising my gaze to his, I rolled my eyes, then went back to buttering my bagel. "Sure, okay, Grayson."

"I don't work all the time," he stated, his voice lowering with annoyance.

I hummed under my breath and fought smiling.

"Last weekend I went and played racquetball."

Through my lashes, I looked up at him. "And did anyone from the office go with you? Did you talk business?"

"It doesn't matter who was there or what we talked about."

"Okay, sir." I laughed, then took a bite of my breakfast. While chewing, I tilted my head to the side and stared at him. For once he wasn't in a suit, but a tee and jeans. How was it possible he looked even better?

"So, you're not going into the office today at all?" I asked after swallowing.

He ignored me until after he came around the counter and got himself a coffee. "I didn't say that exactly."

"Ha!" I shouted. He sighed before he took a sip of his coffee and leaned his hip against the counter next to me. "When was the last day off for you?" I asked. I took another bite and then another while he thought about his answer, which told me enough; he couldn't even remember the last time he'd had a day off. "Don't worry, your silence is enough." I grinned. He grunted in response. Then I added, "I didn't know you wore casual clothing on weekends."

He shrugged. "Unless there is a meeting, I do." We fell into a comfortable silence. I finished my bagel and coffee, and Grayson finished his bland drink. "Tell me what a normal person would do on weekends then?" he asked.

Smiling, I said, "Well, Dylan and I are going to the movies and then dinner later. Before that, I thought about going to the library. I haven't read a good book in some time. The ones I used to read Robert hated. Thought them tasteless, so I stopped." I bit my bottom lip.

"Why a library? Why not one of those Kindle things?"

"I love to hold a book instead of a device. Our lives will soon be ruled by technology, if not already."

"Why not buy the book then? I think I pay you enough to do so."

"Oh, I will. If I truly love the book, I'll buy it so I can reread it."

"You'd reread a book?"

"Heck yes." I grinned. "A story your mind gets lost in, where you feel what the characters feel isn't enough to read just once. It's something you want to experience over and over. The love, lust, betrayal, loss… everything. A good book can get your heart pumping, your belly dipping, and your body tingling. It's something a person can experience, no matter how many times you read it."

"You really love to read." I heard the humor in his voice.

Heat filled my cheeks as I walked back around the counter to the sink. I peeked out the corner of my eye before taking my plate to rinse it.

"Sorry, sometimes I get carried away. Reading is something my mother was passionate about."

"Don't apologize. I've never met anyone so taken with reading."

Nodding, I turned the tap on, rinsed my dishes, then placed them in the dishwasher. I was yet to meet the elves that cleaned the house or did the food shopping. It usually happened when we were both at work.

"You were close with your mother?"

Straightening, I turned and pressed back against the counter, meeting Grayson's stare. "Yes. She was amazing. Kind, smart, beautiful."

"What happened?"

I moved my eyes from his face to the floor. "Cancer."

"Cancer fucking sucks."

A laugh brought my gaze to his. "Yes, it really does. Can I ask… your parents?" I knew they were dead, but that was all.

"Were never really parents. They aren't worth the breath to even talk about them."

"I'm sorry."

"I'm not. Really, it got me to where I am today."

I smiled, teasingly. "A workaholic."

He chuckled. I loved his laugh. It twisted my belly in a pleasant way. When I heard it, I took the time to watch, to listen, and to cherish.

"Something like that," he admitted. "What movie are you going to see with my brother?"

"He said I could pick, and I heard he hated scary movies." I paused to grin. "So we're going to see one."

Grayson smiled. I was so glad he came into the kitchen that morning. Even if he caught me singing and scared me. At least I got to see him smirk, smile, and even laugh.

He wasn't so cold after all.

"That's evil of you."

"Oh, I know."

"The two of you have become close."

I knew my expression softened because I warmed every time I thought of Dylan. He saved me and became my closest friend. He would always hold a place in my heart.

"We have. He came into my life right when I needed him. I would be lost without him."

"I'm glad you have that with him then. Even if he annoys the fuck out of me."

I threw my head back and laughed. Nodding, I admitted, "He does that to everyone. I think it's his charm in a way."

Grayson snorted. "I better let you get ready for the library. Enjoy your day, Makenzie."

"You also, Grayson. Don't work too hard." I winked before exiting the room, giggling to myself over the wink. It was something I never would have thought I'd do to Grayson, but I was more relaxed around him. I only hoped he didn't think it was a twitch instead.

It was the most Grayson and I had spoken, and it had nothing to do with business. I found myself smiling and skipping along with a new spring in my step.

I would not get a crush on my boss though.

Never.

No way.

Still, it didn't stop me from thinking about our chat in the kitchen all day long.

Even after the movie, when Dylan was cursing me black and blue, threatening payback tenfold, I was smiling.

In the elevator after dinner, Dylan curled his arm around my shoulders and said, "I can't help but sense your happiness tonight. Was it from torturing me or is there another reason?"

Shrugging, I grinned. "No reason really, though torturing you was extra fun."

He scoffed. "The way you get your thrills scares me."

"Only because it's at your expense."

"Exactly. Did you enjoy your dinner?"

"I did. Who would have thought a biker bar would serve the best steak in town." Laying my head against his chest, I told him, "You are the best gay friend anyone could ask for."

He hummed and then kissed the top of my head.

The elevator doors opened, and my eyes went right to the man standing at the bar, helping himself to a drink. I stepped out of Dylan's arm and into the room.

Grayson smirked and then asked, "Did you enjoy the movie, brother?"

Dylan groaned, stepping up beside me. "No. I'll be having nightmares all night. So if your phone rings in the middle of the night, and since you're my big brother, you need to take care of me by reading me a bedtime story."

Grayson laughed. "Not happening." His eyes came to me. "Did you have a good night, Makenzie?"

Smiling, I nodded. "I did."

"Did you visit the library today?" he asked.

My face lit up. "Yes, and I got over a billion books."

He lifted his chin at me and grinned. "I'm glad you found some to your liking. I'm off to bed. Good night, Makenzie, Dylan."

"Yeah, night, bro," Dylan answered. His voice seemed strained, so I looked at him as I said my good night to Grayson.

As soon as Grayson was out of the room, I asked, "What?"

He was staring at me strangely. He sighed, rubbed a hand over his face, and said, "You like my brother."

My head jerked back. "What? No! No, nope, nah-uh." I shook my head. "I mean, I like him as a person, but that's all."

Dylan crossed his arms over his chest. His head went back, eyes to the ceiling where he cursed, "Fuck. Fuck me." He pulled his head down, his eyes on mine. "You do like him."

I shook my head, again and again.

Dylan stepped forward. His hands landed on my shoulders. "I get that you do, but remember, Grayson isn't the warmest person, and you just got out of a marriage with a person who didn't give a shit about you."

Dylan, of course, knew everything there was to know about Robert, and he hated him. Even warned me to stay away from Robert or he'd end up dealing with him. Dylan also told me if he ever caught me self-doubting myself in any way, he would deal with me also.

In what way, I wasn't sure. But his tone and expression had told me he was serious.

In a whisper, I said, "It's not like that. I admire him as a person. Honestly, Dylan, there is no way I would start anything with anyone. I'm not ready. I'm only just living again. I want to enjoy me for a while longer and when the time comes, and I feel like dating"—I shrugged—"I don't actually know. It's been a while, and I'm afraid I'll act like a fish out of water, gasping for air."

Dylan sighed again, that time heavier. "I'll help you through it. What are best friends for?"

"Thank you. But it won't be for a long time yet."

"I goddamn hope not. I'm not ready to let you go just yet either. I'm selfish."

"I know." I smiled, patting him on the hard stomach. "Which was why you growled at that biker tonight, saying, 'Mine' like some caveman."

"Yeah." He smiled, but it didn't reach his eyes. "That's right."

Chapter TEN

I WAS MAKING my way into the kitchen for a late lunch, when my phone rang Sunday afternoon. I smiled at the caller ID, my sister. We had been talking regularly, and I enjoyed each call we had. I answered. "Lori, how are you?"

"Good. How have you been?" Her quiet voice came from the other end.

My sister had always been quiet, even growing up she hardly made a sound. She was shy and nervous, which was how Mom was when Dad had met her. He could hardly get a word out of her, and every time he spoke to her, Mom's cheeks would heat and she would look everywhere but at him. Dad told me he knew at first sight Mom was the one for him, so he bided his time until Mom eventually warmed to him, and then he put a ring on her finger. I could only hope Lori would find her special someone. A man who was willing to put in the time and effort and not get frustrated with her shyness.

"Great. Yesterday I went to the library, movies, and had dinner at a biker bar."

Lori gasped. "Really?"

"Yes." I smiled. "Dylan came with me to the movies and dinner." Since starting at Jackson Media, I had also been talking to my dad and Lori each week. She knew all about Dylan and how he helped me get the job and place to live.

"I'm glad he did. How was the dinner with your boss and clients?" Based on the few things I'd told her about Grayson, she thought he was scary. Yes, at first I had also, but not any longer. He was intimidating, could yell, glare, and crack his voice like a harsh whip. However, he was also so much more.

"I only embarrassed myself a couple of times. Sometimes I think I need a muzzle." She giggled. I went on in a hushed voice, "Though, Lori, I can't believe this, but since I've left Robert, men are, God, they're actually taking an interest in *me*. I never thought… it's weird."

"What men? I thought your boss had a girlfriend."

"Oh, no. Not Mr. Jackson. But a client of his who could be my baby brother, I swear he's only your age, and then there's an architect I met one time I was out with Robert. Actually, it was the day I left Robert."

"What are you going to do?"

"Nothing. I'm not ready for anything. I don't think I will be for a while."

Grayson's face flashed in my mind. I quickly got an eraser and scrubbed that out.

"How're things with you on the guy front?"

She snorted. "Nothing new. I'm a bumbling idiot when someone tries to talk to me. Still, there is one guy in my class

I'd like to get to know. If my tongue would unstick from the roof of my mouth, I may actually have a normal conversation with him."

"I'm sure if a guy's really interested he would make an effort and not be fazed by your shyness."

She sighed. "I think I'll die a virgin."

I laughed. "Honey, you're still young, gorgeous, sweet, and smart. You're nothing like how I was back in my college days. Just don't… don't fall for the first one who woos you. Make sure he has the approval of Dad and me. I don't want you to make the same mistake I did."

"Oh, Kenzie."

"No, I really wish I had listened to you and Dad back in the day. Then I wouldn't have wasted six years with a guy who didn't care for me."

"Then you wouldn't have an amazing job, and from what you've said, a sweet pad to go home to every night, and you also wouldn't have met Dylan or Angelia. Some things are meant to happen for a reason. Maybe, just maybe, you were meant to waste six years with him to finally find yourself and eventually find a man who will be your everything, and he'll see the same from within you."

"I can only hope, and I want you to have the same thing, Lori."

"One day, maybe." I could hear the smile in her voice. "Anyway, the reason I called you was to warn you about Dad having a new phone. His texts are worse than before."

Laughing, I said, "That can't be true."

"Wait, let me forward you the text I got from him this afternoon."

Silence and then my phone dinged. I pulled it away from my ear to look at the text.

Jellybean, I need some men. I'm horny. Can you go to the shop and get me some men. Bring home any kind. I'm not funny. Just thinking of men makes me drool I'm that horny. Thanks, JB! Dad.

I burst out laughing, my hand going to my stomach as I reread it and laughed some more. With my phone next to my ear, the first thing I heard was Dad shouting in the background.

"What's she laughing at? You didn't. You showed her. How could you? I told you, Jellybean, you could be my favorite if you didn't show anyone and deleted it." Dad cursed and then into the phone, he said, "Puddin', it was the stupid, fucking phone. It changed my words on me and I didn't look back at that shit. I was thinking of food."

"You sure you weren't thinking of men?"

"Dammit, you're a little shit like your sister."

Snorting through my laugh, I asked, "What was it supposed to say?"

"Nope, convene with the other devil I spawned. I'm not talking to either of you."

I heard Lori call out to Dad. He grumbled something under his breath, and then she was back on the phone saying, "That was hilarious. He went all bright red. When I first read it, I've never laughed so long and loud in class before. It was supposed to say, I need some meat. I'm hungry. Can you go to the shop and get me some meat. Bring home any. I'm not fussy." She giggled. "Just thinking of meat makes me drool I'm that hungry."

"If Dad wouldn't kill you, Aunt Olive would have got a good laugh from it and then given Dad a heap of shit for it."

"I know." She cackled. "Maybe I'll bring it back out at Christmas time. Then at least you'll keep me safe from him."

Christmas. I hadn't spent one with them in such a long time. Thinking of it wiped the smile from my face.

Lori, knowing me well, even after the time apart, ordered, "Don't think about it, Kenzie. We all knew you wished to be with us. We hold *nothing* against you, so you don't need to either. We're looking to the future, sister. Not the past."

"To the future."

"Yes, and we're going to have the best time together."

"As soon as your course is done, you're moving this way still?"

She laughed. "Well, I haven't changed my mind since the last time we talked. Even though Dad doesn't want to let me go, he still understands."

"I can't wait to get a place together."

"Me either."

"Devil spawn, stop gossiping with your sister and come eat dinner."

"Talk soon?" Lori asked into the phone.

"Of course. Love you."

"You too. Bye for now."

Grinning, I finished Dad's saying to her, "But not forever."

It was great having my family back, and I couldn't wait until our first Christmas together. Aunt Olive, Dad's sister, and Uncle Mason usually came all the way from Australia to visit. They loved to give Dad hell. He also gave it back, so the day was always full of laughs.

After a quick bite to eat, I decided to go check out the gym and pool area. Slipping into my one-piece suit, I placed a summer dress over the top and grabbed my towel. I hoped I'd have the floor to myself. I knew a client was staying on the guest floor with their entourage, but I hadn't seen who it was, and I doubted they'd be wanting to swim or use the gym if they were only staying in town for some downtime.

The elevator doors opened, and a gasp slipped past my lips. It was huge. A giant-sized pool greeted me and an area off to the left held the gym with every machine known to mankind, at least I was sure of it.

There was a bang. I stepped further in. That was when I spotted Grayson.

Dear God.

He was in the far corner, lying on a bench lifting weights.

He was also shirtless. I had never seen him in such a way, and I wished I hadn't because I never knew how muscular he was until that moment.

Dang it, he also had freaking abs, eight of them.

Why, oh, why did he have to be so good-looking?

Even his track-pants-covered legs seemed strong.

I needed to back out. Get away from there before my mind supplied me with thoughts I didn't want, and couldn't have.

Stepping back… I slipped on nothing and landed on my butt. Closing my eyes, I lay flat on the floor with my arm over my burning face and prayed my boss hadn't heard my graceful movements.

"Makenzie?"

No, no, no.

I wished I was up in my room away from him and his body.

"Are you all right?" His voice was coming closer.

Maybe I could pretend to have fainted.

No. Then he'd think I fainted over seeing him or he'd call an ambulance, and they'd find out I was a big faker.

"I'm good," I yelled back. I removed my arm and opened my eyes, then screamed. Grayson was leaning over me. "Y-you… have to stop scaring me."

His lips twitched, a gesture I was becoming familiar with, and if I thought about it too hard, which of course I didn't, always left me with hyperactive butterflies in my stomach. His hand came out. Without thinking, I took it and next, with a quick pull—of my hand and nothing else—I was standing next to him.

Shit. Sweat covered his body; he glistened from it.

Look away, Kenzie. Look away.

Still, I couldn't help it. It was like my eyes were glued to his chest and his rock-hard abs.

Robert never had abs. He was never rock-hard. He never looked so good in only track pants like Grayson did.

My eyes widened. Did I just whimper?

Oh, my, fucking, God.

Flicking my eyes to the floor, to the left and then the right, I mumbled through my next words, "Um, I, ah, sorry for interrupting you. I was, um, just thinking of going for a swim."

To possibly drown myself.

Do not lick your lips.

But they're dry.

No. Do not lick them. Grayson may get the wrong idea.

But they're so dry.

I don't care. Don't *lick them.*

Jesus. I licked my lips and shifted back a step, my whole body feeling like it was on fire.

"Enjoy your swim then, Makenzie." His voice was light, as if he thought I was funny for some reason.

Another step back. "Actually, I think, I mean, I just ate, so maybe I should swim later." I laughed nervously and looked at him. Yep, he had a half smile on his face. His eyes were bright, and his hair was a hot mess. I gulped back my laugh and smiled. "I don't want to drown."

"I could keep an eye on you, to make sure you don't."

I rolled my eyes to the left and then the right. Shook my head and again laughed like something was funny, when nothing was. "No, I'll come back."

"Makenzie?"

"Yes?"

"Get in the pool," he ordered in his harsher tone and then stalked off back to the gym.

As soon as he was further enough away and still had his back to me, I quickly slipped off my dress, placed it and the towel on one of the seats by the pool, and got in the water. All before Grayson went back to lifting weights.

Biting my bottom lip, I watched him for a while and then decided to stop eyeballing my boss because it was a bad, bad idea. So I started to do laps, pretending as if I knew how to swim like a professional. Admittedly my favored stroke was the doggy paddle. Not the most graceful of moves, but heck, I rocked it!

After two laps, I was out of breath so flipped over to my back and just floated. My stupid brain kept flashing me images of Grayson over and over. My clit tingled, and I damned it to hell for the inappropriate action and then my mind for the thoughts I was having about my boss, about what it would be like to walk over to the bench and straddle his waist to…. No, I couldn't go there.

Lifting my head from the water, when I thought I heard something, my eyes went to the elevator to see Grayson standing in it with a towel around his shoulders, his gaze already trained on me. I waved. He did nothing but look at me as the doors closed on him.

I then sank under the water and screamed.

Chapter ELEVEN

As usual, Monday was busy with calls, meetings, and e-mails. Grayson was also back to his brooding, darker self. Not that it bothered me. In fact, it helped curb my mind and remind it to stop playing around when it came to my boss. So even when Grayson snarled at me about an e-mail I was supposed to have sent off before lunch and hadn't, I grinned and told him I'd get it done right away. I knew work stressed him; anyone could understand that when his business was worth billions and his clients could be asshats.

Case in point, Zoe Douglas.

She swooped onto the floor with a scowl on her gorgeous face and designer wear on her perfect body.

"I want to see Grayson," she demanded.

"Do you have an appointment?" I asked.

"No," she said with a sneer. "And I don't need one. Tell him I'm here, and he'll let me in."

"I'm sorry, Miss Douglas, but Mr. Jackson is on a very important call right now and is not to be disturbed. If you would like to wait in the waiting area at the front, I'll come and get you when he's free, or I can contact your manager."

She stomped her heel-clad foot. "I need Grayson, and I will not wait, you stupid bitch. When I come here, I demand to be taken care of, not to be pushed aside as if I'm a nobody like you."

Grayson's door swished open. "Zoe. In here now," was clipped out low with a growl.

She sent me a look as if to say "I told you so," and glided into Grayson's office. I didn't look; I didn't need to, not when I could hear just fine. I heard the door close and then… shouting from both sides.

It reminded me of the words Grayson and Harpy had outside the car Friday night. I still wondered what the outcome was.

I didn't have to wonder for long, much to my disappointment. A throat cleared in front of my desk. I looked from the computer up to see a smiling, in a vindictive way, Harper. "I want to see Grayson."

I raised my brows. "I'm sure you can hear he's busy right now." I pointed out, just as his voice boomed something from behind the door.

"Oh, I don't mind waiting. Besides, I have a surprise for you. I found someone downstairs. He seemed lost so I thought I would do the right thing and bring him up." She grinned, while her eyes shone with glee. Then she shifted aside.

With wide eyes, I stood quickly. "Robert," I breathed.

"Makenzie." He smiled, and it was his sweet smile.

"What are you doing here?"

"I came to talk with my wife."

Glancing to Harper, I saw she seemed smug about her findings. "How did you find me?" I asked him.

"I tracked your phone."

I needed a new phone.

"May we speak, please? This nice woman helped me to find your floor, and now I would like a chance to say some things."

Shaking my head, I said, "I don't think there's anything to say."

"Makenzie. Please, darling, six years together and you're willing to throw it all away?"

Was I?

Studying him, his charcoal suit, his gelled back hair, his prim and proper voice, I realized after all the hurtful words, his cheating ways, that I *was* willing to throw it all away without another thought.

I was happy.

I was finally happy with where I was, my job, my place to stay, and becoming more myself than I had been in a long time helped.

"Sorry, Robert, but you showed up expecting something that you won't get. What I said over the phone last time is still where I stand. Have you signed the papers?"

His jaw clenched. "A private word, just for a moment."

"I'm at work. I can't take—"

"Oh, I can cover the desk for you while you speak with your husband." Harper smiled sweetly.

Robert eyed her and grinned back with a nod. "See, the lovely lady is willing to help out."

"My name is Harper." She licked her lips at my ex.

Robert held out his hand to her. She took it, and I watched in disgust when his thumb rubbed over her hand. "I'm Robert Mayfair. It's a pleasure to meet you, Harper."

"Pleasure is all mine," she purred.

To settle my stomach, I needed to get Robert to understand whatever he wanted wasn't going to happen and quickly so he'd leave.

"Robert, if you will follow me," I said and walked around the desk down the hall to the break room where the coffee and snacks were supplied. Turning, I leaned against the counter and asked, "What is it you need?"

He sighed and then smiled. "Darling, I need you. It's always been you, and I'm sorry I lashed out and told a fib, that I cheated. I would never do that to you. I need you to come home." He laughed. "You can't honestly like working here, as an assistant. Yes, it may be flashy, but it's not a job for my wife."

My hands gripped the counter at each side of my hips. "Nothing has changed since I spoke to you last, Robert. I'm not coming back."

His eyes flashed with annoyance. "You care so little for me and what I want?"

"No, it's just that I'm finally putting myself first for once."

He snorted. "Makenzie, this back and forth is getting us nowhere. Come to dinner tonight, and we can talk some more."

Shaking my head, I flicked my eyes to the floor and then back to my ex. "Sign the papers, Robert."

"I will not sign them," he barked. "No wife of mine leaves me."

"Then it's lucky she's not your wife," was snarled behind Robert.

I let out a yip of a squeal, like every time Grayson snuck up on me, and saw him just inside the room, leaning his shoulder against the doorframe with his arms crossed over his chest.

Robert spun around and demanded, "Who do you think you are to interrupt us and say such a thing?"

"Kenzie's boss." His brow rose.

Robert stiffened. "I think it's best you stay out of our business. It's between my wife and me."

Grayson looked bored. "And I think you need to get it through your head she's not your wife anymore."

"Who—"

Grayson straightened and leaned toward Robert. "I'm her boss. I'm the one who saw the pain flash over her face when you told her you cheated. Who told her she was awkward and fat. Let me guess, you used to like going home to a clean, warm house with a cooked meal. You want her back so *you* can have your cake and eat it too."

"You don't know what—"

"I do. I've seen your sort. My father was one of them. Kenzie works for me now. If she wishes for you to sign the papers, you fucking will. If she wishes to never see you again, and I find she has, you will have me to deal with. Do. I. Make. Myself. Clear?"

My heart beat so fast it was hurting, only in a good, wild way. Watching Grayson take Robert down a peg was something I never thought would turn me on, but it was.

Oh, God. Was that sick? Being turned on so much my nipples were hard while my panties were damp because my boss was going head-to-head and winning with my ex?

Robert spun back to me. "Makenzie?"

"I'm sorry, Robert—"

"No, she's not sorry at all," Grayson clipped.

I hid my smile with a cough. "Ah, I would like for you to sign the papers and accept I won't be coming back."

Robert scowled. "You're making a big mistake."

Shrugging, I then shook my head. "See, I don't think I am."

Grayson stepped away from the doorway as Robert stormed from the room.

"Thank you," I whispered.

My boss took me in, my heavy breath, my trembling body. I wondered if he thought it was from being frightened or worried. It wasn't. Not that I would tell him the truth why. Because I was turned on for the first time in years.

He grunted, turned, and stalked from the room. Then he barked loudly, "Get the fuck back to work."

Shortly after, I went from the break room to my desk without meeting anyone's gaze. Only I held my head high and let the tension roll off me when I didn't see Harper or Zoe in sight. I sat down and reread the e-mail I had been working on to send it off to Vice when a message popped up onto my screen.

That was unbelievable. It came from Darby.

I glanced over to her. She nodded, bugged her eyes out at me, and then focused pointedly on her computer.

Another message came through. *After Mr. Jackson finished yelling at Zoe, he opened his door, glared at Harper, and asked where you were. She told him you were dealing with a personal matter during business hours. That girl is vicious. She wants you gone even though she doesn't want your job. Anyway, he said something to Harper, who huffed, then took off. Then Mr. Jackson went searching for you. Was that your douche ex?*

Yes, I replied back.

I think Mr. Jackson is happy with how you do your job to stick up for you like that. He's never done it before.

I guess.

I could hear her laugh. Glancing there, I saw her smile and shake her head.

Well, I'd better get back to work. I sent back a smiley face. I hated the thought of the many questions I was going to get over lunch tomorrow after Darby, who loved to gossip, spread the latest office drama.

Then again, I'd let them think what they wanted. I couldn't let myself worry about it. I'd tell my side, and if they believed it, then they did. If they thought something more of the way Grayson stuck up for me, then I'd let them.

Even if my belly churned with nerves.

I liked my boss. I liked my job and where I was staying and nothing, or no one, was going to ruin it for me when I was for once, on my own two feet.

The intercom buzzed. "Mrs. Mayfair, please bring in a contract form for Ethan."

I scooted my chair back, went to the file cabinet, and grabbed a form out. I paused at his door and took a deep breath. *Body, please behave.*

Opening the door, my gaze landed on Grayson, who gestured for the file with his hand while his eyes were on the computer. I handed him the file and stood back. "Is there anything else?"

"Yes," he bit out coldly. "Next time I would prefer it if you took your personal issues elsewhere. I shouldn't have to interfere."

It was then dread filled my chest, and I deflated like a blow-up doll.

"Of course," I snapped. God, I hadn't even asked him to interfere in the first place. If it weren't for his latest screw, Robert wouldn't have come up to the floor. I ground my teeth together. Grayson was pissed at me because he had caused a fuss in front of his other workers. Well, I was pissed he was taking it out on me.

Men. All the goddamn same.

"Anything else, Mr. Jackson?" I asked emotionlessly. I was good at shutting myself down.

"No, that would be all." He didn't even look at me.

Fine.

It was all fine and fucking dandy.

I went back to my desk, closing the door to his office a little more abruptly than I should, but I didn't care. I wanted him to know I was angry at him for being a dick over a matter he involved *himself* in.

He should have ignored it, left me to deal with it, but he hadn't, and I was not taking the blame for his actions.

Screw him. Screw him and his good-looking face, his hot body, and his deep voice.

I'd go back to calling him Mr. Jackson. I'd go back to dodging him in the kitchen.

In fact, I'd install a fucking mini bar in my stupid, beautiful room, in his ugly, wonderful apartment.

Screw Mr. Jackson.

Chapter TWELVE

"Puddin', Jellybean's got some extra time off from college for the long weekend coming up next month. So since you're all settled with your job, and being away from dickweed, we want to make the drive to come see you. Spend a week maybe."

Smiling, I sat on my bed and coughed up a lung before saying, "I'd love that, Dad. You can both stay here with me. There's enough room."

"You sound as sick as a dog."

I laughed. Dad was never known for his subtlety. After another round of coughing, I replied, "Well, it's lucky it's Friday night and I can spend it recovering." In fact, Mr. Jackson had sent me to the apartment early because people were worried they'd get the flu like I had.

"You make sure you rest, Puddin'."

"I will, Dad, and I'm even going to take some medicine for the cough."

Dad whistled. "You sure that's wise?"

I giggled. "I'm in my room alone, which is where I'll be staying for the rest of the night. Surely nothing can go wrong."

"Hmm, maybe lock yourself in to be sure."

Okay, so every time I had cough medicine, I went a little crazy. It turned me into drunk, happy Kenzie.

However, I had the night to myself. Dylan said he might stop by with some soup if he had time, but I warned him not to. I didn't want to get anyone else sick.

"I will, Dad. Don't worry."

"Do you remember the last time you had some?"

Sighing, I nodded. Not that Dad could see it, so I replied, "Yes."

"And where did I find you?" His voice turned light with humor.

"Outside, singing and dancing in the middle of the street."

"That's right, and then you thought you were invincible and wanted to take on any car that drove down our street. The next day, after some photos landed in the local paper, you wished you never inherited that trait from your mother."

"Luckily, I haven't been this sick in a long time. Plus, I think I'm in the right place to have the medicine, since it's highly guarded. I'm sure one of the security men will catch me if I try to escape."

"I'd warn them, just in case."

"I could have grown out of it by now."

"Puddin'." Dad chuckled. "Get some rest. Bye for now, but not forever."

"Bye, Dad."

"Also, I'll keep an eye out in the paper tomorrow." He laughed.

"Dad." I groaned, but he'd already hung up. I smiled as I placed my cell on the bed. Even though I felt like crap, talking to Dad always eased my mind.

It had been an exhausting couple of weeks, which was how I probably became run down and sick. What didn't help was when Angelia had the damn flu last week at lunch. I was sure she spread it around the whole cafeteria with her coughing fits. Which could be another reason why Grayson had sent me home early after he saw me hacking up a lung. A strange look had appeared on his face, and he'd ordered me upstairs.

Things between us were back to how they had been when I first started. There was no more chatting in the kitchen, lingering looks, and I knew *I* had a lot to do with it. Because the afternoon he'd riled me up, I did go out and buy a mini fridge for my room. I ate my breakfast in the living area off my room. I cooked dinner as soon as I finished work, knowing he would still be busy. The only time I saw him was at work.

I thought it was for the best. I had become confused with my feelings for him, and the bottom line was I didn't want my smutty fantasies risking my job.

Which was why I went online and ordered a monster-sized purple vibrator. The parcel was set to arrive any day, and the company promised discretion so I was confident images of cocks and nipple clamps weren't going to decorate the package.

At the end of the first week, he had called me into his office.

I'd stood in front of his desk and said, "Yes, Mr. Jackson?"

"Can I ask why you haven't been eating breakfast?"

Tensing, I'd replied honestly, "I have."

"Funny, I haven't seen you do it. I don't want you doing something stupid by skipping a meal."

I'd narrowed my eyes. "I'm not being stupid. I've been eating in my living room from the food in *my* fridge in *my* room."

His eyes had flared. "You have a fridge in your room?"

"Yes."

"Why?"

With my hands on my hips, I'd snapped, "Because I would hate it if a personal matter arose and you would have to intervene, even if I never asked you to, and I get my head snapped off like I'm some child. I also don't think you would want such a stupid person around in your area."

He'd sighed, ran a hand over his face, and groaned out my name, "Kenzie."

"Is there anything else, Mr. Jackson?"

Petty, I knew that was how I acted, but I couldn't, wouldn't, let another man walk all over me. He may have felt bad for how he'd acted, so be it. Only, he'd never once apologized. Mr. Jackson and I were better off as employer and employee… not friends who chat, who drank coffee together. No matter how much I missed it.

It was later that day when I'd returned to my desk and heard two male voices in Mr. Jackson's office yelling at one another. I couldn't make out the words, but they seemed harsh just from the volume.

When Dylan walked out, slamming the door behind him, my eyes had widened, and I'd whispered, "Are you okay?" I couldn't help but think I had something to do with the brothers arguing. After all, it had only been a few days before that I'd told Dylan what had happened with Robert, and then Grayson.

He'd leaned in and kissed my cheek. "All good, honey. It was about a property development." Dylan had previously spoken to me about getting his act together, and he thought buying, building, and selling off land was the way to go. I guessed his brother wasn't happy about it. Grayson had always thought Dylan would go back to singing. Though it was something Dylan would never do. He had said he'd partied enough in his younger years and was over that scene.

"It didn't sound like Grayson was up for it."

He'd smiled. "Don't worry, he'll come around. I have to get going. We still on for dinner tomorrow night?"

"Definitely."

Shaking my head at the thoughts, I entered my bathroom and grabbed the bottle of cough medicine off the basin. Pouring the right amount into the supplied measuring cup, I prayed I wouldn't be too dangerous on the stuff and gulped it down.

"KENZIE, PLEASE KEEP your clothes on," Dylan begged for… I wouldn't have a clue how many times.

"My body feels achy. I hate being sick, Dylan. But I love you. Did you know that? You're my bestest friend in the whole wide world." I tackled him to the bed and hugged him tightly.

"Tell me again what you took?" he chuckled from under me.

"Just some cough medicine." Sitting suddenly, I gasped. "Oh my God. It worked. I'm no longer coughing."

"You just had a fit five minutes ago, sweetheart," Dylan mentioned, sitting next to me on the edge of the bed.

Turning to him, I pulled my eyebrows high and asked, "I did?" I couldn't remember. All I knew was that I felt wonderful. Except I was so damn hot.

Dylan's hand came over mine. "Keep your top on," he all but growled.

"But I'm hot."

"Remind me to never pop in when you're high."

"I'm not high. I'm awesome," I cheered, then moaned when Dylan's hands rubbed my shoulders. "That feels so good," I told him.

"Jesus," he mumbled and stopped.

"No!" I cried. "More, please. Pretty please with a penis on top." I bent over laughing. Then stopped. "Penis. Pe-nis. Cock. Dick. Meatstick."

"Kenzie. What in the fuck are you doing?"

"Sitting on the floor between your legs so you can massage me."

"And all the talk about a penis?"

Snorting, I explained, "I just found the word funny coming from my mouth. Like vagina, twat, fanny, meat purse…. Oh, yes, right there."

Dylan's hands kneaded into my shoulders, and it felt amazing.

"Kenzie," Dylan shouted. "Stop trying to take off your clothes, dammit."

"Just my top, please."

"No."

"Dylan," I whined, and quickly leaned forward pulling my top from my body, then unhooking my bra.

"Fuck me. You said top and I didn't want that. Now you have your bra off."

I picked up said bra, flung it around on my finger and then threw it over the other side of the room with a "Woo-hoo." Sitting back, I said, "There, now continue, slave." Glancing up at him, I noticed he wasn't looking down, but his hands still went to my shoulders and started massaging. "Does a woman's body offend you?"

"No."

"Boobs are really like balls, only bigger and less hairy. How can you not like them even if you don't like women?" I grabbed my breast and squeezed. "I think I could fondle another woman's lady bits. Well, maybe just their tits."

"For the love of God, please stop talking."

Sighing, I nodded. "Okay, but only if you keep going."

"Fine." It was bit out through clenched teeth, or at least it sounded like it.

I started humming the tune to Kelis's "Milkshake" until Dylan's hands moved lower on my back, ripping a moan from me. "Dylan, that feels a-ma-zing."

It was then my bedroom door came bursting open, hitting the wall behind it. I screamed, jumped from the floor with my hands going to my heart to try to still it.

"What the fuck is going on?" Grayson snarled. I watched in fascination as his eyes flicked around the room, to the bed, to his brother, to me, back to his brother where they darkened, and then to me once more where they widened.

"Shut the goddamn door," Dylan yelled. He got up from the bed and ran for the door, quickly closing it. "She'll escape otherwise, idiot."

"Tell me why I shouldn't kill you?" Grayson demanded to Dylan and then shoved him.

"Oh, yay. Grayson's here," I cried, my hands going in the air to wave them around.

"Is she drunk?"

"On fucking cough medicine." Dylan sighed. "Kenzie. Turn the hell around and face the wall."

I stopped dancing and placed my hands on my hips. Narrowing my eyes, I asked, "Why? Just because you're gay and my boobs—"

"You told her you were gay?" was boomed so loud I had to cover my ears.

Dylan stomped over to me, picking up my tee on the way, which he tugged over my head, pulling my arms through the holes. "I had to do something. She was skittish with me otherwise. I panicked. Women feel comfortable around gay men."

"Dylan and Grayson are brothers. Hot brothers, one gay and one not. One my boss and one not," I sang, swaying to my own beat.

"Fucking hell," I heard Grayson grumble. "No wonder she's not at the dinner party—"

"There's a party?" I cried. "Yay!"

"Shit," Dylan snapped. He tried to grab for me, but I did a magnificent twirl and got past him. "Grab her," Dylan yelled.

I threw my head back and laughed. I was excited to be joining a party. Only then, something firm and solid came around my waist, and I was pulled back into a sturdy wall. Glancing behind me, I saw my wall was, in fact, my boss.

"Hey, Grayson. What are you doing in here?"

His lips twitched.

Grinning, I said, "I like it when your lips do that. It's cute."

His brow raised. "Cute?"

"And I like it when you do that. Raising one brow like you're He-Man, all strong and mighty." Slowly, I turned in his arms. "Wait one cotton pickin' minute. I'm annoyed with you, you big bossy… boss." I glared up at him.

His lips twitched again.

I pointed my finger at them. "Don't go doing that when I'm cranky." I blinked. "Now, why was I cranky?"

"I'm not sure."

"Nope." I shook my head. "You remember because now I remember. Don't be a big mean person if you get embarrassed."

He snorted. "I promise I won't again."

Smiling, I said, "Okay. Now I'm going to hug you." I wound my arms around his waist and hugged him tightly.

"She's cute like that, hey?" I heard Dylan say from somewhere behind me.

"I think it's best if I leave," Grayson said softly, and then I felt his hands at my waist. He tried to push me back, only he was so warm and hard and amazing, so I wasn't having any of it. Instead, I jumped, making him stumble, but he caught me with his hands on my butt as I wrapped my arms around his neck and my legs around his waist.

"For fuck's sake, Dylan, help me," Grayson barked.

"I'm a monkey," I yelled and then laughed, snuggling my face into his neck.

Dylan chuckled. "Not a chance in hell. I minded her for an hour before you showed up, and now she's all moony eyes for you."

"You had her top off," Grayson snarled.

"*She* took it off. And anyway, I didn't see much. Also, she was only *happy* to see me when I turned up. She didn't scream with joy for me like she did for you. Besides, I'm already late for a date."

"Dylan, I swear to fucking Christ if you walk out of this room…. Stop, you can't—"

"I can and I will."

"I have a party to attend."

Leaning back, I cried, "Party? Yeah, let's rock and roll." I jumped down from my tree and ran for the door, only my hand was snagged on something. Turning, I saw Grayson had a hold of it.

"No, Kenzie. Nothing is going on outside that door. Dylan!"

"Have fun. Don't worry, I'll let the people know you're indisposed."

The door shut with a bang, and then I thought I heard Dylan laugh outside of it.

Glancing back to Grayson, I asked, "So, there's no party?"

"No. No party."

"Hmm," I mumbled. Grayson stepped closer, and I asked, "So, what are we going to do? You look dressed up, all handsome and good-looking…. Are those the same things?"

He sighed, ran his free hand, not holding mine, over his face. "You're going to kill yourself in the morning."

"Why?"

He snorted. "Don't worry."

"Are you sure there's no party we can go to?"

"Yes."

"Then… do you want to massage me like Dylan was?"

"Christ, no."

"Oops, sorry. I forgot you're with Harpy. Not that there's anything wrong with a massage. I mean, you're only touching my shoulders. No harm can come from that, or do you think she won't like it?"

He chuckled. "She would hate it."

"Damn." I thought some more. "Want to dance? Go out to a rave? Water-ski? Oh, I know, let's go to the gym."

"Kenzie?"

"Yes, Grayson?"

"I'm tired."

"Oh, no. That's no good. I can bring you something back while I go to the supermarket."

Grayson tugged on my hand and led me toward the bed. "What are you going there for?" he asked.

"A red bull, no, chocolate. No, condoms. Or some wax. I need to wax first."

"Your legs look waxed already."

Rolling my eyes, I laughed, and when Grayson pushed me back so I was sitting on the side of the bed, I told him, "Not for there, I need it for my—"

"Quiet, Kenzie," Grayson growled low in his throat.

"Okay," I whispered and then watched him walk around the bed. He took off his jacket and tie and then undid the first two buttons of his shirt before he slid onto the bed.

"Come lie down, just for a moment," he ordered with his arm held out flat on the bed.

I twisted, jumped, and lay next to him with my head on his chest. His arm curled around my shoulders.

Yawning, I admitted, "I think I'm sleepy."

"I'm glad."

"Night, Grayson."

"Good night, Kenzie."

Chapter THIRTEEN

My eyes sprang open in panic. Where the panic had come from, I didn't have a clue. I took a deep breath in and tried to calm my fast beating heart. Pulling my hands up from under the blanket, I lay them over my chest.

My eyes widened.

"Oh, shit," I breathed.

There was only one problem with having cough medicine, and that was the next day…. I remembered *everything*.

I closed my eyes as the night played over in my mind. My whole body flushed at the thought of… holy crap, *my boss saw my breasts!* I'd climbed him like a pole. I'd hugged him, I…

My eyes sprang wide. "I'm going to kill him," I snarled and quickly climbed out of bed. Stomping over to my wardrobe, I searched for the right clothes for murder.

Dylan Jackson was going to hurt.

He wasn't gay.

He'd lied to me.

He… I paused and snuck back to the door of my walk-in closet. Peeking around the corner, I saw my bed was empty. Grayson had gone to bed with me the night before, but he was no longer there. Thank God.

Oh shit, my boss had hugged me close because I'd tried to escape a few times wanting to go for a swim. Eventually, I had fallen asleep with Grayson beside me.

Mortification burned my cheeks.

I had to leave my murder plan for another day because there was no way in hell I was walking out of the room in case I ran into Grayson.

He saw my breasts for goodness' sake.

I wanted to curl up in a ball and die of embarrassment.

Could a person die of shame?

There was a high chance I could if I saw Grayson that day.

Leaving my closet, I stalked over to my purse and grabbed my cell. I sent off a quick text to Dylan. **You will die a painful death, and I will smile in glee as I torture you slowly.**

His reply was instant. **Good morning, sunshine. :) Have a good night?**

Clenching my teeth together, I gripped my cell and shot off: **Death. Dooming death, you lying little shit.**

Dylan: I can see you're not in a good mood. Remember I love you.

Me: You lied to me, you sack of crap.

Dylan: All for your own good. If I hadn't, we wouldn't be BFFs now, would we?

Me: Not the same when my BFFF is NOT GAY and saw my boobs.

Dylan: Nice set they are. Why is there an extra F in BFF?

Me: Best fucking friend forever.

Dylan: Now, now sunshine.

Me: You left me with your brother, who is MY BOSS, and he saw my boobs. I said things to him, called him handsome, climbed him, hugged him… YOU SHOULD HAVE STAYED AND SAVED ME.

Dylan: I had a hot date. I couldn't stay. Though I'm sure Gray didn't mind taking care of you.

I snorted. **Yeah right. Anyway, to lessen your pain and right yourself in my world, you are to bring me food. BECAUSE I AM NOT LEAVING MY ROOM.**

Dylan: No need to shout, sunshine. But I can't make it today, sorry :)

Me: Dylan (cue: whiny voice) I need food. I was supposed to go food shopping because I have hardly anything in my room. Pretty please help your supposed BFF out?

Dylan: Love you, sunshine, but you'll have to pull up your sexy panties and head on out. I'm busy (wink, wink)

Me: Fine. I'll send out a notice to the papers so people will know where to attend your funeral.

Dylan: Awesome, you're the best. Have a great day x

Me: You suck x

Dylan: Nope, I lick :P

Throwing my phone to the bed, I let out a frustrated growl, just as my stomach complained of how empty it was. At least there was one good thing. I was feeling better than I had the previous day. My nose still felt a little stuffy and my head a little full, but I wasn't coughing.

I needed a shower, and then I needed to call the secret service to see if they could get me out of the apartment undetected.

My movements were slow. After all, I wasn't in any hurry to get out of the room, even if my stomach was yelling up a storm for me to feed it.

After showering, I dressed in jeans and a soft wooly sweater. I stood at the door with my purse over my shoulder and a grip on the handle. Even with hunger eating at my innards, it still dipped with a jumble of nerves.

This is stupid. He won't even be there. Just open the door and make a run for the elevator.

Sighing, I pulled the door open and strode quickly to the next door that linked to the main living area where my escape route was.

Don't think. Just run, I ordered myself. So I opened that door to find the room still dark. No one had opened the blinds, which I was grateful for. So I made a mad dash to the elevator. When I got there, I pressed the button over and over.

"Come on, come on," I begged the stupid slow contraption.

"Makenzie."

"Eeep," I screamed and spun, leaning back against the elevator doors as I searched the room for the man behind it. "G-Grayson?"

The blinds suddenly opened, and I spotted him right away, standing near the piano. His face was passive, bored even. "Going somewhere?"

"Um, ah, hmm, maybe. Yes. No, I think I'll go back to the room." I rubbed at my forehead. "Boobs, you saw them—Argh," I screamed once again as the elevator doors opened and I stumbled back, landing on my butt. Standing quickly, I pressed Ground Floor and then Close. "Yes, I mean, food, I'm, ah, I need food." The doors started closing. Stupid me and my stupid mouth shouted, "Sorry about last night, climbing you, touching you, and you seeing what you did."

Just as the doors closed, I was sure I saw Grayson smile and his eyes light with humor.

He smiled.

A big one also.

His eyes danced right before me.

Then again, maybe I had imagined it.

Shaking my head, I leaned back against the wall and sighed. My hands were trembling. That man had a thing for scaring me, and one day, I would get him back.

That was if I ever went back to the apartment.

Maybe I could join the circus. Read fortunes.

Then again, I was never good at making things up, and knowing my luck, people would come after me with their pitchforks when what I told them didn't come true.

Leaving my car, I decided to walk the few blocks to a bakery Dylan had shown me a while ago. They had the best coffee and muffins. It was just what I needed to calm my nerves.

Walking in, I smiled at Delia, the owner's daughter, who was around my age. "The usual?" she called. I nodded and went to sit in the window seat.

Taking out my phone, I saw I had a text from my dad. **You weren't on the news. I guess it went okay?**

Shaking my head, I giggled to myself at how wrong he was. It definitely did not go okay. Still, I replied. **Only if you call making a fool of myself in front of my boss who had to hold me down to keep me in the room okay… sure.**

Dad: Shit!

Me: Yep.

Dad: Did he fried you? I can call him, explain a few things.

I was sure he meant fired, instead of fried. At least I hoped he did. **No, well not yet and please do not call him.**

Dad: Call me if need me. I can still kick ass even if I'm orange.

Another text sounded right away from Dad. **Old, not ducking orange. Stew new phone.**

Then another.

Dad: Jesus. Stupid not stew.

Me: LOL. I know, Dad :) Thanks!

Dad: Speaking of kicking ass, some prune at the door for Jellybean. Got 2 go.

And one last text saying: **Ducking hell. I meant punk not prune.**

Laughing, I put my phone on the counter. Poor Lori. I hoped he didn't embarrass her too much. Excitement bubbled up inside of me. I was really looking forward to the week with my family. I had decided to do a million things with them, but most of all take them to a Dodgers game. Dad was a huge fan.

"Here you go, Kenzie." Delia placed my coffee and muffin down.

"You may have just saved my life," I told her.

"Rough night?"

"Roughest."

"Yeah, you don't sound too good."

"Head cold of sorts. At least the hacking up a lung every ten seconds has stopped."

"I'll get a takeaway pack of goodies ready for you."

I whimpered. "Will you marry me?"

She laughed and patted my shoulder. "Sorry, sweetheart, but I promised myself to someone else." She looked across the way and yelled, "Another marriage proposal, Wesley."

Her fiancé's head spun our way. "Makenzie, how could you try and take my woman from me?"

I smiled. "She promised me baked goodies."

He sighed. "Woman, you can't have her, but if you want me…." He winked.

Laughing, I shook my head. "Sorry, Wesley, but I'll keep trying for Delia."

He huffed. "Every man, woman, and dog does."

"He jokes." Delia smiled and rolled her eyes. She kissed my cheek and went back to work.

She may say he joked, but he spoke the truth. Delia was gorgeous. Nearly every day someone would ask her out. However, she'd told me her heart belonged to the man who baked goodies in the back of the cafe. She'd told me as soon as her dad had hired him, she was a goner, and it was the same for him. It was sweet. It was what I would have liked with Robert or even with the next man in my life.

The idea of my purple beast of a vibrator did have its merits. I was glad I'd purchased it.

For one, it didn't talk, it didn't grunt, and it wouldn't sweat a puddle over me. Not that sweat wasn't hot, it was, just not when I could nearly swim in a man's sweat. That was a turnoff.

The vibrator would also get me off each time I wanted it to. It wouldn't care about itself. I would be in control and get what I wanted out of it in the end.

Oh God, what am I doing sitting in the bakery sipping coffee, eating a muffin, and thinking about my soon-to-be-delivered purple friend?

Wiping my mind of sex devices, I finished my breakfast, grabbed my pack of goodies, and headed back to the apartment. Dread swam over me, causing my body to shiver as I rode the elevator up. I prayed he was not there.

Hell, if I wouldn't look like a fool in front of Steve, the man on duty watching the cameras, I would have gotten to my knees and prayed harder.

All I wanted was to drop off the treats and head out again to do some food shopping. Then at least once I got the food I needed for the room, I wouldn't have to leave it. I could even pick up some DVDs to watch for the next day, since it was Sunday, another day free from hell. I blanched, sensing myself pale.

What was I going to do Monday?

I would have to sit outside his office and know, *know* my boss had held me, had seen my tatas, and how I had fondled him. Not in an inappropriate way, but still, I had my hands on him.

If only I had copped a feel—*no, do not go there, Kenzie. Jesus.*

The doors opened, and I froze.

Standing on the other side was Grayson and goddamn Harpy.

I quickly looked everywhere but at them. "Hi, um, just dropping off some cakes and then going shopping. Have a nice day." *Am I talking loud?* "Yep, enjoy it. Nice day to take a walk. Fresh air is amazing for the skin." *Do not talk about skin. He saw too much of my skin last night.* "Not skin." I laughed nervously. "I mean the eyes!" I shouted as I walked across the living room. "Fresh air is good for the eyes, makes them water and get all the icky stuff out of them." *Oh. My. God. What in the fuck am I saying?* "Anyway, be good—" *Shut up, shut up. I need to get out, get away. Her boyfriend, my boss saw my boobs. Abort, abort.* I dropped my pack on the bar and turned back around. With a quick flick of my eyes, I saw Grayson and Harpy were still standing outside the elevator facing my way. They were probably wondering if I was high. "So, I'm just going to leave that there and go out, leave you both to it." To it? Like I thought they were going to have sex. Oh, God, were they? My stomach rolled. Walking back to the elevator, I thanked the high heavens the doors were still open, and entered. Turning, I waved. "See you, ah, later, gators. No, wait, I probably won't see you later. I mean, I could be out all day and night. Anyway—" I let out a squeak when my wrist was taken hold of, and I was tugged out the elevator, noticing Harpy was forced inside.

"I'll set it all up later," Grayson said darkly. "For now, I have to talk to Mrs. Mayfair."

"Is it her?" Harpy snapped as the doors started to close.

"Is what her?" I all but screeched. "I haven't done any-thing," I cried. "I'm innocent, I tell you. Innocent," I shouted as the doors shut all the way.

"Remind me to never partner with you in poker." Grayson sighed, running a hand through his hair.

"I just didn't know what she meant. Do you know?" I shrugged. "That comment was like a puzzle I need to figure out. What could it mean?" I threw my hands up in the air.

"Makenzie."

"Maybe I should go and talk to her? No, that's probably not a good idea. I never know what's going to come out of my mouth."

"Makenzie."

"Anyway, I need to go food shopping and get some, um…." I trailed off to press the elevator button and did so repeatedly.

"Cough medicine?"

I barked out a laugh. "No. No way. I meant something else that will help my stuffy nose. Remember, I'm sick. I'm not really with it at all, and you never know what I'll say or do."

I sensed Grayson take a step closer. Still, there was no way I was going to look at him. I'd made it so far avoiding any discussion. I wasn't going to risk meeting his gaze and… I didn't know what would happen, but still, I wasn't risking anything.

"Are you nervous?" Grayson's voice was low and held something else I didn't understand.

I shuffled closer to my one way of escape and pressed the button once again. "Nope," I squeaked and continued to press the button over and over.

"How are you feeling?"

Nodding, I said, "Good. Great. Busy."

I bit my bottom lip when I heard him chuckle, trying and failing to ignore that his chuckle sent a shudder through me.

"Kenzie," he said low.

"Hmm?"

"I *am* sorry for the way I spoke to you—"

"No! It's all forgiven, all good, nothing to be sorry for… well, except, I'm sorry for—"

"Let me see if I can get this right. Climbing me. Hugging me. Saying certain things to me?"

"Uh-huh."

"Look at me," he ordered gruffly. My head snapped up. He studied my burning face before saying, "You couldn't help being under the influence of"—he smiled—"cough medicine. There is nothing to apologize for."

"So, I still have my job?"

He groaned. "Why do you think I'll fire you every time something happens?"

Shrugging, I mumbled, "I don't know." Finally my escape route arrived, its doors opening. I stepped in quickly. Turning to look back, I saw Grayson watching me with a smirk on his face.

"Um, thank you, for, ah, putting up with me last night." I smiled.

As the doors started to close, I caught his chin lift just before they shut all the way.

"Ohmygod," I said breathlessly.

What just happened? What did Harpy mean? Why was Grayson so nice to me in his demanding, alluring sort of way?

He apologized.

Holy shit, that meant I should forgive him, which also meant I shouldn't really be dodging him in the apartment from then on.

Well, maybe I was going to become too busy to be around the house.

Maybe, I could take up a hobby of duck feeding.

Chapter FOURTEEN

IT WAS JUST over a week later that all sickness had left the building, thank God. There was no chance I would take another dose of cough medicine. Ever. Even if my life depended on it, I'd prefer to rock and groan in the corner with a fever rather than climb hot men inappropriately. Dylan ended up getting sick, so I was yet to get my hands around his neck. Didn't stop him from annoying me though, begging me to come to his house and take care of him. Being the nice person I was, I ended up dropping off some soup, with a threat that I would see him when he was well enough for violence.

He knew I was all talk. There wasn't a chance I could harm one hair on his head. He had helped me take that all-important step to finding myself again. Plus, even though he wasn't gay, he was still my closest friend.

Grayson, of course, didn't get sick. Apparently he was immune to anything and everything.

That first Sunday after my monkey-climbing incident, I had spent in my room resting and watching DVDs. Mainly because I didn't want to take any time off work. When Monday came and then went without any incidents, the tension rolled off my shoulders. I was grateful Grayson was being a decent man and not bringing up Friday night to me at all. It meant the rest of the week passed smoothly.

"Mrs. Mayfair, I need the proofs for Ethan's cover," came his booming voice over the intercom.

Hearing the elevator doors open, I looked that way to see Angelia smiling. She wiggled a file out in front of her. Pressing the button to my boss's office, I said, "They're just arriving. I'll bring them right in."

Standing from my seat. I greeted Ang. "Hi."

"Hey, babe. Sorry for the delay. Let me know if he wants me to change anything."

Leaning in, I whispered, "Shouldn't it be Ethan's manager taking all this on board?"

"Grayson is his manager. Until Ethan can prove himself, he'll stay with Grayson. Though I don't think there'll be any issue at all with Ethan. The other day I walked past recording and let me tell you, that guy's voice it as smooth as butter. If I weren't gay, I'd even spread him all over my—"

"Mrs. Mayfair," was yelled through his office door.

Ang rose her brows. "Yikes, I'll get out of your hair."

"Thanks. See you at lunch," I called and then made my way into Grayson's office. My thoughts were on Ethan and Grayson. Did Grayson take care of all new clients that started out or just the ones who contacted Grayson directly, those who asked for a switch? Maybe Grayson had to pay out Ethan's old music producers to get him over to our side. It could explain why Grayson would personally take Ethan on.

Not that Grayson didn't oversee most clients; he did have the final say on most things after all. However, all the other clients had managers from Grayson's company to themselves.

After placing the file on the desk, I froze because sitting on his desk was an opened box and in it sat my purple vibrator.

My wide eyes flicked to Grayson's amused ones.

"I think it had been addressed incorrectly, because I certainly didn't order it."

No.

Fuck no.

Did autofill screw with me?

"Um…." I laughed nervously. "I-ah, I…." I licked my dry lips and laughed again. "I got it as a joke for Dylan."

"Really?" His brow arched.

I nodded and kept nodding as I picked up the box, turned, and headed back to the door.

"Mrs. Mayfair," Grayson called.

Spinning back, I squeaked, "Yes?"

"Take a seat and tell me what you think of this song from Ethan, please. It's called 'Daylight.'"

My shoulders went back. I was thrilled and proud he wanted *my* opinion on something so important even after something so embarrassing. As soon as I was seated across from him, with my box—the cardboard one—in my lap, he pressed something on the phone and Ethan's voice rang through the speakers. The only instrument accompanying him was a guitar.

"I believe you create your destiny,
At some point chose a path;
Is it one of loneliness,
Or a preconceived fate?

What's normal for the average man,
Did not interest me;
A part of me was longing for,
The gift you gave to me.

With you I'm in the daylight:
The sun is your soul;
I don't have any lonely nights,
When I think of you.
With you I want to stay forever, together
as one;
If time could stand still,
The light in my night.

The life that I've had,
Seemed like such a chore,
But now I surely know,
You're the reward.

It took no time to realize,
I felt alive;
My heart started beating loud,
With you by my side.

With you I'm in the daylight:
The sun is your soul;
I don't have any lonely nights,
When I think of you.
With you I want to stay forever, together
as one;
If time could stand still.
The light in my night."

When it was switched off, I lifted my head and smiled. "It's beautiful."

He studied my face. "It's one of Ethan's original songs. His old producers wouldn't let him place it on the album."

"Seriously? Well, that's ridiculous. Women will go crazy for it, and the way Ethan sang it…. Wow. Are you allowing him to add it?"

"His talent at his age is rare." He nodded, more to himself than me, while he looked at his computer. "The songs he's put forward will be on his album."

Standing, I clutched the box behind my back, hoping he'd forgotten about it and said before I left, "If they're like the one you've just shared with me, Ethan will rock the world."

I backed my way toward his door and spun at the last second, my eyes going to my desk and then they lifted, only to widen.

"Kenzie," Grayson called.

"Makenzie." Randal smiled from in front of my desk.

I heard a chair being pushed back behind me and more shuffling. I needed Randal to get out of the office before I landed in more trouble for bringing "personal matters" into the workplace.

Hurrying out of the room, I placed the box in the bottom drawer and stood behind my desk, my cheeks heating from hiding a vibrator at work and from the way Randal ran his eyes all over me. "Um, hi, what are you doing here?" I asked in a whisper.

"I hadn't heard from you, so I risked making a fool of myself to come ask you to lunch." He smiled, and then his eyes shifted behind me.

I gulped.

"Um," I started, my body tensing from the warmth I felt at my back. "I don't have lunch for another half hour."

"I'm sure you won't mind Makenzie skipping out a little early." Randal grinned at the man standing at my back.

"No. It's fine," Grayson bit out through clenched teeth. I didn't understand why he seemed annoyed… well, other than the fact I was going to have an early lunch, but at least Randal was showing an interest and wanting to spend time with me, not just wanting to fuck me, as Grayson had put it.

"Wonderful," Randal said, his eyes moving to me. "Makenzie, would you like to grab your purse?"

"Ah, sure." I nodded, bending down to the bottom drawer. Only I didn't realize Grayson was so close to me. When I bent, my bottom brushed against his crotch. My face burning, I snapped up straight, and shifted to the side, placing my bag on my shoulder. I walked around my desk and without looking at Grayson, I called, "I'll be back in an hour. If you need anything, just text or call." Of course he didn't reply. So once I was next to Randal, he held his arm out to me. I took it, and we made our way to the elevator.

"CAN I ASK you something personal?" Randal asked. He had taken me to a restaurant down the road from where I worked. On the way, and for the first twenty minutes, we talked about things we liked and disliked. What his business entailed, and if I liked doing what I was doing, which I did. His company was nice and new. His lingering gazes were sweet, and his warm touches to my arm or back were okay. Only, I didn't find myself swooning over them.

After a sip of my Coke, I nodded, and said, "Yes."

He smiled, shifted in his seat so his elbows rested on the table, his chin in his hands as he stared at me. "Is there something going on between you and your boss?"

Laughter burst out of me. "No." I shook my head and bit my bottom lip. Was it hot in there? I lifted my hair up off my neck to air it.

"And you're blushing for?"

"Hot flash. Maybe I'm going through the change of life." I squirmed in my seat.

"I think you're a little young for it." Randal chuckled. "Do you like him?"

"Pfft, nope."

"Hmm." He sat back and smiled.

"Hmm? What does hmm mean?"

Randal shrugged. "Nothing."

My phone buzzed on my lap. I'd kept it out in case I was called back to work. While Randal's attention went back to his food, I checked it.

Grayson: Has he mentioned his house?

My hand tightened around my cell. My eyes were still on the first text I had ever got from Grayson. The way my heart reacted was like I had received my first love note in elementary school.

I quickly replied. **No, why?**

Grayson: He will. Which will mean he wants you back there. In his bed.

Me: Don't be silly.

Grayson: Never am.

Randal cleared his throat. I looked up, and he said, "I live not far from here. You should come around some time and see the view. I have floor-to-ceiling windows."

"Um, maybe." I smiled and then started to sweat, while I ate some more pumpkin risotto. Oh God, was Grayson psychic? Did he have a camera in the restaurant?

Was Grayson right? Did Randal want to have sex with me? How did I feel about that? Honestly, I wasn't sure how I felt, except my stomach churned unpleasantly and my upper lip was wet with more perspiration.

Why did the thought of sex with Randal cause me to want to run?

It was all Grayson's fault. Randal was probably only trying to be nice by asking me to his house to *really* look at the views, and there I thought he wanted sex.

Would sex with Randal be so bad? He was good-looking, smart, nice, and it had been a very long time since I got a bit.

My phone buzzed causing me to jump.

"Are you okay?"

"Yes, no, sorry, it's my sister." I waved the phone in the air. "She's having girl problems." That could mean anything, so I dumbly said, "Tampon problems." I blanched. Not wanting him to think my sister was a novice, because apparently, it mattered in my mind, I added, "Not that she has one stuck up her…. I mean, ah, her nose was bleeding, and her friend said to—because of that movie, she thought it was a good idea—"

"Makenzie." Randal smiled.

"Yes?"

"Do you need to call her?"

Standing, I nodded. "I really should, it will only take a few moments." I smiled and then made my way toward the restrooms. Looking down at my phone, I saw another text from Grayson: **Go to the restroom.**

Why was he telling me to go to the restroom? That was strange. As I started down the hall to the ladies' room, my wrist was seized in a tight grip and I was spun, my back hitting the wall. Looming over me was my boss.

"What are you doing here?" I snapped.

"You need to go back to work," he growled down in my face.

"What? Why? And why did you come here to tell me?"

He straightened. "Just go back to work. Tell him you were called back."

"No." I crossed my arms over my chest.

Grayson's nostrils flared. "Makenzie, as your boss, I'm telling you to go back to work."

"Is there a certain reason why?"

"Yes," he snarled. "That guy out there is a douche. You could do better."

Narrowing my eyes, I jutted my chin out and up, then asked, "And you think you have the right to tell me who I can and can't date? Hell, I will date…" I looked around. I grabbed the waiter by the arm and pulled him close. "Him, if I want to."

"I'm up for it."

Looking at my new friend, I saw he was around eighteen. I quickly let go and said, "Thank you, but I didn't realize you were so young, and I was trying to make a point."

"If you change your mind, come see me again here."

"She won't," Grayson barked low. The boy looked uneasy.

"I will if I want to," I snapped close to Grayson's face and then turned back to the poor waiter. "But I won't, thanks again though." The waiter winked, moved out of Grayson's way, and went back to whatever he was doing before I'd grabbed him.

"Grayson?" a soft female voice called. We both glanced down to the entrance of the hall to see a stunning woman in her early twenties.

I snorted, shook my head, and then snorted again. Glaring at Grayson, I asked, "Does Harpy know you're out with another woman?"

"She no longer has a say since we split."

I waved my hands in front of me. "Whoa, and here you are going for a younger version of her." I slapped my hand over my mouth. "It's none of my business. Your personal life is your own. And so is mine."

"Makenzie—"

"I'll get back to work after I let Randal know I appreciate his offer to see the view at his house, but I realize I'm not ready to date. It's too complicated."

His eyes narrowed. "I told you he would mention his place."

"You did." I nodded. "Am I to expect your new friend to be at the apartment seeing your view?" I gasped. I couldn't seem to keep my mouth shut and my thoughts on the inside.

I shouldn't care what he did.

I shouldn't care at all.

Why was I caring?

God.

I did.

I had to admit it to myself.

I had a huge damn crush on my boss.

Blushing, I offered to the ground, "I'm sorry. Put what I said in the 'it's none of my business' basket, and I'll get going."

He let me go also, because he was busy on a date. Why had he even chosen that place? Had he known I was going to be there?

Walking back to Randal, I suddenly felt guilty over having lunch with him in the first place. I picked up my bag, and said, "Sorry, Randal, but I have to head back to work." I took out some money and tried to hand it to him.

He shook his head and stood, which was when I noticed there was money on the table already. "My treat. Come on,

I'll walk you out." He took my elbow and led me toward the door. I didn't look back nor did I search for Grayson. The last thing I wanted to see was a doe-eyed woman drooling over him.

Standing out front, Randal turned to me and said, "Thank you for joining me. I would like to go for a drink one night. As a friend."

I tilted my head to the side, confused. "Friends?"

"Yes." He grinned. "I saw Grayson arrive. I'm not sure what he was doing with that woman, but if the looks he sent my way were poisonous, I would be dead by now."

I shook my head. "But, he and I aren't… he's on a date, and he's my boss."

He shrugged and winked. "We'll see. Drinks then one night?"

Smiling, I said, "I would like that."

He leaned in and kissed my cheek. As he started to pull back, I noticed his eyes gain a wicked gleam to them and then quickly, he touched his lips to mine. "Just to get the ball rolling."

I threw my head back and laughed. "You're crazy."

"Tell me that in a couple of months."

"Gladly," I said and playfully shoved him away.

"Talk soon, Makenzie."

Nodding, I watched him turn and walk away. His words made me giggle again. There was no chance anything would happen between Grayson and me. I had to accept it and move on. My life was finally in my hands. I wouldn't allow myself to pine for the unattainable.

Life was meant to be enjoyed. Cherished. And I would.

Chapter
FIFTEEN

It had been a little over a month and I was sitting at my desk in the office when I heard the elevator doors open. I looked up and smiled. Standing, I clapped and waved like a wild woman. Then, to top it all off, I jumped up and down. I started for them just as Lori saw me. She threw her hands up and waved, then tugged on Dad's arm and pointed toward me. I was already close when I watched Dad look my way and saw his eyes mist, which of course caused me to get teary.

"Puddin'," he mumbled, right before I threw my arms around him. He hugged me close and whispered with a voice clogged with emotions, "Been too fuckin' long. Shit, girl. Shit."

"I'm sorry, so sorry, Dad."

He let go, pushed me back, and gave me a stern look. "Don't be sorry. You live, you learn, and you find what's good, what's bad, and what stays. Your family will always stay, no matter what."

Nodding up at him, I heard a sniffle beside us. Facing my sister, I cried, "Lori." I wrapped her up in my arms as she wound hers around my waist and buried her face into my neck. "I know I've said it a million times over the phone, but I've missed you like crazy."

She laughed, and in her quiet voice, she said, "You also promised no men would come between any of us again."

Shifting back, I threw one arm around her shoulders, then my other went around Dad's waist, and I walked them toward my desk. I said, "And I'll keep that promise for the rest of my life."

"Well, kid, you'll have to, 'cause we ain't letting go ever again." Dad smiled down at me.

"And I never want either of you to." I stopped at my desk and reached in my bag. "Here is the spare key card. Go up to the top floor and to the right is my side of the apartment. You can pick any room, except the first on the left because it's mine."

"Fancy place, Puddin'."

Nodding, I said, "I was lucky to have found the job with a living arrangement."

"And it was all due to my handsome face," Dylan said as he walked out of Grayson's office and placed his arm around my shoulders.

Dad's eyes narrowed, and Lori blushed.

"Dad, Lori, this is Dylan Jackson. My friend."

"Friend? Not with benefits?" Dad asked, crossing his arms over his chest.

"Dad!" I cried.

Dylan laughed. "No, Mr. Dad. Just friends."

Dad grunted out, "Good. She just got out of a fucked up marriage."

"Dad." I groaned, palming my forehead. "Dylan, this is my father, Trent High, and my sister, Taylor High."

"Sister? There's another one of you. You never told me, sweetheart. You been holding out on me?" He held out his hand to Lori. Reluctantly she took it. He brought her hand up to his mouth and kissed it. "It's a pleasure to meet you, fair maiden."

I elbowed Dylan in the ribs and ordered, "Hands off."

"But—"

"Hell no, kid," Dad said in a stern voice, dragging Lori in to his side so Dylan had to let go of her hand.

A throat cleared behind me. I stiffened when his grumbly voice said, "Mrs. Mayfair, are you having a party at your desk?"

Glancing to him, I saw Grayson just outside his door. The past month had been… where it should always have been: a strict employee-employer relationship, and if I had to admit it, it helped calm my crush to a mild heat that ran through me.

What also helped was that Grayson had disappeared for two weeks right after the restaurant incident and only communicated with me via e-mail.

It had been fine with me. He had probably been busy with the woman he was with at the restaurant, probably whisking her away to some exotic destination.

Not that I cared.

I didn't.

Though, I missed him. I missed his lip twitch, his patronizing eyebrow rise, and his always bored, yet annoyed expression.

Nope. Stop, I didn't miss him.

"No, Mr. Jackson. Dad, Taylor, this is my boss, Mr. Grayson Jackson. Mr. Jackson, this is my father, Trent, and sister, Taylor. I mentioned in an e-mail that they were coming to stay with me."

"Well, damn, this is your boss. You're goddamn huge." Dad stomped his way to Grayson, looked up and reached out to shake his hand. "Good to meet'cha, son. Thanks for taking on my daughter, and sorry if she caused too much trouble when she took cough medicine. Why the last time she took it at home, I had to—"

"Dad! Mr. Jackson doesn't want to hear it."

Dad rolled his eyes. "Anyway, I'm cooking tonight. Said to Puddin' it was the least I could do while I'm here. You wanna stay for dinner?"

Grayson smiled. "Thank you for the offer, but I'll be out most of the night."

"Too bad."

"I'm free," Dylan put in.

Dad looked over his shoulder. "Not you."

Dylan rolled his eyes, and when Dad turned away to talk to Grayson again, Dylan winked and shifted closer to Lori. I gave him a dirty look, which he completely ignored, as he tried to talk with my sister. Only she didn't meet his gaze. Instead, her cheeks went red, and her answers were head shakes or nods.

In general, Lori was shy.

However, with a good-looking guy like Dylan, she would be a mess.

"Well, we'll let you all get back to work. Grayson, son, if you get a chance to get off work early, you come to dinner, yeah?"

"I will, thank you."

Dad slapped Grayson on the back, then gave a scathing look at Dylan as he pulled Lori close once again. I got a quick goodbye from them both before they started for the elevator.

"There're two of you," Dylan commented. "I'm sorry, honey, but I'm totally taken with your sister."

"She's twenty-one, Dylan, and the shyest person I know. Except with me."

"I know." He sighed.

Reaching up, I smacked him in the back of the head to get his attention. When he looked down at me, I said, "You mess with her, I will disown you as my friend. I will also put chili power in all your underwear, and that will only be the start."

"I promise to treat her with the utmost care I have ever given anyone. I'll be on my best behavior, and I swear to you, if she doesn't want anything to do with me, I'll back off. But, Kenzie, I can't not try…. She's stunning, sweet, and shy. Her whole being sings to me."

I groaned. "You only just met her."

He grinned. "It's been said a person can fall in love at first sight." He leaned in and kissed my cheek. "I have a meeting about a property. But do not fear, my dear, I will play it slow and safe." He spun and walked off to the elevator.

With a sigh, I went back to my desk and sat down. "Your family…"

Glancing over my shoulder to Grayson, I narrowed my eyes and warned, "Choose your words carefully, Mr. Jackson."

His expression was back to the bored one. "I was going to say are different, but in a good way."

Smiling, I faced the computer again, and said, "Yes, they are."

AFTER I'D FINISHED work for the day, I went upstairs and walked into the apartment to an amazing smell. No one had cooked for me in such a long time that the scent alone warmed my heart and brought tears to my eyes. I found Dad and Lori in the kitchen, Dad at the stove and Lori sitting at the kitchen table studying.

"Hey, Puddin', dinner's nearly ready."

"Great. Smells wonderful, Dad." I smiled. "I'm just going to change."

"I'll pack up my books and put them in my room," Lori said. I waited for her before I left and we walked together to my side of the apartment.

"What do you think of the place?"

Her eyes lit. "It's incredible. Are you sure you want to move out when I finish school?"

I bumped my shoulder into hers. "Of course." I cleared my throat. "What did you think of Dylan?"

She blushed. "He seems nice."

"He is. He can be annoying sometimes, but he's helped me so much."

"I remember you telling me."

"He looked taken with you."

She scoffed. "I doubt that. No man as handsome as him could be." Her statement hurt my heart because my sister lacked confidence, much the same way I had with Robert, and I didn't like seeing it. I could only hope with time she would eventually find it within herself, with the help of others if need be.

"You think he's handsome?" I teased.

She grinned. "Shut up. There is no female on this earth who wouldn't. Anyway, you get changed, and I'll put these away."

Getting out of my work clothes was always a pleasure. It was like taking off a bra and letting the girls swing free. I dressed in leggings and a sweater. As I opened my door, I found Lori standing there.

"Can I ask you something?" Lori said when we started for the kitchen.

"Of course."

"Your boss, does he treat you okay? He seems… kind of short with people. God, Kenzie, he looked so scary."

Laughing, I nodded. "I know what you mean. He does have a bite, but he's okay with me." When he wasn't confusing me.

"Does he actually have a new girlfriend?"

"What do you mean? I told you he does, that woman from the restaurant."

She shrugged. "Did he actually confirm she was his girl-friend?"

I thought about it for a moment. "Well, no. Why are you asking?"

"I just saw the way he was looking at you," she said as she pushed the door to the kitchen open.

Looking to the floor, I asked, "What do—" I was cut off when I bumped into her back. Lifting my gaze, they landed on the kitchen table where I found Dad, Grayson, and Dylan.

"Don't just stand there staring. Get your butts to the ta-ble. Grayson brought home a stray for dinner," Dad called.

"I'm sure you meant brother, Mr. High." Dylan smiled.

"Nope." Dad shook his head. Grayson laughed and Dylan frowned, until he looked our way and his eyes landed on Lori. Then he smiled while Dad groaned. "Girls, move it, I'm starved."

Confusion swamped my mind. Didn't Grayson have a dinner date? What was he doing there? Why did he want to have dinner with us?

Pushing Lori forward, I said, "You're always hungry, Dad. Lucky we're having meat or did I mean—"

"Not one more word, girl," Dad snapped with a glare my way.

Lori met my gaze, and we both giggled.

Dad turned to Grayson, and said, "Never have girls, son. They're nothing but trouble."

"I'm not sure if I get a say in the end, Mr—"

"None of that, you call me Trent."

Grayson nodded as Dylan said, "Will do, Trent."

"Not you." Dad waved his hand toward Dylan, who was sitting beside Grayson. Dad sat at the end of the table, so I took the seat next to him, which I shouldn't have because it was opposite Grayson. That left Lori sitting opposite Dylan.

"I get a feeling you don't like me, Mr. High."

Dad rolled his eyes. "What I don't like are liars. Heard you told my daughter you were gay, but then she found out you weren't."

Dylan sighed. "That was only one bad thing. I'm certain you've heard many good things about me also." Dad grunted. "Kenzie, you didn't tell your dad how much I've helped you?"

"I have." I looked at Dad to see he was looking at Lori with narrowed eyes. I glanced there to see her eyes were on Dylan. It was obvious Dad's aggression stemmed from worry about his youngest getting a crush on an ex-musician and player. Really it was his own fault googling him and Grayson after I'd told them where I worked and about Dylan being my friend. "Don't worry. He'll warm to you eventually."

"Maybe we should eat?" Grayson suggested.

Straightening, I kind of yelled, "Good idea." Then I started to dish up the casserole Dad had made. Out the corner of my eye, I saw Dad's hand clench around his fork. I glanced to Lori to see her smiling shyly at Dylan, who winked. "Dad," I yelled. His eyes came to me.

"What are you yelling for?"

Besides the fact his thoughts were on forking Dylan in the eye, I shrugged and said, "Um, I don't know. Maybe my hearing is going. Anyway, can you grab the rolls off the counter for me?"

He grumbled something under his breath but got up anyway. I slid down in my seat and kicked out my foot to Dylan.

Grayson suddenly cursed. He glared at me. "Did you just kick me?"

Shit! "Ah, that was meant for Dylan."

"Why would you want to kick me?" Dylan asked.

"Enough or Dad's going to end up killing you," I snarled.

He gave me innocent eyes, then smiled and nodded. "Okay, okay. I'll behave. I can't help but stare at your sister. She gorgeous."

Grayson slapped his brother in the back of the head.

Smiling, I sat up in my seat and said, "Thank you."

Grayson nodded, his lips twitching. Why was I suddenly thinking of licking his lips? Then again, I had heard if a person licked a certain something, it was theirs.

"What're you all whispering about? Thought you were going deaf?" Dad questioned as he slammed the basket of rolls on the table and glared at me.

Waving my hand in the air, I told him, "It comes and goes."

Dad snorted. "You were never good at lying." We all started to dish our own meals up.

"So, Mr. High, tell us some embarrassing things about Kenzie," Dylan asked.

"No!" I screamed.

The roll Dad had in his hand went flying across the table. "Jesus fucking Christ, Puddin'. For the love of God, go get your ears checked."

Nodding, I said, "I will, and Dad, I don't think you should swear so much around my boss."

Dad looked to Grayson. "You mind swearing?"

"Not at all," my boss said before taking a bite of his roll.

Dylan snorted. "Grayson's vocab consists mainly of swear words."

"See, it's fine, Makenzie." He looked to the men. "You two got girls?"

"I'm single." Dylan smiled, then his eyes twitched. I could tell he was dying to look at Lori for her reaction, but he didn't. Hell, I was proud of him.

"Wish you had," Dad mumbled. "What about you, son?" Dad asked Grayson.

A burst of nervous laughter came out of me. I waved my hands around, and said, "I'm sure Mr. Jackson would prefer not to talk about his private life. Let's eat instead. Enjoy our meal in silence."

"It's fine, Makenzie," Grayson said. He looked at Dad and added, "No, I don't have a woman. You make a good casserole, Trent."

"Thanks, I—"

"What do you mean you don't have a woman?" *Shut up mouth, shut up.* All eyes came to me. Dad seemed thoughtful while Dylan grinned, sat back in his seat, and crossed his arms. Was he waiting for a show or something? He wasn't going to get one. And Lori looked… happy. Why was she happy?

Grayson's eyes came to me. They held humor and something else. "Exactly what I said."

I shrugged, laughing and said, before I stuffed my mouth full, "None of my business anyway. Even though I saw her."

Damn it.

"When did you see said woman I'm supposed to be dating?"

Shaking my head, I said, "Nowhere, like I said, none of my business." Glancing down, I forked another mouthful and lifted it to my mouth, but I then stupidly said, "At the restaurant, then I guess you went away with her."

Take that mouth, you stupid, stupid body part. I shoved my food in and started chomping away. I hummed in the back of my throat and nodded at Dad, then gave him the thumbs-up. "Good," I mumbled.

"God, your sister cracks me up." Dylan laughed. I glared over at him.

"Do you mean the day you were on a date with dickhead Randal, and you saw me with Miriam?"

"Who's dickhead Randal?" Dad asked.

"Makenzie?" Grayson clipped. Huh, and there I thought how it was usually only my last name being clipped.

Ignoring Grayson, I said, "No one, Dad."

"I think I need to know about this dickhead Randal." Dad glared.

"Makenzie," Grayson growled out my name.

"There is nothing to know. We're friends, that's all," I told my father.

Grayson snorted. "Friends who kiss each other."

"Oooh, this is getting good," Dylan commented.

Dad's fist came down on the table. "Who the fuck is dickhead Randal?"

"Dad," Lori warned. "Calm down. Kenzie is old enough to do what she likes."

My eyes snapped to Grayson and narrowed. "It was a quick, friendly kiss goodbye. He was playing around."

Grayson leaned forward with his own glare. "He'd like to play around all right, with you."

"Dad," I heard Lori snap. Obviously he was about to insert his two cents, because Lori added, "Stay out of it."

"What's that supposed to mean?" I demanded. "He isn't like that. Well, maybe he could have been if I didn't tell him I wasn't ready for anything."

"Gray—" Dylan tried.

Grayson snorted again. "Did you tell him this before or after he kissed you?"

"Oh, my God. It doesn't matter—"

"Which means before, and yet he was still trying to stick his tongue down your fucking throat," Grayson barked.

"He was not, you… you asshat," I yelled.

"Now, Puddin', you have to remember he's your boss."

"I think," Lori started in a loud voice. We all looked to her. "We got off track. Mr. Jackson, you were saying Miriam wasn't your girlfriend?"

"No," Grayson said through clenched teeth. He took a deep breath and leaned back in his seat. "She's the daughter of a friend who wanted to tell me about a surprise party for her father."

The stunning woman wasn't his new girlfriend.

What did I do with that information?

Store it far away in my mind, because really, it was none of my business.

I suddenly felt awkward. Why had we been bickering in the first place? God, and in front of my father and sister.

"Well, now that it's all straightened out. Let's finish dinner," Dylan suggested.

We all started eating again, then Dad said, "What I want to know is who's dickhead Randal?"

No one replied, and eventually we all went back to small talk. Even Lori added her two cents in every now and then. I was surprised she relaxed so quickly around Grayson and Dylan. Then again, anyone would after her own sister made a fool of herself once again.

At least I wasn't the only one who'd had a crazy overreaction.

Grayson had sure gotten fired up talking about Randal, and I was only defending myself. Why did he care so much when it came to that man?

Would I ever understand Mr. Jackson?

Chapter SIXTEEN

DAD LOVED THE Dodgers game. The tickets Grayson got us were amazing, and once Dad knew my boss was the one who snagged the tickets, he grinned and said, "He's a good guy that one." Then after a bite of his hotdog, he turned to me and asked, "Anything I should know about you and him?"

Lori, on the other side of Dad, starting giggling. "It sure looked it last night."

"What are you both talking about?" I asked, sucking back a drink of my huge Coke.

"The way I saw it. All the yelling, the back and forth shit between the two of you… foreplay," Dad announced.

My Coke wedged in my throat. I choked on it and then spent the next minute trying to breathe again. Finally, I shook my head at my lunatic father and sister. "*First*. Dad, do not ever say foreplay in front of me again."

"Or me." Lori nodded. "Still, he has a point."

"Thank you." Dad smiled. "And I know all about foreplay. How do you think you two—"

"Dad!" we both cried. He chuckled.

"*Second*," I started and glared at them. "You both have lost your minds."

"Kenzie, you're blind if—"

Dad placed his hand on Lori's arm and shook his head at her. "Let her be in her denial world. She's got a lot to learn after living in dweeb world with that ex of hers for a while."

Lori cackled.

I huffed, sat back, and asked, "Dad, how old are you again?"

"Old enough to know when I see a man clearly made for my girl, but she's blind to it."

I gasped. With wide eyes, I looked to my father and asked, "You don't mean Grayson?"

"I certainly don't mean Dylan." He glanced to Lori, and added, "We'll talk about him later."

"He's my boss. He likes to run people's lives. I had enough of that with Robert. I'm—"

"Puddin'." Dad sighed. "Your boss ain't anything like dickface. Just let things keep running the way they are and one day you'll be jogging the same path Grayson wants to lead you down."

Throwing my hands in the air, I yelled, "What does that even mean?"

He patted my shoulder. "Don't worry, you'll understand one day." Dad's cell rang interrupting the confusion swirling around me. He pulled it from his pocket and answered it, "Talk." Pausing to listen to whoever was on the other end, who spoke for a while, he then said, "Got you. Good play, son." Then he hung up, placed the phone back in his pocket, and went back to watching the game.

"Ah, who was that?" I asked.

"Nothing."

I looked to Lori, who gave me wide eyes back. "I didn't ask *what* it was about. I asked *who* it was."

"Right." Dad clapped. "I need to shake the snake." Lori and I both groaned. "Be back in a tick." He stood and walked up the stairs.

"That was strange," Lori commented.

Meeting her gaze, I nodded. "I agree. The only person I know of him calling son is…" My eyes widened. "Why would Grayson call our father?"

She smiled. "I don't know, but I'm looking forward to finding out."

I wasn't.

I knew Dad and Lori thought Grayson had a thing for me, and me for him—okay, so I did have feelings for him when he wasn't being an idiot—but Grayson having one for me? That was crazy. If they got a look at Harpy, the type of women Grayson liked, they'd throw their heads back laughing. Then they'd tell me how loco they were for even thinking it in the first place.

I found my belly twisting with nerves. Why would Grayson call my father?

"Stop worrying. I'm sure it's fine," Lori said, reaching over to take my hand in hers. "Let's beat it out of Dad when he gets back."

I brightened at the suggestion. "Or we could mention letting Aunt Olive see a certain text."

We laughed together. "Even better."

"That laugh sounds kind of evil. What have you both done?" Dad asked as he sat back down between us.

"No line up at the restroom?" I questioned.

"Nope." He shook his head.

"So, who called earlier?"

He stood and shouted, "Yeah, good hit. Run, boy, run."

"Dad," I snapped.

"I'm watching the game, Puddin'."

"If you don't sit down and answer me right now, I'll send that text to Aunt Olive."

His head dipped forward, his chin just about touched his chest. "Fuck." He sat down. "I told him telling me was no good. I told him you're both masters at getting shit outta me. Could never have a surprise party for either of you. One look at me and you both knew I was hiding something."

"Who did you say this to and when?"

"When I went to the restroom."

"You took your phone out in the restroom."

"What? No, this was before I peed."

"Who, Dad?" Lori demanded.

"Grayson."

"Ha! We knew it," I shouted.

"Then why in the hell did you both just give me shit?"

Lori shrugged. "We wanted you to confirm it."

"Will you lot take your family matters out of here? It's distracting." A middle-aged man said from behind us. When we all turned slowly, the man pulled back from whatever the expression he saw on our faces, and said, "Don't worry, talk away."

"Damn right we will," Dad grumbled.

"Are you going to tell us what Grayson said?" I asked.

"He wants you to work tonight."

My eyes narrowed. "And he called to tell you… why?"

"Your cell must be dead."

Taking it out of my bag, I pressed it. Immediately, it lit up. "Nope. Try again."

"He wanted to talk about a man thing."

"With you?" Lori questioned.

"Yes. I am a goddamn man."

Sighing, I rubbed my temples. "In five seconds you tell me the truth, or I'm posting your text to Lori to Facebook."

"You little… Fine," he snarled. "He's taking you to some music award night tonight. Wanted to make sure you'll be home in time to get ready."

My eyes flicked to my sister. Hers were wide with surprise. My body stilled, only to tremble with nerves.

"I can't. I won't. I'll make a fool out of myself and him. Why would he want to take me? I'm just his assistant. I'm sure he could find someone else." I sat back on the seat, only to shift to the side, and then I moved forward again. "This is… crazy. Doesn't he see what could happen? People will take… Oh my God, people take photos at this type of thing. I don't want my photo taken." I stood, then sat again. "I have to call him." I reached into my bag for my cell. "He has to find someone else." I paused and looked to Lori and Dad. "Maybe he couldn't find someone else, and that's why he asked me, and then if I don't go, I'd be letting him down." I bit my bottom lip, looked to my hands wrapped around my cell and sighed. I then added, "But I can't go. I'll say or do something that will embarrass both of us." Looking to my family again, I said, "You both know what I'm like when I'm nervous, and Grayson makes me nervous all the time."

Dad grunted. "Good."

"Good? How can that be good? When I'm nervous, my brain doesn't function right, and I blurt out whatever's on my mind without my knowing." I sat back in the seat and crossed my arms over my chest. "I won't go." I thrust my cell out to Dad. "Here, you call him and tell him I was abducted. No, I ran away."

Dad rolled his eyes at me. "Makenzie, no. I won't call him. This is why I wasn't supposed to say anything. He knew you'd freak."

"He did?"

"Shit, yeah."

"Okay." I nodded. "Then if he knew, he will understand why I can't make it." Leaning over Dad, I pushed the phone at Lori. "You call him and tell him I'm sick."

"No way, Kenzie."

"But we were supposed to have a movie night. A *family* movie night. I'm not backing out of that. I was looking forward to it. We were going to torture Dad with a *Bridget Jones* marathon."

"Like hell I would sit through those movies. Don't matter now, you're busy. So Lori and I'll find something else to watch."

Shaking my head, I slumped back in the seat and stated, "I'm not going, and that's final."

I watched Dad and Lori share a look, with a smile playing on their lips.

"Seriously, I'm not," I snapped.

"GO AND GET ready, Makenzie," Grayson ordered from where he sat in the formal living room. He tipped his scotch back and just stared at me. We'd just arrived back from the Dodgers game—where Dad nearly had to drag me into the apartment—and exited the elevator to find Grayson waiting for us.

Covering my mouth, I coughed, and then said in a croaky voice, "I can't go anywhere. I'm sick."

He raised his brow at me. Damn that brow.

I straightened and glared. "I'm not going. I'll do or say something to embarrass us both."

He kept staring, saying nothing.

Dad and Lori were both silent beside me, taking it all in. My hands went to my hips. "Grayson, you've been around me enough to know something is going to go wrong."

He stood. His eyes still on me.

I clenched my teeth together, shook my head and then said, "You'll regret it. I'm sure you can easily find another woman to go with you. You're not so hard up you had to have your assistant attend this thing. Hell, I could go out on the street and ask the next woman walking by. Or I could call Helena. She'd be happy to go with you."

He took another step closer and raised his brow again.

"Damn it, Grayson." I stomped my foot. He sat his drink on the small table next to him, straightened, and crossed his arms over his chest. Narrowing my eyes further, I growled in the back of my throat and then snapped, "Fine. But don't say I didn't warn you."

As I walked off, I heard Dad whistle and say, "Well shit, I've been her dad for twenty-eight years, and I could never get her to give in like that." He sounded ridiculously impressed. "And hell, all without saying a single word."

Spinning around, I pointed a finger at Dad. "I'm not giving in." Then my finger went to Grayson. "Be warned, I'm fighting on the inside, and I'll be annoyed the whole time I'm there."

"Would it help to know your sister is also accompanying you?"

"What?" Lori gasped.

"Now, hey, I never agreed to that," Dad said.

Grayson didn't look away from me. I smiled and nodded. "Yes, actually it does help. Come on, Lori. Let's go and get changed." I stalked back to my comatose sister, took her hand in mine, and dragged her from the room.

Still, I didn't miss Dad asking, "Who's gonna be Lori's date?"

"Dylan."

Lori's panicked eyes met mine. I squeezed her hand and whispered, "You'll be fine."

"Now I can't have—"

"I assure you, Trent, I'll make sure Dylan is on his best behavior."

Dad grumbled something before he spat, "Fine."

I took Lori into my room. She looked like she wanted to throw up. "I-I don't think this is wise," she stuttered. "Why would Grayson do this to his brother? I'm not good company."

She slumped down on my bed, while I walked into my closet. "You were great last night."

"I think you bickering with Grayson helped relax me."

Sticking my head out the door, I smiled and said, "Well, I'll just fight with him again."

She laughed. "You would for me, wouldn't you?"

"Of course."

"But I won't have you do that. Be yourself, but don't pick a fight just to help me out. Enjoy yourself. After all, you're on a handsome man's arm tonight."

"I will, if you do the same."

She rolled her eyes. "I'll try, but if you see me struggling, please come to my rescue."

"Promise. Though I honestly think Dylan could talk enough for the both of you, and he wouldn't mind at all." Taking a few dresses off the hooks, I walked back into the room and laid them on the bed. "In fact, even if you didn't speak one word, I'm sure Dylan would still enjoy having you at his side."

She snorted. "Then he must be crazy."

Rolling my eyes, I told her, "You just don't see what everyone else does. You're a beautiful young woman, and men would fight for a chance for your attention and company."

She looked at me skeptically. "Are you drunk?"

I slapped her arm. "Stop it."

"How did we get ourselves into this mess?" She lay flat on the bed with a sigh.

"Blame my boss. All he has to do is stare, raise his brow, cross his arms, and I'm willing to do anything he wants."

She giggled. "I'll have to mention you'd be willing to do *anything*."

"Pfft. Okay, I'm willing to agree to crazy things like attending a music award night." My belly fluttered.

Lori sat quickly. Her voice held fear when she whispered, "Kenzie, we're going to a music award ceremony."

Gulping, I nodded. "I know."

She stood. "Oh God. I better go get ready. I'm so glad I brought my bridesmaid dress I wore to Aunt Olive's wedding. How should I do my hair?"

"Any way," I said, because I honestly couldn't help her out when I was trying not to panic over my own hair. At least I knew I'd find a dress fine enough because Robert had liked me to dress over the top to some functions.

"Okay." She nodded. "Okay," she said again on the way to the door. She turned back and admitted, "This is way out of my comfort zone."

Smiling, I nodded and agreed, "Mine also. At least I have you to do this with."

She grinned. "That's what sisters are for."

"Exactly. We go through tortuous nights together. Now go get your clothes and come back in here to get ready with me."

"I'll be back soon."

As soon as the door closed, I lifted my hand to the back of my neck. Shit, I was sweating already. *Right, remember to put in my bag, lipstick, baby wipes, deodorant, perfume, and a gun.*

To shoot myself with when the night went to the crap house.

Chapter SEVENTEEN

"I TOLD YOU," I cried to Grayson, who sat next to me in the limousine on the way back to the apartment. Looking at Lori, who was beside a smiling Dylan on the side seats, I asked, "Didn't I tell him? I knew it. I did. I knew somehow I would do something."

"It's wasn't that bad," Lori commented quietly and then winced.

Her wince said it all.

Scoffing, I slumped back in the seat and into my sour mood.

"I thought it was awesome. You got up like a skillful ninja. Never seen you move so fast." Dylan chuckled.

"I will slice you open if you mention it again," I warned.

"Come on, Kenzie, relax. It probably won't even make TV."

Leaning forward, I rested my elbows on my knees, buried my head in my hands, and groaned. I knew it would make

TV. I just knew the whole of America would have seen me making a fool out of myself. I couldn't face anyone.

"No one will see it besides the people who were there tonight, and even if people did, you shouldn't let it worry you," Grayson's deep, sober voice said beside me.

Turning my head, I asked, "How can you be so sure? And how are you so calm?"

Ignoring my first question, which told me he wasn't sure people wouldn't see it, he stated, "I have nothing to get worked up over."

Nothing to get worked up over.

Well, really.

If I hadn't have made an idiot of myself, then I knew I'd be worked up over what happened just before my slipup.

THREE HOURS EARLIER

As soon as the limousine stopped on the red carpet, my body started shaking. "We have to get out here? In front of everyone?" I asked, my voice at a higher octave.

Grayson's lips twitched. "Yes."

Dylan patted my back. "Don't worry, we'll take care of you."

"Why are you doing this to me?" I cried as the door suddenly opened. Flashes of cameras started snapping in our faces, and we hadn't even climbed out of the vehicle.

"Hey," Dylan started. "You remember that time you took me to a scary movie when you knew I hated them?"

Slowly, I turned my head to see the wicked gleam in his eyes. "Yes," I hissed.

His smile was big. "Payback's a bitch. Grayson was kind enough to help his brother out for once."

As Grayson started to climb out, I punched him in the back. I heard his grunt, and then it was all too late to back out of anything. Dylan knew this whole scene would freak me out, the ass. Grayson's hand came in. I took it, squeezed it, and then he was helping me out of the car.

As soon as I was beside him, he got in close, while we waited for Dylan and Lori to hop out, and whispered in my ear, "You punch me again, there will be consequences."

Smiling, I said out the corner of my mouth, "Oh, I don't think so, boss. That was payback for helping Dylan torture me."

He curled my hand in the crook of his arm and started down the red carpet. People called his name and Dylan's, who was behind us with Lori, my poor sister. She would be going out of her mind with everything.

Both men ignored all the calls for interviews or questions. They headed right for the entrance. Once we were through, I turned and stopped still, my brows low. Lori was laughing at something Dylan had whispered into her ear. She saw my gaze and came forward.

"Isn't this amazing? I saw Pink, Keith Urban, and John Legend. No one is going to believe I was here."

"They will if they watched it on TV." Dylan smiled down at her.

"I wish I'd thought to DVR it."

"What have you done to my sister?" I demanded in Dylan's face.

Lori grabbed my hand. "Stop it. He's done nothing. I'm just having a great time. I never even thought I would get to see someone like Beyoncé, Taylor Swift, and…. Oh, wow, there's Adele."

I felt Grayson's heat before he whispered into my ear, "Do you even know who she's talking about?"

Looking up at him, I smiled. "Nope."

He threw his head back and laughed. I turned fully his way so I could watch; he looked amazing. His dark hair was neat and styled back from his face. It didn't matter he had stubble because he rocked it. His tux was nicely fitted to his large body.

"Well, fuck me," I heard Dylan say behind me. I looked over my shoulder to see him watching his brother.

After Grayson's laughter waned, he said, "Shall we find our seats?"

"Sounds like a plan." I nodded. My body jolted when I felt his warm hand on my lower back. I glanced up as he looked down. His eyes were light, and his lips twitched. Damn that delectable lip twitch. He was enjoying himself, and for that alone, I was happy to have been there to see it.

It was then I settled. Relaxing, I leaned into his touch. We found our seats, which were about the fourth row from the stage. Grayson was on the end. I sat next to him, then Lori and Dylan. What was also great to see was Lori relaxing as well. She was currently huddled close to Dylan as they talked about his musical past. Her cheeks were flushed, but she was asking questions and seemed excited to find out everything she could.

The ceremony started and people quieted. There were awards for everything and musicians who performed, I enjoyed a lot. Some I liked so much I was going to google them when I got home to buy their work.

Grayson leaned in every now and then to let me know who his clients were, and each time I would sit up and pay closer attention. If anyone were to ask me, I would have to say Grayson's clients were better than the rest.

Tipping my chin up, I whispered, "Do we get snacks like at the movies?" Hell, I was starting to get hungry and earlier I couldn't eat because I'd been so nervous about the whole event.

Grayson started shaking next to me. I pulled back and smiled when I realized he was chuckling. After he calmed, he shook his head and said, "Unfortunately, no."

I frowned, only to grin up at him. Then I went back to watching the stage. Still, I could feel a heat on my face and wondered if Grayson was watching me and not what was going on in front of us. Then I thought I could have something on my face, so I slyly swiped at it.

Grayson laughed.

Moving into him, I asked, "What? Did I have something on my face?"

He looked down at me. His eyes seemed to touch each inch of my face as they roamed. My breath caught and then took off at a rapid pace. My chest rose and fell quickly when I noticed Grayson's eyes heat, and then he licked his lips. My clit pulsed and I really didn't think getting turned on at an award ceremony was a great idea.

Finally, his eyes met mine and he rumbled low, "No, it's perfect."

What was that?

I bit my bottom lip. He watched and then met my stare.

Something was going on.

Something, which heated my body, pebbled my nipples, and clenched my lower stomach.

"Hey," Dylan called, breaking our connection.

Unless it wasn't a connection and I'd dreamed it all.

Then again, the way Grayson looked around me to his brother was very hostile.

"Your category is up next," Dylan said, ignoring Grayson's look altogether.

"Category?" I asked. "You're up for an award?" I whisper hissed. "Why didn't you tell me?"

He shrugged. "It's nothing."

My attention was pulled to the stage when the singer said, "And the winner for producer of the year is… Grayson Jackson."

Clapping started. People around us started to congratulate Grayson. He turned to me.

My hand went over my mouth. Behind it, I mumbled, "You won."

"Sorry?" he asked, smiling.

He started to stand. Until I grabbed the front of his jacket in my fists and cried, "You won. Oh my God." Then I kissed him.

I kissed Grayson right there in front of millions. When he finished standing, I was up with him, and when his arms wrapped around my waist bringing me flush against him, I moaned.

He pulled back suddenly, looked down to me, and clipped low, "Fuck."

Fuck?

What did fuck mean?

"Gray, get your ass up to the stage."

He nodded, only his eyes never left my face, and then he was gone.

Like someone controlled my body, I sat down. I was sure shock had started to set in. Lori's hand came down on mine. I jumped and glanced at her.

There was clapping, I heard Grayson's voice in the background, but my ears were ringing as my heart pumped harder than it had before.

"Kenzie? Kenzie, are you okay?" Lori asked.

I nodded and then shook my head.

I'd kissed my boss.

Kissed him.

My lips were sealed against his.

Oh, shit. I stuck my tongue in his mouth.

"I have to go," I whispered.

People were laughing about something, I didn't know what.

"What?" Lori asked.

"I have to go." Next, I was standing, making my way out into the aisle. Then I was falling, my knees still weak from the kiss. At least that was what I thought it was. I landed on the ground hard, only the mortification didn't stop there. There was a slant in the room, and it went down toward the stage, which was the way my body started rolling as soon as I landed on the ground.

"You're lucky you didn't hurt yourself too much," Lori offered as we pulled up in front of the apartment. That was true. I knew I'd wake up with a few sore spots, but other than that, and a torn dress, I was okay.

"Except I hurt my ego and Grayson's," I muttered, more to myself than anyone.

"You didn't hurt mine," Grayson said. He had to leave the ceremony early because of me. I kissed him, then had fallen and rolled down the aisle. How could he say his ego was still intact? I thought he was just trying to be nice.

When the driver opened the door, I patted his leg for trying to make me feel better. Then I realized I shouldn't touch him at all. I quickly pulled my hand back and got out of the car. I was already halfway to the door when Lori called my name.

Turning, I could see the blush coating her cheeks before she said, "I'm just going to talk to Dylan for a few moments. I'll be up soon."

I gave Dylan a warning look. He saluted me and grinned. Sighing, I said, "I'll try and keep Dad upstairs, but I doubt I will for long."

She nodded. I went on ahead to the elevator with my head hung low and my thoughts of everyone's face as I'd scrambled to my shaky legs after my tumble. A few chuckled; most asked if I was okay. I'd apologized and quickly ran up the aisle away from my disaster. God, I hoped Grayson was right, and no one would have seen it on TV. However, it was doubtful. After googling it in the car, I discovered it was televised live.

"I'll have to walk around the town with a bag over my head."

"It wasn't that bad," Grayson said, causing me to jump. I hadn't realized he'd followed me onto the elevator.

"Wasn't that bad?" I near screeched. "I-I, ah, you know, kissed my boss for everyone to see and somehow my tongue got an idea of its own and ended up in your mouth, then I fell on my face and rolled, *rolled*, Grayson, down the aisle in front of millions." My eyes widened. My hand went over my mouth as I gasped. "What about work? Oh…" I bent over at the waist, taking a deep breath. "They're going to think… think…. No, they're going to see I mauled you like a starving lioness." I sank to my bottom on the floor of the elevator. "Just leave me here to die. I can't face anyone."

Grayson sighed. "Get up, Makenzie, and don't worry about what people will think."

Thumping my head back into the wall, I looked up at him. "How can you say that when you were embarrassed for sticking up for me with Robert in front of everyone at work?"

He rolled his hardened eyes. "I was a dick then. I don't give a flying fuck what anyone will say or think."

What did *he* think?

I wanted to know, but there was no way in hell I was going to ask.

The doors opened, and I spotted Dad right away. He stood at the bar helping himself to a drink. "Puddin', didn't you have dinner tonight, because it looked like you were ready to devour your boss there?"

Groaning, I closed my eyes and buried my head in my hands.

"You okay after the tumble?"

I let out a whimper, then cried, "See. Everyone saw it."

Heat hit my side. I pulled my face away from my hands to see Grayson crouch beside me. "So what? None of them matter. Something else will happen, and then they'll focus on that. Besides, I'll kill anyone who says shit."

I nodded.

"Come on, Puddin', chin up and fuck the lot of them."

They were both right. I knew they were. If Grayson didn't care, then I shouldn't, right?

"I think I'll wallow in my pity for the night at least," I said.

Grayson's lips twitched, and somehow, despite my embarrassment, my hoo-ha still took notice. When he stood, he held out a hand to me. I took it and rose. We both then stepped off the elevator.

"Trent," Grayson started. "Lori's still downstairs with my brother."

"The fuck?" Dad bellowed. "Outta my way. Even though he's your brother, I'm gonna take him down."

Dad got in the elevator and pushed the button for the doors to close. I turned to Grayson and giggled. "That was evil of you."

"Let that be payback for having you go tonight."

"Thank you. That's sweet." I started for my side of the apartment, and Grayson headed to his. "And sorry again for, you know, infusing my mouth to yours. I was just really happy for you, and yay, you won. I never did say congrats. Well, good night." I laughed nervously.

"Makenzie," he called.

Turning, I said, "Yes?"

"You definitely do not have to be sorry for that kiss." He winked. My boss actually winked at me and left through the door.

Oh. My. God.

Chapter
EIGHTEEN

THE NEXT DAY, Lori and I were in my bedroom talking about the night before. Well, Lori was doing the talking, trying to keep my mind off things. I'd checked the papers and the news. My mishap had made it everywhere. I was dubbed the girl who collapsed after kissing Grayson Jackson, billionaire music producer.

That morning my phone hadn't stopped ringing. All of my lunch friends wanted to know what was going on between Grayson and me. Ignoring their calls, I sent off a text to all, stating how it was a onetime act for the camera—of course it was all staged. I wasn't sure if they believed me or not, but I then went on saying I couldn't talk about it and was spending time with my family while they were in town.

Like my father and Grayson had said, they could believe what they wanted. I'd walk into the office come Tuesday with my head held high and pray I didn't vomit from nerves.

"All we were doing was talking and then Dad has to come downstairs and embarrass me." Lori sighed.

Smiling sadly, I said, "Don't worry about it. I had a talk with Dad earlier and told him to back off. That he should be proud you're coming out of your shell around a guy in the first place. I think he just needs to see that Dylan genuinely likes you."

She bit her bottom lip and looked at me through her lashes. "Do you think he does?"

"Dylan?" I asked, and she nodded. "I really think so, sweetie."

"He's so nice, sweet, and handsome."

"I can see some swooning going on," I teased.

"There is, but I'm not sure how it could work with me going back home to finish college. There're a lot of women who would kill for his time."

"As far as I can see, he only has eyes for you."

She shrugged. "All I can do is see how it goes. Now, what about you and Grayson."

I laughed. "No. Nothing there."

Her head tilted to the side and she raised her brows at me. "That kiss last night wasn't nothing."

Groaning, I flopped back onto the bed. "I can't believe I attacked him like that."

"He didn't seem to mind. After all, he was the one who dragged you up to continue."

"Lori," I started, as I sat back up. "I've just come out of a marriage. I'm not looking for anything."

"Doesn't mean you can't have fun. Besides, when was the last time you and Robert… you know?"

"Before I left him, it was about eight months."

"Really?"

I nodded. "He wasn't interested. And honestly, neither was I."

"And tell me, when was the last time he showed any lovingness for you? When he took you out without a client being present? Bought you flowers, or any type of present?"

Biting my bottom lip, I thought about it. "At least nine months or more."

She took my hand in hers. "Honestly, I think your marriage ended a long time ago. It's okay to move on if you want to. No one will think badly of you for it."

Shaking my head, I told her, "I don't want to move on yet anyway."

Lori rolled her eyes. "Sister to sister. Do you have feelings for Grayson?"

Dropping my eyes, I thought about it. I had a crush. I just wasn't sure if the desire I felt for him was more than a fantasy. He was the most handsome man I had ever met. His height, his voice, body… everything about him appealed to me. But then we argued. He was stubborn, pigheaded, and a workaholic.

Yet… I admired him for getting to where he was, and I knew his stubbornness and such helped him accomplish his goals.

He was also sweet and caring at times.

He sent my nerves, body, and my heart into a tailspin every time he was around, and for the life of me, I couldn't get the kiss out of my head. The way he did drag me up, the way his hands then splayed across my hips and held me tightly to him.

Meeting my sister's gaze, I nodded. "I'm pretty sure I do, when he isn't being a bossy bastard."

"Then just see how things go. Be brave and don't let anyone get to you when it comes to what happened last night. All that matters is you being happy."

"What happens if he crazily has feelings for me also and we try a relationship only to then break up? I'd lose my job, my friend, since Dylan's his brother, and I'd lose him."

God, I sounded like a scared, whiny teen.

"Do you know something someone taught me?" she asked.

"What?"

She smiled. "Life is all about chance. People need to take them. Sometimes they work, and then sometimes they don't. It's the what-ifs that aren't worth worrying about. Because even when the chances you take don't work out, you learn from them. You even become a better person from them."

"Who taught you this?"

"You."

Laughing, I asked, "How?"

"You took a chance on Robert. You were fearless enough to have a good try at it. Even though Robert was a chance that didn't work out, you learned from it, and you're a better person for it. You're even stronger from it. Tell me, would you have argued back with Robert like you do Grayson?"

I shook my head. There was no way I would have. I was all about conceding when anything came to my ex. With Grayson, I felt… Lori was right, I felt stronger in myself to share my piece of mind and damn the consequences.

"How did you become smarter than me?"

"She takes after me," Dad said, entering the room. "Now what are we talking about?"

"Men."

He stopped and his hands went to his hips. "Do I need to kill anyone?"

We both giggled. "Not today, Dad."

"Good," he huffed. "Grayson was just showing me the gym floor. Get your swimsuits on. We're gonna head down there."

"Can't," I said. "I got a visit from Aunt Flow this morning." Lori hid her snicker behind her hand.

Then, of course my luck was still down the crap hole, because Grayson appeared behind my father as he boomed, "You don't have a fuckin' Aunt Flo. What are you talking about?"

Grayson's eyes widened. He then spun back around and walked out.

"Dad," I whined, shaking my head at him. "I was talking about my period."

Dad paled and then it was his turn to shift back around and walk out the door. What was it with men and periods? At least they didn't have to go through it. They only had to put up with our mood swings, but shove a chocolate bar down my throat, and I was back to being happy.

"Son," we heard Dad call. "We need to get to the shops pronto. Buy the fuckin' store out of chocolate. It's the only thing that soothes the wild beast."

"Dad!" I screamed. "Shut the hell up."

"See what I mean. Let's go."

Lori looked at me; we both bulged our eyes out at one another and then burst into a fit of giggles.

It wasn't until later, when Grayson and Dad got back from wherever they went, that Dad appeared in my doorway. Lori and I were watching a movie. He threw a box of Baby Ruths onto the bed and backed out of the room. "That should keep you satisfied for a while. There's more in the kitchen. I'm heading out with Grayson."

"Where are you going?" I asked.

"For a drink," he yelled from outside the door and then disappeared.

I snorted. "Trust Grayson to actually take time off to spend with our father. God knows what Dad's telling him."

"I think Grayson knows by now you can be a little mental at times."

The cough medicine.

The speaking my mind when it should have stayed in my head in the first place.

The kissing him.

"Yeah, I suppose you're right."

"Dad will put fear in him for whenever you have your period though." Lori giggled.

"If I get chocolate out of it, I don't mind at all," I said, reaching for the box.

"Remember the first time you got it and how Dad re-acted?"

Laughing, I nodded. "Yes. He'd just gotten home from work and Mom told him his firstborn was growing up. I was lying in the living room on the couch. He came in and asked if I was okay. God, I can't believe I yelled at him and said,

'I'm bleeding out of my vagina, Dad. How do you think I am?'"

Lori fell back laughing, holding her stomach. "I never knew Dad could run that fast."

Nodding, I added, "Then he went outside and threw his fists to the air yelling, 'You couldn't have given me one boy?'"

"I don't think he'd have it any other way though. He loves us."

"He does, and even when he's too overprotective, we love him back." After talking a bit, and moaning around my Baby Ruth, I asked, "Do you think he's happy back home?"

"You're worried about when I leave him also?"

"Kind of."

"I think he loves his job cooking, but I'm not sure how much he'll love it after I'm not there. We did a lot together. He's not only my dad but a friend, you know?"

"Maybe we can convince him to move? We could all get a house together."

Lori scrunched up her nose. "I-I can't live with him forever," she said quietly, no doubt guilt eating her up.

"That's true. How would you bring guys home otherwise?" I winked. She blushed. "We'll think of something before the time comes. I'd love to have Dad close, but I agree having him living with us could be a problem in the long run." I gripped her hand, passed her a chocolate with my free hand, and said, "We'll figure it out."

She smiled and nodded. "We will."

Chapter

NINETEEN

THE TUESDAY AFTER my screw-up on TV and the long weekend, things weren't good. Some work colleagues laughed it off with me, others ignored it altogether, and then there were the whispers from others who accused me of sleeping with the boss to get my job and to steal his money. Which was ridiculous. Besides, it was Dylan who got me the job in the first place, and couldn't they see it was one excited congratulatory kiss that would never happen again?

By the end of the week, people were no longer speaking of it. At least, if they did, it was nothing I heard about. I think what helped was how Grayson was his usual brooding self with me. He even yelled at me a few times in front of people. Which helped a lot and brought a smile to my face. Only, next time I had to make sure I smiled *after* Grayson had left because he caught it, causing his jaw to clench, his nostrils to flare, and his eyes to narrow. Then he'd stormed back into his office, slamming the door behind him. At first, I thought he could have ignored my little mistakes of e-mailing the wrong person in the company. Then again, when people witnessed his outburst, it helped my case by having them realize nothing had been going on between Grayson and me. So in the end, I was grateful for his temper.

To confirm people were dropping the subject, Friday at lunch, I was sitting with the usual people when Darby said, "Talk's died down about you and Grayson. What helped was when you tripped over your own two feet the other day. Now they think you accidently fell onto his lips and then rolled down the aisle."

Earlier, as I made my way down to the cafeteria, I'd also heard whispered from Kim, "There is no way a man like Grayson would like something like that."

A friend of hers replied, "The poor guy probably went home to wash her away."

Kim laughed. "I know I'd like to help him wash her away. Wouldn't be the first time either."

What the hell? Had Grayson been with Kim? Where was a barf bag when I needed it? Did he gag her to shut her up while they…. Shaking my head, I threw the unwanted, icky thoughts out of my head and glared over my shoulder before walking off.

Ryan snorted, bringing me back from my thoughts, and then he said, "Idiots. I guess they didn't see the way boss man clung to our Kenzie here. Like she was his air and he needed her oxygen to live."

All eyes, including my wide ones, turned to him.

"What?" he asked around his mouthful.

"There was no clinging going on. It was an excited, congrats touch of the lips and that was all."

Ryan and Hudson shared a look.

Pointing my finger at them, I snapped, "What? What was that look?"

Ryan shrugged. Hudson shook his head.

"Babe," Angelia started. I glanced at her. "The meatheads, like us, still think something will happen with the two of you."

"Me and who?" I dumbly asked.

Angelia rolled her eyes. "Grayson."

I snorted, then laughed. "You're all crazy, like my family."

Ryan arched his brows. "So your dad and sister think you and Grayson will get it on?" My dad and Lori had come to lunch a couple of times during the week, so they got to meet everyone.

Rubbing my forehead, I shrugged and told them, "I think so."

"New bet," Hudson called and everyone quickly threw money on the table placing a date on when Grayson and I would wake up and get together.

They didn't know what I knew.

Actually, they should. Grayson had a type, and I certainly wasn't it.

WE HAD JUST stepped into the restaurant when I froze. Earlier, Dad, Lori, and I were on our way out for our last dinner together before they left the next day, when Dylan and Grayson had caught us in the underground garage heading to my car. As soon as Dad had seen Grayson, he asked my boss to come along. Dylan, who had already been on his way up to see Lori, tagged along. I was surprised when Grayson agreed also and took his car with his brother in it.

So when we showed up at the restaurant and walked in, my heart jumped into my throat, and my ears started ringing with nerves when I spotted Harper sitting at the bar with a few friends.

Harper.

Grayson's ex.

Had she seen the award show?

Had she seen me kiss him?

God, I felt like a bitch all of a sudden.

Spinning around, and since I was the first one through the door, I threw my hands up and frantically said, "This place looks full. Maybe we should go somewhere else."

Like to hell, which was where I was sure Harper would be wishing me to.

"Puddin', what in the hell are you talking about? The place has heaps of tables left." He tried to shove past me, but I pushed back.

"Maybe they're empty because the food here isn't good? Did you think of that? You don't want food poisoning when you drive back tomorrow. You could poop your pants."

Shit. I just said poop aloud.

I winced. Dylan laughed, and I saw Grayson's lips twitch, and then he looked over my shoulder.

"No!" I cried and forced myself between Dad and Lori, then shoved Dylan sideways to grip Grayson's cheeks in my hands, forcing his face down, so his eyes met mine. "I think I saw something heading for your eye." I lifted one hand and swiped my finger under his right eye. "There, it was just an eyelash. Now, let's get out of here." Forcibly, I turned him and pushed his back to get him walking. Only he didn't move. Not even an inch.

Under my hands on his hard back, I felt him sigh.

He'd seen her.

My shoulders sagged as I placed my arms back down to my sides. Grayson turned. "I'm not sure why you're hiding us from Harper."

My eyes bulged. "Ah, in case she saw the awards show."

His brow arched.

"The, um." I laughed nervously. Had it suddenly become hot? "When, you know, I congratulated you. She may think… that you broke up with her." I laughed again. "For me." I rolled my eyes. "Ridiculous I know. But I don't want to cause a scene."

"Then maybe it's best she doesn't walk over to us like she is right now?" he questioned.

"Ya think?" I snapped, my eyes narrowing on him. His lips twitched as I mumbled to myself, "I would have had us out of there, but nooo."

"Grayson," Harper called in a sweet soft tone. Then I turned and her smile morphed into a scowl.

"Let's go grab a table," Dylan suggested.

Grayson nodded. "I'll be there shortly."

My gaze swung back to him. He was going to stay and talk to her. The knowledge didn't sit well with me, but I refused to analyze it.

Harper arrived next to us. She went to her toes to kiss Grayson on the cheek. Completely ignoring me, she beamed up at him. "It's great to see you. I never did get to thank you properly for the modeling job."

Modeling job?

Grayson had got her one?

"No need to thank me." Grayson smiled tightly.

"Kenzie, you coming?" Lori asked.

Harper shifted to look with a glare at me. "Did you have fun at the awards show the other night?"

For some reason, I had an urge to yell, "I didn't do it." And I was about to open my mouth when a hand covered it.

Glancing up, I saw Grayson was right next to me. He probably knew I was about to blurt out something that would have been inappropriate. "Makenzie, go and sit," he ordered. I narrowed my eyes at him as he removed his hand and gently ushered me into Dylan's arms.

I had to bite the inside of my cheek to keep from saying anything to Harper as we walked off. Her smile was smug and I wanted to knock it off her face.

"Come on, honey, retract those claws and sit." Dylan gestured to the seat next to Lori. As soon as I sat, he took the spare one on the other side of my sister.

"Dylan, I have no claws to retract. It's fine. I'm fine. Harpy doesn't get to me." I snorted, moving my eyes to Grayson and Harper as she threw her head back and laughed. I clenched my jaw and then muttered, "She's nothing special, only a model, who looks fucking good in her designer gear. And that hair, all glossy, shiny, and long. I mean, he broke up with her… I think, or did she break up with him?" I laughed nervously. Pulling the collar of my shirt away from my neck, I felt hot again. "Maybe he misses her if she broke up with him? He looks happy to see her." I slumped in my seat and picked up a fork, twisting it in my hand. "Not that I care. I don't. He's my boss. He can do what he wants."

"Puddin', put the fork down before you throw it."

Blinking, I looked at my dad, who sat on the other side of the table. Then I looked down to the fork and discovered it was stabbed into the table. Blushing, I pulled it free with a hard yank.

Sitting straighter, I smiled. "All good. I won't kill anyone today."

Unless I heard Harpy laugh one more time.

"So that's his ex?" Lori asked.

"Yep," Dylan answered. "Gold digging bi-ah-witch."

"She looks like a stick of celery," Dad offered.

Lori and I laughed.

"She just kissed him," Lori whispered.

"Puddin', let the knife go," Dad warned.

"It was only a peck," Dylan said quickly. "Like I'm sure you and dickhead Randal did."

Scoffing, I shook my head, dropped the knife, and wiped at my forehead. "I don't know why you're all running a commentary. It's not like I care." All eyes turned to me. "I don't." Damn them and their raised brows. "Let's look at the menu. I'm starved."

"She's hugging him," Lori said.

I swore under my breath.

"Jellybean, I can't afford to bail your sister out of jail. Best not tell her what's going on."

"Damn it," I snapped, picking up the knife again and waving it around at the people at the table. "This is our last dinner together. We're going to enjoy it. Everyone look at their goddamn menu."

The table fell silent. I put the knife down and picked up the menu, my movements jerky. Stupid Harpy. Stupid Grayson. Stupid fucking kiss. Not only the one she laid on him but the one I gave him.

Out of my league. He always had been.

My chest ached over the fact I made a fool of myself, not only from kissing him in the first place but also for letting my family and Dylan know of my crush.

Taking a deep breath, I had to calm my leaping heart. I needed to calm my twisting stomach and hope Grayson had insurance. There was no way of knowing if a knife or fork would end up in his eye by the end of dinner.

My body jolted when the chair beside my dad was pulled out. "Sorry about that."

The table stayed silent. For God's sake, someone speak.

"She was just telling me about the job I got her."

No one said anything, our heads buried in our menus.

Rolling my eyes, I guessed it was up to me, so I mumbled, "Uh-huh." And flicked my eyes around the menu, not really reading it though.

"She just got back in yesterday."

"Hmm," I muttered.

"I couldn't exactly walk away from her."

"Uh-huh."

Will someone else speak already before I stab the lot of you?

"It would be rude to have ignored her."

That was when I laughed. I threw my head back and laughed loud and long, my hand going over my belly. I wiped my eyes as my laughter waned. "Oh, that was precious. You being rude." I narrowed my eyes at him. "It's like your middle name."

"Boss," Dad coughed into his hand.

Clenching my jaw, I picked up the menu again.

He was my boss, and I had no right to be annoyed… like I was jealous.

I'm not jealous.

I'm not.

Fuck. I am.

Harpy was his type, and I wasn't.

"Makenzie—"

"Let's order," I virtually shouted. Looking around, I waved a waitress over. "Hi, I'd like the steak and fries."

"Okay. Would you like a drink?" she asked.

"Yes. I'd like… um, just make up any cocktail, and I'll drink it." I handed her the menu and turned to Lori. "Are you going to have a drink with me?"

"Jesus," Dad muttered.

"I'd love to." Lori smiled. "Make that two cocktails, and I'll have the mushroom risotto."

The men ordered after us. I turned to Lori and started a conversation about her exams coming up. She answered, only every now and then her eyes would flick to Grayson opposite me. She knew I was diverting the situation by not talking to him or looking at him.

In other words, she knew I was being childish.

I had to get over my crush. I had to find someone who could help me get over it.

THREE HOURS LATER

"NO, NOPE, I'M really gonna do it," I drunkenly yelled. We were sitting in the kitchen, chatting and just having fun. I had tried to get them into my living room, in case Grayson got home, but Dad thought it safer to be in the kitchen. I'd only spilled a few drinks in the past. Suddenly, I stood from my seat, only to stand on it and then the table with my drink in my hand. "I declare that all men are idiots." My sister clapped and cheered. "Men are no good for nothing. Men can kiss my round ass because I'm turning gay."

"That means I won't get grandkids from you," I heard Dad shout from wherever he was.

"I'll get them for you, Dad. Kidnapping is out so my girl-friend and I will use a turkey baster because, from this day forth, men no longer do it for me."

After dinner, Grayson had said he had to be somewhere and disappeared, taking Dylan with him. When Dylan said he'd catch up to us later at the apartment, Grayson said nothing. He was probably going off to see some other woman, or he'd planned to catch up with Harpy, who had left the restaurant an hour before us with a smile and a wink to Grayson. Not that I was looking.

"We need T-shirts made saying *Men suck*. Wouldn't that be cool?" I asked Lori.

"Totally." Lori grinned and took another sip of her cocktail. She was drinking more than she would have because she was upset that Dylan couldn't make it back. Something had happened with a business deal of his, and he had to work it out before the shit hit the fan. Which was what he said. He also promised my sister he would see her bright and early to say goodbye. Lori admitted she didn't want to say goodbye. She wanted to wrap Dylan up and take him home with her, which was when Dad had left the room to leave us to drink.

"Son, I wouldn't go in there."

I shook my head. Looking down to Lori, I asked, "Did Dad just say something."

"Nope," she replied with a happy drunk smile, probably much like my own.

"Right, where was I?"

"Men don't do it for you. You're turning gay." She giggled.

"Okay." I nodded and threw my hand up in the air, sloshing my drink around, then yelled, "Men suck."

"K-Kenzie."

"That's right, sista. Men suck, and I'm gonna get grandkids for Dad from a turkey baster." I looked down at her. She seemed pale. "Hey, hey, hey." I got to my knees on the table. "You okay? You don't have to turn gay with me. You just let me know if some guy fucks with you, you tell'em your big sista is gonna beat their ass." I reached out and patted her head. "Okay?" I asked.

"I see you're having a good night, Makenzie."

My hand froze on Lori's head. I leaned in and whispered, "My boss is standing behind me, isn't he? I did hear his voice, right?"

She nodded.

Closing my eyes, I sighed loudly before I sat back on my knees and glanced over my shoulder. "Good evening, Mr. Jackson." I raked my eyes over his body. Damn him for looking good. How was I supposed to get over my crush when he looked so bloody delicious?

"I never would have thought to return home to find my assistant standing on the dining room table," he commented, leaning against the doorframe, only to straighten and step in as Dad came into the kitchen from behind him.

"Ladies, I think it's time for bed. Lori, we've got a big drive tomorrow, and I ain't pulling over every half hour for you to puke."

I blinked slowly. Bed did sound wonderful. At least there my mouth wouldn't open where I'd say stupid stuff that should stay in my head. I got down from the table and straightened. "I'm angry at you."

"What did I do?" Dad asked.

"Not you. Him." I pointed at Grayson, then walked right up in front of him.

"Puddin', I wouldn't say any more," Dad suggested.

Grayson's lips twitched right before he said, "It's fine, Trent. No matter what she says, she won't lose her job."

Well, that was nice.

"That's nice," I cooed, patting his chest. "See, you can be sweet." I smiled and then narrowed my eyes. "But I'm still angry."

He sighed but did it with a smirk on his lips.

Lips I had kissed.

Lips I felt I was swaying toward.

Shaking my head, I stood tall and muttered, "I think I should go to bed." *Want to join me?* Was on the tip of my tongue. I bit down on my bottom lip and whimpered when I saw Grayson looking at my lips.

Spinning, I went to Lori and hugged her tightly. "I love you so freaking much, Lori, Tori, Pori."

"I love you more." She sniffed into my shoulder.

Hands on her shoulders, I pushed her back and cried, "I can't wait for you to move here. Then we can get a place to-gether." Leaning in, I whisper-yelled, "You work on Dad moving too, but not in with us. We want to bring guys home and all."

There was choking behind us.

Kissing her cheek, I said, "Sleep well, my beauty."

Next, I moved to Dad and hugged him just as tightly. "Daddy, Dad, Dad. I have missed you so, so much." Pulling back, I added, "But no more. I'll be calling all the time and Skyping and other shit, like all the time and you'll be like, 'I wish Kenzie would shut the hell up and stop calling.' So you'll just have to move here, and then I can visit instead of calling, so at least you won't hear *bring, bring, bring* like every hour."

Dad chuckled. "I'll think about it."

I pointed in his face and warned, "You do it or *bring, bring, bring* every second."

"See you in the morning, Puddin'."

Smiling, I nodded. "You will. But I'll be sad to see you both go."

"We'll be sad to leave."

"Now I feel like crying," I whispered.

"Makenzie," Grayson clipped. Jumping, I looked at him. "Get to bed."

Saluting him, I said, "Yes, sir." Under my breath, I added, "Mr. Bossy."

At least I didn't feel like crying, so I went to bed a happy drunk. Waking had been another story altogether. After a tearful goodbye, Dad and Lori left.

Dylan placed his arm around my shoulders and said, "I'm a goner, honey."

I could see it. The way he had been so attentive to Lori, leading up to the final second, and now he seemed like his light had been snubbed out. He wasn't smiling. His eyes weren't shining, and he sighed sadly.

Patting his stomach, I said, "She'll be back soon."

"Not soon enough," he grumbled.

Chapter TWENTY

Over the next month, a lot had changed, and I wasn't talking about work.

Grayson had changed.

It was only in small ways, but still, I could see them.

Actually, I could feel them.

For some reason he seemed happier, and whenever I was close to him, he would reach out to touch me in some way.

A hand to the back or arm. A finger graze here or there. Each time, my body would light with fire, and each time I would become confused by it.

He couldn't actually like me, right?

Maybe he would be like that if he had a sister or something.

Though another thought had occurred to me. In the weeks after my family had left, he'd seen how sad I had become, so it could be his way to show he cared, to show his support.

Whatever it was, it was driving me insane and made it impossible to get over my crush. He was everywhere I went in the building when I wasn't working. If I went for a swim, he'd show up. If I were in the kitchen, he would waltz in with a smirk on his face.

Worst of all, just the previous day, he came into the kitchen when I was having breakfast and informed me he was having his side of the apartments renovated. My body stiffened with a spoon halfway to my mouth.

"Pardon?" I'd asked.

"Tomorrow, I'm moving to one of the rooms on your side while they redo my side."

"But… you have a whole guest floor you could stay in."

His brow arched as he took a sip of his coffee. "You would kick me out of my own apartment rather than share your side?"

I paled. Would it be rude if I said yes? Just the thought of having him close to my room sent my emotions wild.

"Um, no?"

He chuckled before he walked out of the room.

All I had to do was hope I didn't somehow sleepwalk for the first time in my life right into his room and climb into bed with him. Then again, maybe having him in the room next door was a good idea. He could snore. I hated snoring. I was a light sleeper so little sounds woke me. He could also have night terrors and scare the crap out of me. Then I would move to the guest floor… after I comforted him, of course.

Shaking my head, I stirred the pumpkin soup on the stove. I opted out on music that night because it was payback time. As soon as I heard him coming, which I knew he would, because he was getting to the apartment earlier to have dinner with me, I was going to hide and jump out at him. I wanted to film it, his girly scream, but I thought just knowing I'd finally got one up on him would be enough.

"Hey, honey. What's for dinner?"

Jumping, I squawked out a scream and turned with my hand over my chest. "Dylan, you shit. You scared me. Wait, you can't be here. Did you see your brother on the way up? Is he coming soon?"

"Why? You planning on having a romantic dinner with him?"

I snorted, then laughed and blushed. "No. Don't be stupid."

He rolled his eyes. "Then why can't I have dinner here?"

"I was planning on payback."

"You're going to poison him?"

"What?" I cried. "No, why would I want to do that?"

He shrugged, walked over to my side, and grabbed the wooden spoon out of my hand. "That was the only thing that popped into my head." He took a taste of the soup and moaned. "You're not getting rid of me now. What else are we having with it?"

Sighing, I said, "Roast lamb."

"Yeah, baby. Now we're talking." He leaned into the counter and kept stirring the soup for me. "So what payback were you talking about?"

"Scaring him. Every day, without a doubt, I jump out of my skin when he sneaks up on me. I was going to do it to him, and then if he got angry, I'd show him what's for dinner."

"Oh, I'm staying for this." His smile was a little wicked.

"Good, you can play lookout then. Get over near the door, and when you hear him, I'll hide beside the door. Once he's through, I'll jump out."

"Pure evil. Good to see you're working it on my brother instead of having me watch a scary movie," he said as he walked over to the door and opened it a crack.

"It was one time. One movie, Dylan, and you still haven't got over it?"

"Nope."

"Have you spoken to Lori lately?" I asked, glancing over my shoulder at him to see his grin. I turned down the heat and faced him.

"I have. I'm thinking of taking some time away to go see her."

He really was taken with my sister. It was wonderful to see and hear about. Especially when all I heard from Lori was Dylan this and that.

"She'd love to see you, and Dad would love to castrate you."

He chuckled. "I can handle your father."

"Uh-huh, sure."

Dylan opened his mouth to say something when he suddenly looked back out the door. "He's coming," he whispered, his eyes lit with humor and something else I couldn't quite pinpoint.

Still, whatever it was, I put it to the back of my mind and quickly dashed for the door. I stood beside it, and Dylan moved around the corner more near the kitchen table.

As Grayson grew closer to the room, I thought I heard him talking, but then it fell silent. My heart raced in my chest. I shifted from one foot to another as a thrill ran through my body. I was giddy with adrenaline, and I nearly giggled from it.

Finally payback.

The door opened. His face was turned away. Still, I jumped out and screamed.

He yelled back and faced me, still yelling.

That was when I realized it wasn't Grayson.

Oh shit, oh shit.

The man clutched his chest and stumbled back. Grayson, who was behind the man, caught him, and helped him lie on the floor.

"Oh my God. Oh my God. I'm so sorry. So, so, sorry." I got to my knees on the floor beside him as Grayson shifted to his other side, also on his knees. I told the stranger, "I thought you were Grayson. He's always scaring me and I wanted to pay him back."

The man gasped for breath, terrifying me when he grabbed at his chest again. Was he going to have a heart attack? My stomach dropped, my hands shaking with fear.

Dylan's laughter registered.

Spinning my head toward him in the doorway, I snapped, "Now's not the time to laugh, Dylan." Meeting Grayson's eyes, I ordered on a yell, "Grayson, do something. Does he have a bad heart?" I got close to the man and begged, "Please, please be okay. Do you need something? I'm sure Grayson's got something to help. Heart pills, Advil, Viagra? Something? Anything? Please, please be okay."

"Why in the hell would you think I have Viagra and heart pills?" Grayson snarled from the other side. "I don't need either of those."

"Grayson, don't snarl at me. He's dying, and it's all my fault." My bottom lip trembled.

Grayson scoffed. "You can stop acting now, Vice."

The man on the floor quickly ceased struggling and grinned up at me.

My eyes sprang wide. My mouth dropped open. "W-what is this?"

"Oh hell, I think I'm going to piss myself." Dylan grabbed his stomach and rushed from the room.

I sat back on my knees and narrowed my eyes at the two remaining men. "*What* is this?"

Grayson stood. His hand went out to Vice and pulled him to stand beside him. Slowly, I got to my feet. My hands went to my waist, and I leaned in to hiss, "What *is* this?" Straightening, I huffed and walked into the kitchen making my way to the stove. "Stupid men and their stupid games."

"And you weren't about to play a game on me?" Grayson questioned, coming to stand beside me. He leaned into the counter and raised his stupid sexy brow up at me.

"Of course I was. You get your kicks scaring me. I thought it was about time I did it to you." I shifted to the side of the stove and leaned my butt against the counter. "How did you both know?"

"What I want to know is why you thought I would have Viagra in my bathroom? Also, why in the hell would you suggest it to someone who could be having a heart attack?"

Heat hit my cheeks. "I was just throwing the idea out there. Doesn't it help men's heart race while they… I mean, men can go all night on the stuff. I thought it could help pump—"

"Makenzie." Grayson shook his head. "I don't have any, and I can still go all night."

"Eep," I squeaked like a damn mouse. My belly fluttered happily. Though, that information I didn't need to know because it only fed my crush that much more.

Grayson's lips twitched. He looked to Vice, so I looked there also. "Vice Salvatore, business associate and old friend, I'd like you to meet my assistant, Makenzie Mayfair."

Vice sent me a chin lift while he sat at the table. He also smiled, and then said, "Good to finally meet the woman behind the voice."

"Ah, you also, though it could have been under better circumstances. How did you two find out?"

Grayson raised a brow and Vice's smile widened.

"Dylan," I bit out through clenched teeth.

"You called?" Dylan grinned as he came back into the kitchen.

"You." I pointed. He froze. "You told them? How? You were in the kitchen the whole time."

He winked. "Honey, don't be too mad. But we brothers have to stick together, and I'm a whiz at texting without anyone seeing."

"He never saved you from the horror film," I pointed out.

"True. But I always enjoy your reaction. No one ever knows what will come out of your mouth. It always makes me laugh. Viagra. Brilliant."

"Right," I said, nodding to myself. "Okay, that's fine." I nodded again and turned back to the stove. "Who would like some soup?"

"Now, Kenzie. Whatever you have drafting up in that sweet noggin of yours, don't even think about it."

Glancing over my shoulder, I asked, "Is this when I should be cackling like a mad woman with a plan to scare you?"

"No, no it's not. I'm already scared from the look in your eyes. Cutie-pie, come on now. You don't want to harm your future brother-in-law." He was referring to Lori, right, not me and Grayson? He came over to my side and threw his arm around my shoulders. "Kenzie, you're my BFF, babe."

"Aw." I patted his hand and took the pot off the stove, turned, and placed it on the mat on the island counter near the bowls. Dylan moved with me, then behind me so he could wrap both arms around my chest.

His nose nuzzled my neck. "You don't want to upset your sister by harming her man?"

"Pfft, please. Lori will be on my side once I tell her what you did."

"Dylan," Grayson clipped.

We both looked up. His eyes were hard. My brow dipped in confusion, but then I was distracted by Dylan stepping away from me to grab some spoons.

"Anyway," he started, "dinner smells amazing."

It was after dinner and business talk, I received high praises for the soup and roast. Dylan then quickly slipped out saying he needed to make some calls, no doubt to my sister.

Grayson stood a few moments after his brother left to grab me a glass of wine and a Fat Tire for himself and Vice.

"Sweetheart, did Grayson ever tell you about the time he ran naked through the courtyard at college?"

My eyes widened and laughter spilled from me. "What? No. This I have to hear."

"Vice," Grayson warned. Were his cheeks pinking?

Thank God Vice ignored his friend and told me how Grayson used to play football and as a tradition, rookies were locked out of the locker room naked.

Grayson groaned and sank into his chair. "Makenzie, don't listen to a thing he says."

Smiling, I ended up laughing. "Sorry, boss. But I think we'll have Vice around for dinner more often. What else did young Grayson get up to?"

Vice told me a few more stories, which had me laughing aloud. Grayson seemed to like getting into a bit of trouble. He even attended a rally against animal testing, which I thought was sweet. Until I found out he only did it to get the girl he was after. Only in the end, he went on one date with her and returned to his dorm pale faced. She was a "natural" woman, who didn't like to shave. Grayson had told Vice he swore she was part yeti.

After some time, Vice leaned forward, his elbows on the table. He winked and said, "I'll have to save some stories for next time. Just to make sure I get invited back over."

"You won't," Grayson bit out. He'd been quiet through-out the tales of his college days. I was surprised he didn't wade in to stop Vice, but his small smile told me he was hav-ing fun listening to the old times.

"You will. Ignore him."

Grayson rolled his eyes and grinned. After a swig of his second beer, he said, "I think I'll have to call your father for more stories about you when you were younger."

Snorting, I told him, "I was an angel compared to you."

"Not what I heard when you're on cough medicine." Vice chuckled as I gasped, then choked on my sip of wine.

Pounding my chest, I glared over at Grayson. "You told him?"

"It's not every day my assistant flashes herself and climbs me."

My whole body flushed. Groaning, I hid my face behind my hands. "I can't believe you said that."

Both men laughed.

To change the subject, I said the one thing that had been on my mind. Only it should have probably stayed in my head. Removing my hands, I said, "Vice, you were very… abrupt on the phone the first few times. I could even say you were an ass, but in person, you seem like a nice guy." I covered my hand with my mouth as both men stared at me. Then Vice threw his head back and roared with laughter.

Calming, he patted Grayson on the shoulder and said, "Now I see what you mean. No filter on this one. It's refreshing."

Grayson had said I was refreshing?

That was sweet, in a way.

"Babe, Grayson and I are so much alike. If we're having a stressful time at work we—"

"Become an ass," I offered with a smile.

He chuckled and nodded. "Yeah. What you've got to learn is to not take our shit and give it back if we're in the wrong."

Grayson snorted. "Believe me, she's getting there. She either ignores me, snaps back, or rolls her eyes."

"Which I'm sure drives you fucking insane." Vice smiled.

Grayson looked to me, grinning. He glanced back to Vice and said, "It does."

"Shit, Gray." Vice chuckled, shaking his head.

Shit?

What did shit mean?

"I am in the room." I glared.

They again laughed.

Harrumphing, I sat back in my seat and took another sip of wine. Thankfully, they brought up another subject, only it was back to work, which bored me, mainly because I was tired.

Standing, I said, "I'm going to head to bed. Vice, it was a pleasure to have your company. I look forward to the next time to hear more stories of Grayson."

My boss snorted.

"Babe, been an amazing meal and company. Best night in a while. I'll be back soon."

"Good to hear it, and maybe when you call next, you'll remember not to snap my head off."

He chuckled once again. "I'll try."

Smiling, I nodded. "Thank you and good night."

"Night, babe."

I shifted my eyes to the other man. "Good night, Grayson."

He gave me a chin lift, his eyes warm, though that could be from the beer. "Good night, Makenzie."

It wasn't until later as I lay in bed that I remembered Grayson was only a few feet away sleeping… naked maybe.

Did I get any sleep after that thought?

No.

Chapter
TWENTY-ONE

SIGHING, I RUBBED a hand at the back of my neck and checked the tour dates for James Carter once again. It was still the same. Whatever James's manager had worked out, the venues had screwed them all up. I was surprised Micha, James's manager, hadn't already picked up on it. Or his assistant at least. Grayson was going to be pissed.

Standing, I walked to his door and knocked. It had been a few weeks since the night I met Vice and at least I knew things between Grayson and me were at the stage where I knew he wouldn't get pissed and yell at me for the screw-up. It was the other people who needed to fear for their lives.

"Yes?" he called. I opened the door to find him where he always was, sitting behind his desk.

"We have a problem."

He huffed out a deep breath and leaned back in his seat. I made my way around his desk and laid the paperwork out before him.

"The venues for James's concerts don't match what Micha sent us. If we keep this one here and that one there, then they'll run over each other…." I trailed off when Grayson stood, one hand went to his desk and the other rested against my lower back. Not only that, but his side was up against mine. Feeling him, his heat, made it hard for me to concentrate.

"Why didn't Micha or his assistant find this?" he asked.

Licking my suddenly dry lips, I said in a breathless tone as his fingers dug into my flesh, "I-I don't know."

He turned his head to mine. "Call Micha, let him know, and then tell him once he fixes it, I want to talk to him."

"Okay," I whispered.

If I just pushed a little, our lips would meet. Everything inside of me urged me forward. At least a small part of me was still sane and knew kissing him would be a bad idea.

Clearing my throat, I straightened and stepped back, taking the papers with me. Clutching them to my chest, I told him, "I'll call him now."

"Thank you, Kenzie, for finding it."

Shrugging, I smiled. "It's part of my job."

"How's that?"

"I help make your life easier, and then you won't have to kill any employees."

He chuckled. He was doing that more often and I loved hearing it. In fact, I enjoyed it so much my belly fluttered from it. I started for the door when he called my name.

"Yes?" I asked.

"You do."

Tilting my head to the side, I asked, "I do what?"

“Make my life easier.”

Stiffening, I bit my bottom lip. He was really making it hard for me to not run back and jump him like a tree again.

“Um, thank you?”

He smirked as my cheeks heated. “Can you do another thing for me?”

“Of course.”

“Check everything is set for the dinner party tonight. The catering and waiters. Then double check Coco’s recording schedule. I was worried it crossed over with Ethan’s when I booked it in.”

Nodding, I saluted. He rolled his eyes. Then I said, “On it, boss.”

Exiting the office, I closed the door and turned, finding Bob, the office lawyer, standing at my desk.

“Bob.” I smiled. “How can I help you?”

“Actually, it’s I who can help you. He finally signed them.”

My feet halted. “He did?” I breathed.

Bob smiled and shook the folder he had in his hand out. “He did.”

Robert had signed the divorce papers.

I was free.

Single and ready to mingle.

Still, the only man I wanted to mingle with was my boss. He was the only one who caused my heart to race, my skin to tingle, my body to shiver. It was his smile, smirk, lip twitch, and even when his brow arched at me. I loved his chuckle, his eyes, his jaw, hands, feet when I saw them bare in the apartment. I loved…

Oh shit.

I loved my boss.

"Mrs. Mayfair. Are you okay?"

I knew my face drained of color, but I also felt a sudden rush of heat all over me. Nodding, I stumbled over to my desk and quickly sat down. My legs felt weak.

"Are you sure?" Bob asked again.

Sniffing, I nodded once more and then smiled up at him. It wasn't his fault I just realized I was in love with a man who wasn't mine. Who was my boss… my employer.

Oh God, I would lose my job.

If Grayson found out, I could lose everything.

I rubbed my chest. Then I realized I still held the papers against it and they started to crinkle. I put them down and offered Bob a shaky smile. "Sorry, I'm good. It was just a shock, but a good one." I laughed nervously. "Yay, I'm no longer married." I pumped the air above me with my fists.

Bob gave me a strange look, like he thought I'd lost it. He didn't know it was just how I was.

"Thanks for bringing them up to me, Bob. I really appreciate it."

"Yeah, sure. No problem." He put the folder on the desk and backed away. He was soon out of my sight once he turned and made a mad dash for the elevator.

I was divorced.

And I was in love with my boss.

Fantastic on the first part.

Holy hell on the second.

Still, right then I didn't have time to celebrate my divorce or worry about my love. I had work to do. Grayson was having a small formal dinner party for Ethan in our apartment. I had to make sure everything would be perfect for it. Actually, I was even excited to see Ethan, and I hoped Monty would be there also. It had been too long since I'd seen them last, and I was sure they would help keep my mind occupied.

There was no chance I would slip up and blurt out my devotion to Grayson… no way in hell.

I hoped.

A FEW HOURS later, I was in the formal living room dressed in an elegant dress and mingling with the rich and famous… or so I'd heard. I didn't actually have a clue who most of them were.

Then out of the corner of my eyes, I spotted Ethan, who was actually wearing a suit, with his tie undone and it hanging around his neck. I quickly made my way toward him. He was in the middle of a conversation when he spotted me and stopped talking to smile widely. He excused himself and was at my side in seconds.

"Kenzie, it's so good to see you here tonight among these stuffy people," he said with warmth in his voice as he hugged me.

Pulling back, I laughed and told him, "These stuffy people are who will help promote you."

"Oh, I know that. Doesn't mean I have to like them."

Linking my arm through his, I asked, "How has everything been? I thought I would have seen you around a lot more."

He tilted his head down to look at me. "Are you serious?"

My head jerked back. "What do you mean, am I serious?"

He threw his head back and laughed, which caused a lot of people to turn and stare. "Ethan," I snapped, only with a smile plastered on my face.

"Sweetheart," Ethan started, shaking his head while a smirk played on his lips. "Come and get a drink. I'll tell you a little story. That's if the big bad wolf doesn't find you at my side and drag you away."

Frowning, I said as we started for the bar, "You're making no sense."

"I know." He grinned and then turned to the waiter to order us a scotch and Coke. "You do drink scotch, right?"

"Yes. But only one. I want to make sure everything runs smoothly tonight." I took the drink he handed me and then glanced around to see if I could spot Grayson. When I didn't, I looked back to Ethan, who leaned against the bar and mentioned, "I heard you're singing tonight."

He grunted. "A duo in fact. Evelyn should be here shortly. Grayson matched us up since she's seasoned and also a country singer."

"Do I detect a little bit of awe in your voice?" I smiled.

Ethan snorted into his glass, took a gulp, and then said, "That woman drives me insane."

"Don't all the best women?"

Laughing, he nodded. "I suppose you're right."

"I can't wait to hear it—"

Hands landed on my waist, and then I heard, "Darlin'," whispered into my ear.

Smiling, I turned and pulled Monty into a hug. "It's great to see you, Monty."

"You too, darlin', you too." He grinned and moved to stand beside me, leaning in he added, "Get me a drink, Ethe. Gonna need to get drunk to put up with these stuffy shits all night."

"Monty," I scolded with a slap to his arm and quickly looked around. Thank God no one was near us. "You can't say things like that."

He shrugged and took a large mouthful. He wiped his lips with the back of his hand. "I'll always be myself, said the same to Ethan. Don't let any of this go to your head, I said. They're all about money. We're not." I raised my brows. He chuckled. "Truly, darlin'. I'm here to support my nephew. Ethe's here to live his dream. Always loved to sing, always had a voice for it. Now all we have to do for his dream to come true is put up with people like this. We ain't silly though, Kenzie. We know when to keep our mouths closed. We also know when a person is being themselves and won't share any shit we dribble. Like you."

"Of course I wouldn't."

He chuckled again at my shocked look. "You're a good woman, Makenzie Mayfair. Would'a been happy if you and Ethe got together. You would have kept him grounded. Too bad your boss saw it another way."

"I was about to tell her about it, Uncle."

Monty leaned into the bar, much like his nephew, on the other side of me and said, "This'll be good."

Smiling, Ethan turned his eyes to me. "The reason you haven't seen us around is because Grayson made sure of it."

My head jerked back. "What?" I breathed.

"Sweetheart, Grayson knew I wasn't messing with you. If you gave me an in, I would have snapped you up in seconds."

My heart beat erratically behind my ribs. I lifted a hand to my neck. "What?" I whispered.

Ethan chuckled. He glanced to his uncle, and I followed his gaze to see Monty fighting a laugh. "She's cute being all clueless," Ethan said to his uncle. Monty nodded. "Kenzie. Grayson didn't want me around you because he wants you to himself."

My body stiffened. My hand at my neck gripped tighter. No, he had it all wrong. Grayson couldn't want me.

"Breathe, woman," Monty ordered on a chuckle.

I sucked back a huge lungful of air and coughed. Then laughed, and slapped Ethan on the arm. "You jokester."

He took my hand in his. "Kenzie, I'm not messing around. Grayson came to me and warned me away from you. Said about how you just got out of a marriage and wasn't ready for anything."

"Well, that's right. But that doesn't mean he's confessing his need for me in *that* way."

Ethan and Monty looked at each other and then burst out laughing. Ethan finally said, "Anyone with eyes can see Grayson Jackson wants you for himself."

There was something wrong with my heart.

It was beating too fast.

My legs weren't doing great either.

"I… ah, no. I… he and I, and I… you can't be right."

He couldn't be.

I wasn't his type.

Harper was.

Not me.

Ethan patted my hand. "You'll see one day."

I scoffed, then snorted and finally laughed nervously.

What was Ethan doing to me? Didn't he know he'd feed my feelings for Grayson by giving me false hope my boss actually liked me also? "You're crazy," I told him. I couldn't think about it. Not then, not even the next day or a million years from then.

"Makenzie," was said low and right behind me.

First I jumped, caught my scream with my hand over my mouth, and then quickly spun, dropping Ethan's hand to face my boss.

Grayson Jackson.

Who apparently had a thing for me.

I giggled behind my hand. *He doesn't. He wouldn't.* He was sane, I was not. He was stern, I was not.

My laughter died when I saw his body was tense, his eyes hard, and his jaw clenching. Even though he looked pissed, he still sent my stomach fluttery.

"We have a problem," he clipped.

"What? Where? The catering? The guest list? Has someone not shown? Have we run out of alcohol? Do you need me to run to the store?"

He shook his head and looked over my head to Ethan. His eyes narrowed even more.

Oh shit. Had he heard Ethan's fantastical tale of Grayson wanting me?

"Evelyn can't make it tonight."

"What's happened?" Ethan asked, his tone filled with what seemed to be genuine concern.

"She's come down with strep throat. I've told her to stay in and get better. She'll need to be well for the final recording of the song next week."

"What are we gonna do tonight?" Monty asked.

"Makenzie will have to sing her part."

"What?" I screeched, before gasping and sliding sideways so Grayson's large form blocked me from any prying eyes. "Are you crazy? You are. You're completely out of your mind." I reached up to feel his forehead. "You don't have a temp. Did you have any cough medicine by any chance?" His hand came up and gripped my wrist, lowering them down to his side.

He tugged me closer, his face suddenly in mine. "You can do this. You have a beautiful voice, and if you don't do this, then the party was all for nothing."

"Bull," I snapped, not caring he was my boss. "Ethan can sing one of his songs on his own. That's who they're here for anyway. He'll melt the ice off all the women in the room, and the men will know talent when they see it. Then they'll see dollar signs going up in their eyes."

"I brought them here to sell them on the duo song, Kenzie. They want to hear it. Ethan will also be doing one on his own."

My free hand went to my rapidly rising and falling chest. "You're killing me," I told him. "My nerves will get the best of me. I'll screw it all up and make Ethan look like a fool. Damn it, Grayson. Look at what happened at the awards night."

His lips twitched. Why in the fuck were they twitching when I was slowly dying of a panic attack?

"Nothing too bad happened that night, and I know nothing will this night. Think of the business. Help me out, Kenzie. Please."

He said please.

Please in that deep, sexy voice of his was what won me over.

"Okay." I nodded. I heard Ethan and Monty laughing behind me. Ignoring them, I said, "But we better do this now or I'll either run screaming or cry."

"I'll get it set up. Ethan will be playing the piano. You'll stand next to him, and I'll make sure the words will be right in front of you," he said and then disappeared.

"Sweetheart," Ethan started. His arm wrapped around my shoulders. "If you get scared, just look at me and no one else." He kissed the side of my head and started us toward the piano. "Thank you for doing this for me and Evelyn."

"Yep," I mumbled. I couldn't say too much; my body and mind were in freak-out mode. I wanted to run and hide. I wanted to drop to the floor and scream. Though I couldn't do any of it because I would make Grayson look like a fool, and this was his business, his livelihood, and there was no way I would jeopardize it… at least I would try not to.

Grayson's voice rang out over a microphone from somewhere. I didn't know where because I wasn't looking up. I had my eyes glued on Ethan, who placed me next to the piano, and then I watched him take his seat. I flicked my gaze down to the sheet music and tried to stop my body from shivering as Grayson announced, "Unfortunately, due to sickness,

Evelyn won't be able to make it tonight. Though, you are still able to hear the song Ethan and she are collaborating together on, it's called 'Making Changes.' For tonight, my assistant, Makenzie Mayfair, will be filling in for Evelyn. Then Ethan will be singing his first song on the album, which I'm sure you will know, as well as I already do, will top the charts as soon as it's released."

People clapped. Then I felt their eyes shift toward Ethan and me. *Shit, shit, shit.* I was really going to do this. Grayson was going to owe me big-time.

"Ready?" Ethan asked. I jumped but smiled shakily down at him. Once I nodded, his fingers flew over the piano, and as he sang the first words, I shifted my gaze to the sheet music. As we sang, the tension rolled off me.

Ethan's voice was silky smooth with a twang to it.

> "Why did I love to hate,
> Wishing all around me some ill fate?
> Couldn't catch a break,
> Thinking all the world was just so fake.
>
> The same things every day,
> Alone in bed, I did lay;
> Something's gotta give,
> I just want to start to live.
>
> I'm making changes,
> So we can live;
> I'm making changes,
> It's time to forgive;

Now we've opened our eyes,
There's so much more to see."

With a big gulp of air, I opened my mouth and started, "My story has only just begun;

Up till now, there's not much to be told,
I want to live my dreams,
But nothing was ever quite what it seemed.

The same things every day,
Alone in bed, I did lay,
Something's gotta give,
I just want to start to live.

I'm making changes,
So we can live;
I'm making changes,
It's time to forgive;
Now we've opened our eyes,
There's so much more to see."

Then together we sang while looking at each other smiling. "We'll write our own stories,

We'll sing songs, together you and me,
Changing our destiny,
Our lives entwined together, for all eternity.

It's always a brand-new day,
Together in bed, we do lay;

We've got so much to give,
Now we know, how to live.

I'm making changes,
So we can live;
I'm making changes,
It's time to forgive;
Now we've opened our eyes,
There's so much more to see.

I'd done it and actually enjoyed it. I didn't fumble the words. I didn't make a fool of myself or the company. Ethan stood and hugged me, thanking me once again before I made a quick escape and he started his other song, only that time on guitar.

I moved off toward Monty at the bar. He stood beside Grayson. Both of them smiled at me.

Stopping just in front of them, I looked up at Grayson and said, "You owe me."

He grinned. "I know."

"Good." I harrumphed.

Chapter
TWENTY-TWO

THE LAST PERSON walked into the elevator as Grayson stood just outside it saying good night. I started collecting the few stray glasses scattered around that the catering company had missed after we'd sent them home. I would clean them and call the company to collect what was left in the morning.

"Leave them," Grayson demanded. He sounded just as tired as I felt. Slowly, I turned to watch him make his way toward me. Of course I didn't move an inch so I could enjoy the scene of my boss still in his dark suit, with his tie loosened, stalking his large, glorious form my way.

Then I remembered what Ethan had said.

My body stiffened.

I bit my bottom lip and wished it were true.

There was a whimper, and I think it came from me as Grayson took his last step, halting right in front of me. I tipped my head back to see his lips twitch.

"You're beyond tired," he commented.

"No, I'm fine."

"Let's have one drink to celebrate how well the night went and then get to bed." He took the glass I still held in his hand and placed it back on the table beside me. My eyes moved with it.

"I was going to clean them," I said to the glass. My hand was captured next, and I was tugged toward the kitchen.

"I'll have someone do it tomorrow," he said over his shoulder. When he left me at the kitchen counter, I climbed onto the stool and watched him walk to the refrigerator where I kept my favorite wine. He took out the bottle and poured me one, while he grabbed himself a beer. Grayson came back around the counter and sat next to me on another stool, though I would have shared mine if he had asked.

Stop.

Picking up the glass he placed before me, I took a large sip and drank it down with a sigh at the end.

"So it was a good night?" I asked. Grayson had spent the rest of the night mingling and talking, while I'd stayed close to Monty and then Ethan. Only every now and then did I find the strength to venture among the rich and famous to smile, wave, and talk to those who approached me. They wanted to tell me what a wonderful job I had done singing with Ethan. They also mentioned I was wasting my time being Grayson's assistant. I reassured them, I wasn't. It would be better off if I stayed out of the spotlight. Which was when they recognized me as the woman at the awards night mauling my boss and falling over my own feet. Not that they put it like that. In the end, they'd given me an understanding look and walked off.

"It was. Mostly everyone is on board to promote Ethan, which was what we hoped for."

"That's great news." I smiled.

"It is." He grinned and then took a gulp of his beer. Of course my eyes lasered in on his neck muscles working as the beer slid down his throat. The *gulp, gulp, gulp* motion went in time with my *zing, zing, zing* action as my clit pulsed.

I needed to get out of that room.

"You're good at what you do," I announced instead of fleeing.

He smirked, placing his beer on the counter. "Even though I can make my employees cry?"

Shrugging, I smiled and said, "Well, you could be a little gentler. But you do seem to get what you want in the end."

His eyes ran over my face. He nodded. "I do get what I want."

My eyes flared while my belly tingled.

What did that mean?

The way he said it, as he looked directly into my eyes… was Ethan right?

Did Grayson feel something for me?

I honestly never would have thought his feelings could surpass anything other than a thought to strangle me at times. But maybe I was wrong.

Which caused my body to tense.

It was worse if I knew a guy liked me. I was a mess when Robert had made his intentions clear.

God. I really needed to get out of the room.

"Bed," I shouted. "Maybe we should go to bed." I stood, and my words ran through my head. I gasped and looked to Grayson. His one stupid, sexy brow was raised. "Alone," I screeched. Then laughed nervously. "Of course I meant alone. Not that my mind went there. It didn't. I mean, you're my boss and I'm me… but, ah, you know… I, um, I think I know everything about you."

What in the hell did I say that for?

Was I trying to give him the green light to go by telling him we knew each other so it would be okay to sleep together?

"Do you?" he asked.

"Yes?"

His smirked. "You don't seem so sure."

"Um." I bit my bottom lip and thought about it. "I do." I nodded, my gaze meeting his. I knew just about everything about him. His favorite drink, food, pastime. The way he had his coffee, the way he liked to eat his pasta, which was to twirl on the fork instead of scooping. I knew what aftershave he wore. I knew when he was angry, annoyed, amused. His workout routine. When he got frustrated, he'd run a hand through his hair or at the back of his neck.

"And I you, Kenzie."

"Sorry?" I asked. I forgot what was being said. I was lost in my thoughts of the man I loved.

Jesus, there I went again.

Love. Him.

My cheeks heated. I knew he saw it when his brow arched in question from it.

"Ah, what did you say?"

Before he answered, he took another sip of his beer, while his eyes stayed on me. The intensity kind of made me sweat. I shifted from one foot to the other while I waited for his answer.

He smiled and then placed his bottle on the counter. Finally, he said, "I know you also."

"You do?" I breathed.

"You like your coffee with milk and one sugar while you eat your morning bagel with cream cheese. You enjoy swimming and reading, and you love your family passionately. You would do anything for them and will no longer let anything come between you again. You're good at what you do. You're strong when you need to be. You're a good friend. You're funny, warm, and sweet. You think less of yourself than what other people think of you." He stood, and my pulse jumped. "Sometimes you don't have a brain-to-mouth filter, which you think is terrible, but most people find it charming." He took a step toward me. I didn't move. I couldn't. I was frozen by his words. "You also become nervous, a lot," he added as he stood right before me. His voice lowered when he said, "Especially around me, when we're alone." His eyes flicked all over my face. "Breathe, Kenzie," he ordered with a smile. I took in a lungful of air, only I didn't release it because his hands cupped my face. He leaned in and gently touched his lips to mine. Against them, he said, "Which I like, a lot." I felt him smile. He touched his lips to mine once more before he pulled back and told me, "I think it's time for bed." My eyes widened. He chuckled. "God, woman. You make me crazy, but I'm trying to be the good guy here. So it will be in separate beds."

Jump, jump, jump.

My heart was trying to jump out of my body. It wanted in Grayson's. It wanted to curl around his heart and become one.

With another gentle kiss, where if I weren't still frozen, I would have climbed him and pulled him in for a tongue-lashing, he pulled back, stepped away, smiled and then left the room. With a, "Turn the light off once you're done," he was gone.

I fought with myself to stop from yelling out, "Come back and be the bad guy. Be the bad, bad man with me because I suddenly feel like being a very naughty woman."

However, I didn't. I was *still* frozen by the time he left. Suddenly, I took another deep breath and nearly sagged to the floor. Reaching out, I took hold of the counter. There was no chance I would be able to sleep. On shaky legs, and after I had grabbed my glass of wine, I walked to the door leading to my side, and shut off all the lights along the way before making my way to my quarters. Only, I didn't go to my room. Instead, I went into my living room and sat on the couch watching the fire still burning in the hearth.

He'd kissed me.

My boss had kissed me without my forcing a kiss on him.

He did it of his own free will.

A smile curved my lips up. Ethan was right. Grayson did like me.

Closing my eyes, I rested my head back and played the visual over, of the heated look in his eyes, the way he got close and cupped my cheeks right before his lips pressed against mine.

My nipples hardened, my clit pulsing.

Why was he trying to be a good guy? Why did he walk away? I would have been an easy lay. He could have done anything to me, and I would have let him, enjoyed it in fact. At least I hoped to have enjoyed it.

When had his feelings changed for me?

Pulling my head up, I took a sip of my wine as an unwanted thought bombarded my mind. Did Grayson only want a one-night stand with me? Was I an itch to scratch? Have a quick lay with the assistant before he got rid of her?

My head flicked around… had I heard a noise?

There, again, something was coming from the other side of the living room wall.

Where Grayson's bedroom was.

What was he doing?

Quietly, I set my glass on the table next to the couch and stood. I was in stealth mode as I crept over to the wall beside the fireplace.

Leaning my ear against the wall, I strained to hear something, anything.

Maybe he was a snorer.

Was that a moan?

Pulling my lips between my teeth, I stopped breathing to listen more. I swore I heard a groan that time.

Holy shit. I stood straight and took a breath; my eyes grew wide. Was Grayson touching himself only a few feet away?

Was he stroking his cock in his hand?

My pussy clenched at the thought.

I spun, wanting to hear more. I wanted to hear it all. I searched the room and then ran from it to my bathroom. I grabbed the small glass my toothbrush was in and tipped it out. I rushed back into the living room and over to the wall. I remembered seeing somewhere that if you placed a glass against the wall and then put your ear against it, you could hear more.

So I tried it, and I was sure I heard another groan and then… was that my name falling from his lips as he jerked the salami?

Straightening, my pulse raced. I covered my mouth to hide my excited giggle.

Only, as I placed the glass against the wall again, it slipped from my fingers. I fumbled it, but I was useless, and it fell to the ground, smashing on the hard floor near the fire.

"Shit," I whispered, placing my hands on my hips and glaring down at the glass. There went my chance to spy. Unless I could do it without the glass. Just as I was about to place my ear against the wall, the living room door burst open and in it stood Grayson, his chest heaving.

He was also only wearing black boxers.

"What happened?" he asked.

I hoped he didn't expect an answer because I was incapable of one when he was standing there in nothing but boxers. Form-fitting boxers. So of course I would see the outline of his hard penis.

Huh, it didn't go down after getting a scare from the glass breaking.

He must have been really turned on.

"Makenzie?"

Wait. I narrowed my gaze to laser in on his penis. Was it growing? It seemed to be; his boxers were twitching.

"Woman," he groaned.

It *was* growing. No way. That man was huge. My walls clenched at the thought of his penis visiting my center.

His boxers were now tented, the slit in the boxers widening and my new friend was just poking out to say hi.

"Did you just wave at my dick?" Grayson asked, his voice light with humor.

I looked at my hand to see it suspended up and out in the air, like I had been waving. I quickly placed it down.

"Well, um." I licked my suddenly dry lips and then gestured with my hand to his boxer region. "He was coming out to say hi."

Grayson looked down and then up at me. I gulped. His eyes were hot and hooded. "He can't actually help it when you've been staring at him the whole time."

"I wasn't," I lied.

He raised his brow and leaned against the doorframe, crossing his arms, as if his cock weren't tenting his boxers excited to see me… at least, I hoped he was.

"Tell me something, Kenzie."

"Hmm?"

"Woman, eyes up here," he ordered with a chuckle behind it. I met his gaze, and he went on, "What were you doing with an empty glass over by the wall?"

I rolled my eyes around in my head, looking everywhere but at him as I thought of the best lie. Only I couldn't come up with one, so I asked him a question instead. "How do you know the glass was empty?"

"There's nothing spilled on the floor."

"Oh." I nodded, looking down at the floor.

"Makenzie, were you listening to me in the next room?"

I stiffened. "No." I laughed, only it was more like I was choking.

"You were."

Scoffing, I crossed my own arms over my chest and glared at him. He had a smug smile on his luscious lips. Jerk.

"Whatever," I snapped.

"Did you like listening to me?"

"*What*?" I breathed.

Straightening from the door, he took a step into the room. "Did you like hearing me, Kenzie?"

"I-um, I mean…." What was I supposed to say? I wanted to say yes because I did like hearing him and thinking of him touching himself. However, then he would catch me in a lie when I said I wasn't listening in.

"Makenzie?" he growled my name low in this throat.

"Yes," I whispered.

"Fuck it," he bit out and strode toward me while talking. "This is happening, Kenzie. I won't wait any longer. Are you over your dickhead of a husband? Do you want this? Me?"

When he stopped just in front of me, I looked up through teary eyes and said, "Yes."

"Why are you crying?"

My heart raced; it was confession time. I shook my head and smiled. "Because I've been over him since the day I first saw you, and I have wanted you for a long time now."

"Fuck," he clipped. "Fucking hell," he added right before curling his hand in my hair, pulling me against him, and slamming his lips down on mine.

I moaned against him as his other hand wound around my waist, and his teeth bit into my bottom lip. I gasped, and his tongue found its way into my mouth to play with mine.

My stomach was a jumble of… everything: nerves, heat, lust, desire. My hands shook when I reached them up to his shoulders. I stood on my tippy-toes to deepen the kiss, drawing out a groan from Grayson.

"You're digging into me," I mumbled against his lips. He pulled back enough to arch his brow in question. His cock was digging into my stomach.

I gripped his length and squeezed. Grayson clenched his jaw. "You were digging into my stomach," I told him. He grunted. "Maybe if I stroked him a bit, he'll go down?"

He snorted. "You're crazy if you think that will help him go down." I kept running my fist up and down his length. Grayson threw his head back and cursed. "You keep doing that I won't fucking last."

I paused my action. "We can't have that." I smiled.

His eyes met mine. His hand in my hair slid to my cheek. "You're fucking stunning, Makenzie."

My heart skipped a beat. "Thank you."

"You're mine," he demanded.

Moving both of my hands to his waist, I asked, "What about work?"

"Fuck work. Fuck what anyone thinks."

Well, okay then.

I laughed. "So this isn't a one-night thing?"

His eyes flared, along with his nostrils as he sucked in a deep breath through them.

"Christ, no. I don't care how slow you want to take it. I don't care who knows about it, but woman, you drive me fucking insane. Your little nervous laughs, when you fidget, smile, get a mischievous look in your eyes. Hell, even when you roll your eyes at me. This is happening, Kenzie. We're happening."

Grinning, I said, "I'd like the right to refrain from agreeing until I know how good you are in bed."

Never had I been so bold.

It was a new side to my old self, and I was liking it.

He laughed loud. After he had settled, he kissed my nose and said, "Well, I better do my best then."

Pulling my lips together, I sighed and nodded. "You better."

He took my chin between his finger and thumb and then tilted my chin so he had my eyes.

"Only you," he started. "Only you can make me laugh, even when I'm turned the fuck on. Only you who can roll your eyes at me when I'm yelling in your face, and I find it cute instead of firing you, and it's only you who will get all of me. We were meant for this, for us to become an *us*. No one and nothing will stop it from happening." My hands bit into his sides as his words crashed into me. Tears filled my eyes. He smiled. "And it's only you who has been clueless to my feelings for you for so long."

"Hey," I snapped, only doing it grinning.

"Now tell me something, are you on the pill?"

My lower gut clenched. My clit pulsed.

"Yes," I whispered.

"Good," he growled low before biting my bottom lip. "I'm clean, and I overheard you telling your sister when she asked if you'd been tested so I know you are."

"Grayson," I snapped.

"Which got me so fucking hard that day. It's why I tried to get you to go swimming with your family. I wanted to see you again in your sweet as hell swimsuit."

"Oh my God." I laughed. "And to think, I didn't even have my period that day. I was just messing with Dad."

He groaned, and next his hands were on my ass pulling me into him. "Woman, you are dangerous sometimes."

"Only to those I care about."

"Why not to me then?" he asked.

"Who said I care about you?" I teased.

"You did not that long ago."

"That's right. I have a bad memory, so bad I forgot why we aren't already in bed with you inside me."

"Shit," he hissed, spun, and took my hand in his, leading me into my bedroom.

Chapter
TWENTY-THREE

OH SHIT, OH *shit, oh shit.* We were really going to do it. I was about to have sex with Grayson Jackson. I felt giddy like a schoolgirl with her first boyfriend. I wanted to call my sister and giggle into the phone about having sex with Grayson.

I wondered if he would wait while I did it?

He stood me beside my bed and stepped around to my back. After twirling my hair around his fist, he tugged my head back and then to the side. He leaned in from behind and kissed my neck.

And all thoughts of calling my sister fled my mind.

His other hand pressed to my back, on my dress zipper. Slowly, he slid the zipper down. My dress loosened around me, and his lips and tongue paid special attention to the other side of my neck.

I was panting, I knew I was. But he was driving me insane with his slow, sensual movements.

His fist let go of my hair, and I rested my head back against his shoulder as I felt him run his hand around the front of me, to my stomach. He flattened his palm against it, then ran his hand over it and up so slowly, stopping just under my breast. I whimpered.

"You want my hand on your breast?" His voice was deeper than usual. When I didn't answer, he thrust his hardness into my back and growled low in his throat, "Answer me."

"Yes."

I hummed when his hand finally cupped me. He ran his hand around it, applying pressure here and there. Then his fingers pinched my nipple.

"You like this?"

"Y-yes."

"Fuck, Kenzie. Your breasts are fucking beautiful." He bit my neck. "I want to see them."

A bolt of nerves had me stiffening when his hands landed on my shoulders, and he slowly lowered the dress. Instinctively, as the dress pooled around my feet, I placed one arm over my breasts, still hidden behind my bra, and then my other arm went across my stomach.

"Don't," he ordered. His chin on my shoulder, he slid his hands onto my arms and took hold of my wrists, tugging them down to my sides. "Never be self-conscious around me. You make me rock hard." As if to prove his point, he again thrust his length into my back. "Everything about you makes me want you. But especially your goddamn, stunning body."

I shivered, not only from his words but his breath on my neck. My chest rose and fell rapidly. His hands slid up my arms and then around to my back to unhook my bra. He pulled it free from my body and threw it to the side. With his chin on my shoulder again, he swore, and slid his hands to my breasts, cupping them. "Fucking gorgeous."

My belly dipped and swirled as Grayson massaged my sensitive breasts. The air seemed thick in the room, or I just wasn't getting enough oxygen in my body. My ex had never made me feel so wanted. Desired. My panties were soaked and we'd hardly even done anything.

If Grayson kept up his seduction, I was going to be a mess on the floor shortly.

My teeth carved into my bottom lip when he pinched my nipples. Still, I moaned. His lips touched my neck and shoulder over and over. Then he nipped at each spot as well.

"I swear, Grayson, if you don't stop, I'm going to come soon."

His hands and mouth paused, and I felt his smile against my shoulder. He lifted his head and whispered on a growl into my ear, "Not yet you're not. I want to taste your first climax."

My eyes widened. He didn't mean… he couldn't mean what I thought he meant, could he?

"Turn around," he ordered after standing tall and removing his hands and mouth from me. Suddenly, I felt cold. I wanted his heat back, but I wasn't sure if I could go through with what he was wanting.

Heat ran up my neck and lit my cheeks on fire. "Um…."

"Kenzie," Grayson clipped.

Slowly, I turned, my arms coming up to cover my chest. When he saw me hiding, he glared. "Wait," I started. "Um, we need to have a serious conversation, and I don't feel right doing it with my boobs swinging in the breeze."

He snorted out a laugh. "A serious conversation? Now?"

"Yes." I nodded.

He crossed his arms over his delicious chest and quirked his brow at me.

"Okay, I don't know how to say this, but… I don't like that sort of thing."

His head jerked back. "What sort of thing?"

"You, um, wanting to go visit my forest."

"Your forest?"

"Yes." I nodded down toward my girl bits. "You know."

His lips twitched. "Can I ask why?"

Letting out a breath through my nose, I told him, "Because that kind of thing doesn't do anything for me."

Both his brows shot right up. "I'm sorry?"

"I don't like the, you know." Lifting one hand, I spread two fingers and stuck my tongue between them. When he just stared and finally blinked slowly, I sighed. "I'm defective in that area. It doesn't do anything for me. I won't, ah, climax."

His shoulders went back, and a smug smile appeared on his lips right before he said, "It's obvious the fuckhead didn't know what he was doing with you. Unlike me, Kenzie, I know exactly what to do."

Glancing sideways, I asked, "Are you sure you're that good? What happens when nothing *happens*?"

He closed the gap between us and brought me tightly against him. First he kissed my forehead and chuckled; then he kissed my cheek.

"It *will* happen because I know I can be that good for you." His hand threaded into my hair, tugging my head back. "You trust me?"

"Yes."

He winked, smiling. "Good," he mumbled just before his lips took mine in what I could only call a possessive kiss.

Lost.

As soon as he commanded my body, even just by his lips touching me, no, *possessing* mine, I was lost. No thought touched my mind. All I could do was feel, and what I felt was more than I had ever before.

The slight glide of his fingers over my body as his mouth played with mine drove my senses insane. I moaned into his lips and was rewarded with a smile back. He liked he was pulling a reaction out of me.

"More?" he asked against my neck.

"Uh-huh," was all I could manage. His lips made their way down to my breast, while his hands slid from my back to my sides and down further to the top of my panties.

Maybe it was because as he licked, sucked, and bit each breast and paid special attention to my nipples, I didn't notice I had somehow lost my underwear.

Not true, I knew where they were—pooled at my feet.

The coolness of the room caused me to shiver while the rough hands gliding down and around my thighs caused me to tremble.

With my palms on his back, I flexed my fingers against him. He looked up and whatever he saw, maybe the fact I was worried I would fail in this area, he ordered, "Lie on the bed, Kenzie."

He was taking control. Then again, he'd had control right from the start.

Sitting back on the bed, I scooted all the way on and into the middle. Grayson's eyes followed every move. They were low and heated. He pulled his bottom lip between his teeth and bit. I'd never seen a man do that before, but it was the sexiest thing I had ever witnessed. Besides his chest, butt, legs… I had to face it; I was a goner for the man standing beside the bed looking at me as though he wanted to devour me.

"You look fucking amazing lying before me."

Heat filled my cheeks, and I smiled shyly up at him.

"Relax," he demanded.

Rolling my eyes, when they landed back on him, I said, "You can't just demand me to relax."

He smiled. "Then I'll *make* you relax." Leisurely, he leaned over and gripped an ankle in each hand. He forced my legs apart—though they happily complied—his eyes watching his work, and then gradually he trailed them up my legs to my center. After his hungry gaze checked me out, his knees came up on the bed and then his fingers played along my sensitive skin, traveling up until his hands tightened around my waist before he sat back on his haunches. I stretched, and his jaw clenched. Grayson reached out one hand, and my body twitched when I felt his fingers teasingly run up and down my lower lips.

"So wet," the smug man commented. He leaned over me, his free hand resting to the side of my head. My lips parted on a gasp when he inserted a finger inside me. "Fuck, so sweet, so goddamn sexy." He pulled his finger free and then quickly thrust it back in. "I never stood a chance."

I opened my eyes, which I hadn't realized I closed, and looked up at him.

"Never stood a chance against you breaking through my walls. You're right where you're meant to be."

Spreading my legs more, I nodded and told him, "S-so are you." His finger drove in and out of me the whole time, my belly tensing in that tingly way right before… "I'm going to—" He stopped. "Hey," I yelled.

He chuckled and kissed me. The anger I felt from being deprived left. Grayson Jackson's mouth was a wonder. His lips trailed down to my neck, then my shoulder, where he bit. He leaned up over me again and said, "You don't come unless it's on my mouth or cock."

I gaped at him, but he shut my mouth with a kiss, and then I lost his lips as he moved down the bed, his arms going under my butt, lifting my lower area up to his face. A blush overtook my cheeks and neck. I was completely on view for him. I willed my embarrassment to disappear and focused instead on Grayson. He didn't seem fazed. In fact, as I looked down my body to him, he looked satisfied. Then he kissed my mound, bit my thigh, and breathed over my entrance right before he licked from top to bottom.

Gripping the sheets, I placed my head back on the bed and gasped with a heavy breath.

Maybe because my ex had made it seem like a chore or maybe it was because he didn't like doing it, but never in my life with him did I experience even the tiniest of thrills. Nothing compared to the feeling of Grayson, a gorgeous man lapping at me, sucking and kissing and taking his time with doing it all.

I ground down on Grayson's mouth, and he hummed against me, ripping a moan from me.

"Grayson," I breathed. He picked up his pace. I was close and surprised to find myself on the verge of coming.

When he twirled his tongue over my clit, pressing down on it more and inserting two fingers inside me, which curled up in just the right spot, I cried out his name over and over as my walls clenched around his fingers.

He kissed his way back up my body and finally my lips. I didn't care he had just been eating me. I was in a blissfully relaxed state. In fact, when he shifted back to look down at me, I smiled and said, "Your mouth is the holy grail."

Grayson blinked. He then threw his head back and laughed. I stayed where I was and enjoyed the show. His eyes had been warmer for some days and even more so when he smiled or laughed.

Shaking his head, his laugh died, and he told me, "You're crazy, but in a good way."

Reaching up, I ran my hand over his stubbly cheek, smiling. My heart was melting because I never would have expected to have Grayson in my bed. To see him leaning over me, doing wicked things to me, and suddenly, it all felt too much, but also in a good way.

"Kenzie, are you okay?"

Meeting his eyes, I grinned. "I'm fine. Good, no, grand actually. I'm just… happily nervous, yet excited to have you in here. In my bedroom and my bed. I never thought it would happen, yet here you are."

Grinning back, he nodded. "Here I am. Where I've wanted to be since the day you strolled into the office."

Snorting, I rolled my eyes and said, "Yeah, right."

"It's true. You were nervous, flustered, yet everything you did, everything you said, I found myself being charmed by it all." He winked. "What also helped were those fucking high heels you wore, the way you had your hair and clothes that hid what I wanted to run my hands over underneath."

My eyes were wide from his confession. "Even with… you know… Harper was there that day."

"Yes, and we had been arguing for months before and after you arrived. As soon as you showed though, I wanted her gone. I may have acted like a dick toward you, but it was because I wanted you too much just from one look at you."

"You have acted like a dick," I threw out there.

"I have, and I regret it. I'm possessive. I like what's mine to be only mine. I know work stresses me, yet I can't see myself doing anything else because I like the challenge. You're the only woman who has stayed by my side through all the yelling and demanding. You roll your eyes, and if I'm in the wrong, you let me have it, which I appreciate and respect."

"So, I can keep my job after this?"

His brows shot up. "After this. You say it as if it's one fucking night. Like I said, it's not, Makenzie. We'll work out how it will be in the workplace. But up here, anywhere else, but the office, you are mine."

Smiling, I confessed, "I like the sound of that."

"Good. And I can promise you I will never want you to change in any way."

Tears blurred my vision. "I'd appreciate that." Shaking my head, I added, "But we seem to have gotten off track." Sliding my hand down from his around his waist, I gripped his half-mast cock in his boxers. His jaw clenched, his eyes growing lazy, and then he kissed me. Quickly, he hardened in my hand. Still, I wanted to touch him without anything between us. I pulled away enough to reach up and push him on the bed to lie flat. I kneeled, winked, and said, "It's my turn now."

Reaching up, he tightened his fist into my hair and brought me down for another kiss before loosening his grip to cup my cheek. "Go for it." He smiled.

"Oh, I will." I laughed giddily. I had free rein of his body, and I was going to enjoy every inch.

I touched my lips to his neck, and then up, where I took his earlobe between my teeth and bit. He cursed. I sucked on it and blew against it.

"Kenzie," he growled out.

Smiling, I slid my tongue down his neck to his chest and then around his left nipple. Tensing, his hand on my leg bit in. I worked my mouth down, nipping as I went, and finally, I reached the top of his boxers where I licked from one hip to the other. He cursed again. Shifting, I took hold of the fabric and slowly slid them down. Grayson lifted his sexy ass off the bed to help. As soon as they were free, I straddled his thighs and looked down.

My eyes widened, my lips parting. I met his gaze and asked, "Are you related to a dinosaur? Because you are huge."

He snorted, then chuckled. "Baby, I'm all man."

Nodding, I gulped. "A man-made god." He smirked and shrugged. Shaking my head a little, I admitted, "I feel like I need to pet him and just appreciate his awesomeness."

He rolled his eyes, lips twitching. "I'm sure he'd enjoy some petting, as long as there's a happy ending when you're finished."

"Oh, there will be."

Dipping my upper body down, I kissed his stomach, which quivered under my lips from Grayson sucking in a deep breath. I kissed my way lower and lower until I was eye level with his massive cock and neatly trimmed pubic hair.

There I breathed him in. No matter where on his body, he always smelled amazing. He flinched when I first touched my tongue to the base of his length. Then he groaned when I ran my tongue up to the tip, circling around the edge.

I felt him move and looked up to see him up on his elbows so he could watch everything I was doing. Winking, emboldened by his reaction, I took the end of his cock in my mouth and sank my mouth down slowly, swirling my tongue as I went.

"Fuck," he bit out. His eyes more heated and hooded than I'd ever seen them. "Faster," he demanded. Only he wasn't the one in charge right then. I smiled around his cock. He glared as I gradually withdrew my mouth and tongue up to the tip and then back down again leisurely.

"Kenzie," he clipped low. Picking up the speed, I cupped his balls and rolled them gently in my hand. He threw his head back and cursed to the roof. I hummed around the base of his cock and watched his hands fist the sheets. Then he reached one hand up and gripped my hair. I was expecting him to push my head down on himself, but he never did. Instead, he loosened his grip and slid his hand around to cup my cheek while he watched me work his cock in my mouth. Grayson hissed out a breath when he also snuck a finger inside my mouth. I let his cock fall to his stomach and sucked on his finger like I would somewhere else.

"Fuck this," he said with a grumble to his voice. Next, he knifed up and pulled me over him, so I straddled his waist. "Need your pussy, Kenzie. You going to give it to me?"

I gasped, his words sending a quiver to my center. "Yes," I whispered.

On my knees, I straddled him and grabbed him in my hand, guiding him to my entrance. He was so long and thick, I was worried he wouldn't fit, but as I slowly sank down on him, I knew I was wet enough for it not to hurt. I felt stretched but good. I sank all the way down and moaned.

"Fucking made for me," he clipped through gritted teeth.

"You feel so good inside me." I gasped as I withdrew and sank back down. His hands clasped my waist, and I looked down, his eyes already on my face. We smiled, just before he took control once again. He held me up, so I was on my knees more, and he thrust himself up and down into me. I threw my head back, my lips parted, and my breath uneven.

It was heaven.

Already another climax was building.

"Shit, fuck," he cursed. His hand slid to the side of my neck, forcing my upper body down, so our mouths met in an urgent kiss. I ground my hips down hard onto him, pulling a grunted-moan from him, which fell into my mouth. I couldn't quite catch my breath, but I didn't care. I cupped his face and kissed him deeper. My heart beat frantically behind my chest, and I felt his beating just as hard.

It was more than I could have ever imagined with Grayson Jackson.

My walls quivered and compressed around him. Crying out, I threw my head back. I closed my eyes tightly as I rode my orgasm out. It kept coming and intensified when he swelled inside of me. My belly dipped again when I heard him curse and then, "Fuck, yes. Yes, I'm coming."

With one final thrust into me, he stayed all the way in. My hands on his shoulders, I opened my eyes and looked down to the man who had stolen my heart.

"Can I lock you up and keep you as my sex slave now?" My eyes widened; the words had just popped out.

His lazy, smug smile lit his face, right before he curled me in tightly against him and laughed into my neck.

Chapter
TWENTY-FOUR

WAKING BEFORE MY alarm, I stretched. My body was sore in all the right places, and I smiled as the night before rushed into my mind.

I felt heat across my stomach. I pulled the blanket up to see Grayson's arm slung over my waist. Shifting my head to the side, I found Grayson's head close to mine, and he was still sound asleep.

Just to make sure he was real and not a figment of my imagination, I reached out and poked him on the nose.

His eyes opened, his lips already twitching when he asked, "Did you just poke me?"

"I sure did." I smiled and then quickly covered my mouth with the blanket. I wasn't ready to kill him with my morning breath.

"Can I ask why?"

"Just to make sure I didn't imagine you," I mumbled behind the sheet.

"Not sure your imagination can be that good with what we did last night in the bed, shower, and the living room couch."

"Oh, it can and it has multiple times."

He chuckled. "You'll have to tell me what else and where you've imagined it for it to become a reality. Now, can I ask why you're hiding your sweet mouth from me?"

"Morning breath. Deadly."

"Baby." He grinned. "I have it also, and I don't give a fuck because when I want your mouth, I want it, and nothing will get in my way." He grasped the sheet, pulled it out of my grip, then planted his mouth over mine. When he swiped his tongue over the seam of my lips, I was a goner, so I opened eagerly. He pulled back. "No, you're right. That is deadly."

Glaring, I swatted his arm. "You—"

He laughed heartily. "Baby," he murmured against my temple, "I'm messing with you."

"Yes, well…" I didn't have anything to say really, because I found myself liking this teasing side of Grayson a whole lot. "We'd better get ready for work."

"After a shower."

"Of course." I nodded.

He bit my neck and said, "Together."

My clit pulsed as my body heated. "Okay," I breathed.

"Then I want you wearing the red heels today, Kenzie. You going to do that for your man?"

Oh my God. I'd died. Dead. Or at least melted.

He was my man.

Grayson Jackson was mine.

He'd said it, and there were no takebacks.

Tears threatened, I blinked them quickly away and smiled big up at *my* man. "Since you asked so nicely, I suppose I could do that."

"Good." He grunted and kissed me again, only that time it was gentle, tender. "And since you're doing that for me, I guess I'll make you come in my mouth in the shower."

Another belly flutter.

"Um, deal?"

He chuckled, flipped back the sheets, and pulled me from the bed. Then he made true on his words. We both ended up going to work with a smile on our faces.

AT FIRST, I wasn't sure how to act around Grayson at work. Our final kiss was upstairs in the apartment before Grayson left earlier than me, since he'd only had a coffee for breakfast. I made sure to grab him some fruit to put on his desk for later if he got hungry. My heart beat like a nervous canary flying from a cat on the way down to the floor, and I kind of wished I had called in sick. The only problem with that was Grayson definitely knew I wasn't sick. As the elevator doors opened, I looked down to the floor and quickly made my way to my desk. It was as though I felt guilty, like I'd dipped into the cookie jar too many times, and everyone could tell it was me.

A few work colleagues called out, I waved my greeting, but other than that, I kept going. I placed my bag under the desk and sat in my chair. Turning on the computer, I drummed my fingers into the desktop and waited for it to load.

The door behind me opened, and I bit my tongue to try to refrain from saying anything suspicious or stupid.

"Makenzie, we have a meeting in the boardroom."

"Yes, sir. I mean, Mr. Jackson." I stood, grabbing my notebook and pen, a blush filled my cheeks and neck.

"Mr. Jackson," Lexi called, appearing out of nowhere.

"Nothing," I yelled.

She eyed me like I had lost it, which I sort of had. Especially if my heart rate didn't slow down, and if I didn't stop clicking on and off the stinking pen she was currently staring at. I placed my arms behind my back and laughed nervously. There was no way I could look at Grayson. I would probably swoon like a lovesick girlfriend. After all, I knew what he looked like naked.

God. Naked Grayson.

"Hmm," I hummed and smiled to myself.

Grayson cleared his throat. Swiftly, I looked up with wide eyes. "Why don't we start for the boardroom," he suggested, his sexy, very kissable lips twitching. I had to get a grip. Grayson again cleared this throat. "Makenzie, after you. And Lexi, you can speak along the way."

"Right." I nodded. "Yes, good idea." I smiled. His eyes twinkled with humor as he threw his arm out and gestured for me to walk.

"Sorry," I offered Lexi and then started off. "Had a rough night, hardly got any sleep."

I heard Grayson choke on a breath. He coughed and said, "So, Lexi, what can I do for you?"

I clenched my jaw tightly shut, so I didn't yell anything out and kept walking while she talked about her next project. Actually, at the start all I heard was whine, whine, whine and then a bit of blah, blah, blah. Her voice was irritating, and I flinched every time it grew an octave.

"I'll deal with it, Lexi. You should have come to me about Michael sooner though, before it got to this."

Oh, come on.

I punched my thigh to stop from groaning in frustration. Michael was one of her clients, and everyone knew she had a thing for him. Only he wasn't interested, and she was pissed over it. I couldn't see Michael out drinking every night and not listening to her instructions, causing problems with his up-and-coming album.

It was something I would mention to Grayson. I didn't want him looking like a fool if he went to Michael to chew him a new one.

As soon as we arrived at the boardroom, Lexi quickly disappeared to the back. Grayson sat up in the front, and I was seated just behind him. The meeting wasn't long, which I was grateful for because I was sure people were staring at Grayson and then me with extra care. Which got my mind conjuring up thoughts that they knew I had slept with the boss.

Had Grayson placed my panties in his top pocket of his jacket instead of a handkerchief? Then I remembered he never wore anything in his top pocket.

Did Grayson look or act differently after a night of hanky-panky? When he snapped at William about a certain cover that was supposed to be ready by the end of the day, I second thought that one.

When the meeting was adjourned, I made my way out of the room and quickly back to my desk, avoiding Angelia in case she could pick up anything from me.

I was already sitting at my desk when Grayson strolled up. "A word, Makenzie."

"Yep," I squeaked.

Standing, I followed him into his office. "Close the door," he ordered. I did and turned to find him right in front of me. "You wore the heels." His hand curled around my neck and he brought me in close.

"I did," I whispered.

"It was all I could stare at when you walked in front of me. I hope you heard what Lexi was saying because I certainly didn't."

Giggling, I smiled. "I heard some."

"Good." He grinned down at me before he slowly leaned in and kissed me senseless. Against my lips, he said, "You really need to stop acting and looking so guilty." He touched my lips briefly with his before pulling back. "No one knows, for now, while we enjoy sneaking around. When they do, you will not care."

Snorting, I said, "You can't just order me to not care."

He shrugged and said with a smirk, "I did. Though I'm sure they'll work it out soon enough from the way you can't meet my eyes or your blushes."

Groaning, I thumped my head against his chest and felt his laughter before I heard his chuckle. "I'm really bad at acting."

"I would have never guessed," he deadpanned.

Looking up, I told him, "I'll try. I like that it's just us knowing for now. So I'd like to keep it that way for a while."

"So do I."

"Okay." Getting to my toes, I kissed him quickly and then stepped back. "I have to get an e-mail off to Kevin before eleven, but I also wanted to let you know… um…."

"Just tell me, Kenzie. *You* can tell me anything."

Nodding, I smiled and told him what I heard about Lexi from the others.

He grunted. "I guessed as much. I'll talk to Michael."

"Great." I was just nearing the door when it suddenly opened, making me jump back. Dylan entered, closing the door behind him.

"Hey, you two. I was in the area when…." He trailed off and looked at his brother then to me, to Grayson and then back to me. "What's going on?" His eyes narrowed.

What did he mean?

"What?" I snorted and heard Grayson sigh behind me. While my cheeks burned, I went on, "Nothing, nothing at all. What do you mean by 'what's going on?' We're talking business, that's all—"

"Makenzie," Grayson called. I looked over my shoulder to see he was amused, no doubt with me. He shook his head.

"Finally," Dylan shouted.

I swung my gaze back to Dylan to find him grinning like a fool. "Finally what? There is nothing finally about anything."

Dylan rolled his eyes and glanced at his brother. "Is she for real?" He thumbed my way. I shifted so I could see both men.

Sighing, Grayson nodded, his lips twitching. "Unfortunately, yes."

Dylan laughed. "Brother, make sure she's never your partner in cards."

"What? I'm fine. Everything is fine," I cried, throwing my arms up in the air.

Grayson stood and came around his desk. He grasped my arm and pulled me close. "Grayson," I hissed.

"He knows." He smiled, right before he kissed me.

Dylan clapped, I jumped, and then Grayson brought my back to his front, curling his arms around my chest. Dylan whistled. "It's goddamn great to see, but keep all the PDA for the bedroom." His eyes widened. "Does anyone else know?"

"No," Grayson answered. "And we'd prefer to keep it that way for some time."

"Yeah, of course." He nodded; however, there was a glint in his eyes I didn't trust.

"Dylan," I warned.

"Nope, my lips are sealed. Anyway, I had better go. This"—he waved his hands at us—"is great to see. About time my brother got his head out of his ass." He stepped up and kissed my cheek, held out his hand to Grayson, and they shook. Stepping back, he nodded. "Good to see." Then he was out the door before either of us could say anything.

"What did he come here for in the first place?" I wondered more to myself.

"With Dylan you never know," Grayson replied and kissed my neck.

"The door's open," I whispered and slipped out of his hold. "I've really got to get that e-mail off. Um, I'll see you when I see you." I turned to smile and watch Grayson's tight ass as he walked back around the desk.

"If you keep looking at me like that, Kenzie, you can close the door while I take you over my desk."

My body shivered at the thought.

Grayson chuckled; he knew I was thinking about it. "E-mail, now."

"Yes, sir." I winked and closed his door.

My phone started ringing in my bag just as I sat down. I pulled it out and saw Lori's name on the screen.

Placing it to my ear, I said, "I can't talk long. I'm at work. What's up?"

"Dylan just rang." I could hear the smile in her voice.

"No," I whispered out harshly.

"Yes." She giggled. "So you and Grayson. Tell me everything, when it happened, how it happened, and was it good?"

"I'm going to kill that man."

"Who, Grayson or Dylan?"

"Dylan."

"Don't be too hard on him." She laughed.

"We asked him not to say anything."

"But we're family. Of course it's our right when you both finally figure out your feelings for one another."

"But still—"

"No buts about it. We're happy for you both. We can see how happy he makes you and how crazy you drive him."

"What exactly do you mean by we?"

Please don't say Dad knows. Please.

"Well… I mean, um, me and Dylan and—"

The office door behind me opened abruptly. I jolted and swung around in my seat to find Grayson standing there with his cell to his ear and… he was blushing.

"Right, yes. Of course. Okay." He held out his phone to me. "Your father wants to talk to you."

"*No.*" I breathed.

"Yes. And pencil me in for this afternoon to kill my brother."

I snorted. "Is two o'clock okay?"

"Sounds great."

Once I took his phone, Grayson quickly disappeared into his office.

First, I said into my own cell, "Lori, I'll call you back tonight. Dad phoned Grayson and he's waiting to speak with me."

Lori gasped. "He didn't."

Sighing, I nodded and said, "He really did."

"Talk soon," she replied and hung up.

I took a deep breath to prepare myself for whatever Dad was about to say.

"Dad, why, oh, why would you ring Grayson?" I whispered, and quickly looked around to make sure no one was in hearing distance. Which there wasn't.

"Your line was busy. Thought you may be with him. So I tried his."

“Did Dylan tell you?”

“Nope, overheard Lori talkin’ to her shmuck.”

“Can I ask what you said to my boss?”

He chuckled. “Hey now, he’s not only your boss any longer, right? I didn’t get that wrong, right? You two an item?”

“I can’t really talk. I’m at work.”

“Yes or no, Puddin’. That’s all you have to answer with. Actually, you don’t. Grayson pretty much confirmed it. I told him I was ready when he was to ask for my permission for your hand in marriage.”

I gasped. “You didn’t?”

“I sure damn did. He said he’d come to me when it came to that time. Means he thinks you’re a keeper even if you are a bit nuts around him.”

“I’m not nuts.”

“Puddin’.” He chuckled. “Don’t matter. You two suit each other. Best fucking news I’ve heard since I found out they deliver groceries instead of me heading to the stupid store and putting up with running into people I know and have them asking stupid questions I don’t got time to answer.”

“So, you’re sure about Grayson?”

“Right from the first sight of the big guy. He couldn’t keep his eyes off you. Knew right away what would happen. You two just took your goddamn time. I need grandkids before I drop dead.”

“Dad. We’re—”

“Yeah, yeah. I know. Grayson said you two are just starting out. He doesn’t want any added pressure on you to scare you off.”

Oh wow. He said that?

I snorted. There was no chance he could scare me off. If anything, I thought I would be the one to scare him away.

"Dad, I have to get back to work."

"Right. Let you do it, just wanted to tell you I'm happy for you both. Really happy, Puddin'."

"Thanks."

"Bye for now, but not forever," he called before the line ended.

My family was crazy, but I wouldn't have them any other way.

I quickly took Grayson's cell back to him with a quick apology kiss, where he told me not to worry about it, and then I went back to work.

Chapter
TWENTY-FIVE

OVER THE NEXT few weeks, Grayson and I had settled into the relationship. When we worked, I soon realized I was the only one who could give away the fact I was dating the boss by my actions. So I had calmed my heart and did as I had before boinking the boss.

So far, no one had looked at us with curious eyes. No one had mentioned anything to me, and even everything had been dropped about the awards night. There were too many other things going on to talk about at work. Like the fact Grayson had fired Lexi. Not only had she been lying about Michael, but when Grayson spoke with him, he discovered Lexi had sabotaged many things to hold Michael back.

Then there was also the fact Angelia was now dating Darby from my floor. Of course we gave them a lot of flak for it, but we were all happy they seemed to be totally taken with each other. I had asked Darby one day as we rode the elevator together how it happened. Apparently one night they had seen each other out, and things escalated from there.

I glanced to Grayson's door for the millionth time. He was in there, and I had an urge to be very naughty. I just wasn't sure how he would take it, but there was one way I could find out. I had been… excited all morning since I had a sex dream and woke up alone. Grayson and I shared my bed every night since the first night, and I looked forward to the end of the day every day. We ate dinner together, talked, watched movies, and just enjoyed each other.

However, that morning I woke to a note saying he forgot to mention he was meeting with Vice. Usually we showered together every morning. I never thought I would enjoy sex so much, but I did, and I couldn't get enough of him.

You can do this, Kenzie. Just go in there and seduce your man. It's that simple. I took another look at his appointment book and knew he had no one coming in for a while. Then again, he may be too busy returning calls or e-mails.

He could say no.

So what if he did? I may be embarrassed for a little while, but I would get over it.

"Right," I muttered to myself. My hands went to the desk, and I pushed myself up. Striding to the door, I then knocked.

"Come in," he called.

Opening the door, Grayson smiled over at me. I quickly entered and shut the door again. Grayson went to talk, but I held up my hand and said, "You know, I have an urge to suck your co—"

"Vice," Grayson near shouted.

My eyes widened.

"Hello, sweetheart." Vice's voice light with humor came from the phone speaker on Grayson's desk. "And thanks for the offer, but I think Grayson would actually kill me."

"Cobbler," I shouted. "I was going to say cobbler."

Vice's laughter came loud and long. Grayson chuckled with him and shook his head with a smile on his lips.

Groaning, I stepped back against the closed door. "I think, ah, I need… Yes, I heard my phone ringing."

"Vice, I'll call you later."

He snorted. "Of course, you lucky bastard. Enjoy your cobbler, Makenzie."

Grayson reached over and pressed a button.

Looking to the floor, I said, "I'm never going to be able to face him again."

Grayson scoffed, stood, and then came toward me. "You'll be fine. Not sure I will be though. Now he'll be thinking of you… sucking a cobbler." He chuckled again.

Banging my head back into the door, I groaned at my foolishness. "I should have made sure you weren't busy."

"Probably," he admitted from right in front of me. "However, what's done is done, and what I really want to know is did you mean what you said?"

I met his eyes and smiled, ignoring my blushing. "What? Sucking your cobbler?"

"Yes." His eyes lowered to my lips, and I nodded. "Right. Let's go then." He shifted me away from the door and went to open it.

I called, "Wait. Where are we going?"

"Lunch."

"You want me to suck you off at lunch?"

His eyes widened before he laughed. "No, though I am as hard as fuck. But I'm taking you to lunch because if I don't, I'll have your skirt up and you bent over my desk in seconds."

"The problem in that is?" I queried.

"Jesus. I don't know. I can't think straight right now."

A knock sounded at the door. "Grayson, is Makenzie in there? I'm here to relieve her for lunch."

Grayson sighed. "That's right. I'd called Helena before I was speaking to Vice to come take over for your lunch because I was planning to take you out."

I smiled, my body warming at his thoughtfulness. Then teasingly, I whispered, "So sex is out of the question right now?"

"Woman," he growled out low before he opened the door and gestured me out. Over his shoulder, while I grabbed my bag, Grayson said, "Mrs. Mayfair and I'll be gone for over an hour for a business lunch, Helena. Any problems, phone one of us." He strode off to the elevator. I said a fast thank-you to Helena and quickened my pace to catch him.

Grayson ended up pressing the button and swiping his card to hit our apartments. He'd said he had to grab something before we went out. As soon as we were on our floor, he took my hand, kissing the back of it before leading us into the kitchen. When I stepped in, I froze.

Set out on the table were already lit candles, place mats, two plates, and cutlery.

"I had a friend come up and set it up for us."

Tears welled. No one had ever done something so romantic for me. Ever.

With one leap, I was in Grayson's arms and kissing him. He groaned against my mouth and sat my ass on the kitchen counter behind him.

Parting, he smiled and asked, "I guess you like my idea?"

"Very much so." I nipped at his neck. "Was this friend the one who you were on the phone to?"

"That could be the one. He brought takeout. It's in the refrigerator. However, I'd like to get back to what you wanted in my office."

Giggling, I asked, "And what was that?"

He smirked. "Sucking my cobbler."

"I'll gladly suck your anything anytime."

His eyes shone. "I'll have to remember that and test it out."

"I can promise you I won't back out."

His brow quirked, his eyes flashing in challenge. "We will see. But for now, I'd like to do some sucking before I fuck you so hard you'll have trouble returning to work."

"I'll have to let my boss know."

His hands drifted up under my skirt. I lifted my hips as he grabbed my panties and pulled them all the way down and off. "He's very unforgiving. He'll want to know exactly why you aren't returning to work." His hands slid back up under my skirt. However, only one was between my legs, the other was on my hip. I gasped as a finger tested how wet I was. He smiled. "In fact, your boss could end up punishing you."

Panting, I nodded. "I-I think that would be okay."

"Spread your legs, Kenzie. Put your feet on the chairs and bare yourself to me."

I did as I was told, and still, Grayson didn't relent on stroking me, up and down, then swirling around my clit.

Leaning in, he raised his gaze to mine, and said, "This is the best lunch I have ever had."

I threw my head back and moaned when he sucked my clit into his mouth and rolled his tongue over it before two of his fingers dipped right into me. In and out they went, faster and faster.

"Grayson," I breathed.

His hand on my hip disappeared. I heard his belt buckle and then the swoosh of his pants hitting the floor. Next, he was up and over me, the tip of his cock at my entrance instead of his finger and he thrust inside of me all the way. I cried out as he swore. He pulled back and pushed all the way in again, over and over.

"Shit, fuck. You feel so good," he muttered into my neck. A breeze hit my chest; my bra was forced down, and his mouth was on my breast, his teeth sinking into my nipple.

"Yes," I yelled. He pumped his cock faster into me. I gripped his head, and he lapped at my other exposed nipple.

"Jesus," he cursed. I mewed in complaint when he pulled all the way out. He cupped my pussy, slid a finger in and left it there. Through hooded eyes, I met his heated ones. "Can't get enough of this pussy. Mine. All fucking mine."

I nodded. "All yours."

"Christ." He straightened, shrugged off his jacket, then shirt and kicked off the rest of his pants and boxers. "Get naked," he ordered, reaching out a hand to me.

I took it and hopped off the counter.

Standing, I slipped out of my skirt and top. Unhooking my bra, I threw it to the counter and stood before him naked. I ran my gaze over his body and licked my lips.

Perfection.

All of him was.

He took hold of his cock and pumped it in his hand once, twice, all while staring at me. A small smile played on his lips.

My pussy already throbbed from the way he fucked me hard before. I was soaked and wanted more. I needed him inside of me.

When his phone rang, I looked to the counter to see it there. Grinning, I said, "You'd better take it. Could be important." I held it out to him.

Snorting, he said, "There is no way in hell—"

"It could be Helena with something major going on."

"Fuck." He ground his teeth together, snapped the phone from my hand and placed it to his ear. "What?" he snarled.

I could hear a female voice on the other side, which did sound like Helena.

Stepping forward, I kissed his chest as he grumbled through whatever he was saying. I didn't take notice what it was because I got to my knees before him and placed the tip of his cock to my lips. Glancing up, I saw Grayson's eyes on me, his brow arched, and he kept on talking, only faltering his words when I sucked him all the way into my mouth.

I slid him all the way out again and waited to see if he wanted me to stop while he concentrated on the call. Apparently, something had gone wrong with Ethan's album. Other than that, I knew nothing else because I felt his hand grip my hair and he watched me as he forced my mouth back down onto his erection.

"Yes. Find out from Carlson where the file is."

As I got my rhythm going, his grip in my hair loosened. Still, he never let go.

"Hmm," he said into the phone. His jaw clenching. "Fine," he grunted. His head fell back, his eyes to the ceiling. "I'll be back when I can." He stepped back, his dick dropping from my mouth. "That was evil." He smiled down at me.

"But, did you like it?"

"Hell yes." He strode to the table and pulled out a chair as I got to my feet. I was surprised when he sat down on it. He crooked his finger at me, while he pressed something into his phone. "I have to make another call, but I want you riding me while I do it."

My eyes widened. "Are you serious?"

"Yes. Get over here, Kenzie. Now."

He placed the phone to his ear and spoke to someone by the name of Nick. I didn't know who he was and I didn't care. Excitement burst through me and my belly fluttered from it, my skin breaking out in goose bumps.

What we were doing was wrong, yet thrilling.

My walls clenched, my clit pulsed, and my nipples hardened even more. With my chest rising and falling rapidly, Grayson took it all in and smiled as I walked slowly over to him. He kept talking, but my ears were ringing from the adrenaline rush so I didn't hear what was being said.

Straddling his legs, I shifted forward more as Grayson's free hand came up to grip my waist. Reaching between us, I held Grayson's leaking cock and lined it up with my entrance.

Slowly, I pressed down. He filled and stretched me like always. I bit my bottom lip to stop my moan. With my feet firmly on the floor, I pushed up and then back down. Over and over I rocked myself on Grayson.

His responses were curt, his voice hard, and his eyes lazy as he watched between our bodies, entering me again and again.

Suddenly, he let go of my hip. It was lucky I had hold of his shoulders, or I would have fallen. I gasped when he pressed a finger against my clit.

"Yes, do that. I have to go," he bit out, hung up the phone, and threw it to the table. "Fucking hell. I'm so close," he groaned, bringing me against him and latching his teeth into my neck.

"Grayson," I whispered, resting my forehead on his shoulder.

"Yes, fuck me, baby. Fuck me."

"God, yes," I cried. My walls shook, tightening around him. His hands going to my ass, he then stood with me, still inside of me and I was still coming. Then, he fucked me.

As in, fucked me hard.

With his hands on my ass, he pulled me back and thrust me down hard onto his cock.

"Fuck, shit," he yelled, swelling inside of me as he exploded.

Two more times he thrust into me before he stopped, our breaths mixed in with one another as his forehead touched mine.

I let my unsteady legs drop to the floor. He slipped out of me, causing both of us to shudder. Then he gripped my leg and pulled it up, placing my foot on the chair, his hand moved between my legs, his finger inside of me. I was soaked with both of our releases.

"Perfect. Fucking perfect."

My chest ached with an overload of emotions for the man before me. The intensity of his eyes making my heart beat that much harder.

Still, the words weren't shared between us. We both felt it, I could see it written all over him, and I was sure he could from me as well.

Soon, the love I had for him would burst out of me. What was holding me back, I wasn't sure.

Maybe I thought it too soon.

Didn't matter though. We saw it, felt it, and we would enjoy it all until the day the words were finally spoken between us.

Chapter
TWENTY-SIX

IT WAS NATURAL in every relationship that people argued. Grayson and I both expected it, and when they came, they were big. Even if it was only over little things. What made a relationship was if you're able to work through the fighting, and I was happy to say Grayson and I could.

It was the weekend a month after we got together, and we were in my living room watching TV. Actually, I was watching a movie, while Grayson was going over some paperwork.

Suddenly, the door opened and Dylan appeared. The fearful look in his eyes had us both standing.

"Don't either of you answer a fucking goddamn phone?" he yelled.

"What's wrong?" Grayson asked.

"Our cells are in another room," I explained, even though I had worry coursing through me. "We didn't hear the home phone."

Shaking his head, he started for my room. "Grab a bag, pack. Lori's been in an accident."

My body seized. My breath caught in my throat, and my heart stopped.

I heard the brothers shouting, but it sounded in the distance. I blinked hard as Grayson's face popped in front of mine.

"Kenzie, baby, you're okay."

"Lori…." My bottom lip trembled.

"She'll be okay," Grayson reassured me, despite not knowing for sure. He pulled me into a tight hug, then got me moving toward the door. "You get her to the car, and I'll grab some things."

"Come on, honey," Dylan said beside me, his arm coming around my shoulders. In a daze, he led me to the elevator, got me in it, and we were on our way down to the garage.

Sniffing, I steadied my heart and tucked my shaky hands under my arms. I couldn't break, not until I had answers. "How?" I whispered.

"A car smashed into hers. I didn't get much out of your dad. All I know is she's in surgery." He sighed, his arm squeezing around me. "She's a fighter. She'll be fine. S-she *has* to be fine." His voice broke at the end.

It was then I knew Dylan was feeling the same devastation I was.

He loved my sister.

Leaning into him, I said, "She will be. Dad's probably yelling through the hospital corridors telling her to get better."

He chuckled. "True."

Dylan and I waited in Grayson's car. It didn't take him long to show. When he did, he threw the bag into the trunk and climbed into the driver seat. He reached over, took my hand and then looked to his brother, so I glanced there also. Dylan was biting his thumbnail in the back and bouncing his leg up and down.

"Let's go see your sister." Grayson tried for a smile, but it wasn't his normal one. It was sweet for him to try for me though.

Nodding, I leaned in and gave him a quick kiss. He started the car and began driving. The two-hour drive was quiet, but I was glad I wasn't doing it alone.

Grayson and Dylan were a part of my family. They meant more to me than my husband ever had. Especially the man beside me, who kept flicking his worried gaze my way. After the fiftieth time, I laid my hand on his thigh and told him, "I'm okay. Until I know everything, I'll be okay."

He nodded and placed his hand over mine, bringing them up to kiss my wrist. "You're strong, baby."

I half laughed. "Just wait, you'll need to catch me later when I do break."

"Always will."

Glancing behind me, I went to give Dylan a smile, but he was busy in his own world doing something on his phone. I wasn't sure if he had even heard us talk.

Looking back to Grayson, I saw his eyes had also been on his brother in the rearview mirror. Grayson's brows pinched together, concern etched on his face for his brother.

Hell, all of us were concerned for each other, but mostly Lori and my dad. If anything… happened, I wasn't sure how Dad would be.

No, I couldn't think like that.

Some time later, we finally pulled up to the local hospital. Grayson parked in a loading zone. I was about to say something when he shook his head. "They can tow it, give me a ticket, I don't care. I'm coming in with you."

We were out of the car and in through the doors quickly. I spotted Dad pacing the floor and called his name. When he turned, his face crumbled, his arms coming out wide, and I ran into them.

"How is she? Where is she? What's happening?"

He took a deep, shuddering breath and pulled back. Dylan and Grayson were at our sides. "She's out of surgery, had some internal bleeding. They're taking her to recovery. They think she'll be okay."

My hand went to my chest, and I sagged with relief. Grayson closed in, his arm coming around my waist.

Dylan's head tipped back. "Thank fuck." He straightened and moved away, mumbling and cursing. He kept rubbing the back of his neck as he paced.

Lifting my head to Grayson, I said, "Go to him."

His brows dipped. "Are you sure?"

"Yes." I nodded.

He kissed me, then walked over to his brother. They had words, and next Grayson grabbed Dylan and hugged him.

Turning back to Dad, I asked, "How are you doing?"

He shook his head, tears pooling again. "Never thought I'd be scared again as much as the night I lost your mom.

Until now." He clenched his jaw. Shaking his head, his eyes went to the floor, but I didn't miss the tears that fell.

"Dad," I whimpered, curling my arm around his waist. He stayed tense. His hands fisting and releasing at his sides.

"Scared me, Puddin'." Seeing my dad crack wasn't helping me stay in control of my emotions. I swiped at my cheek as Dad took in a shuddering breath. "When the hospital called, I lost it, Kenzie. I don't know how I managed to get here, but I found myself standing out here yelling for someone to listen. I wanted to see her with my own eyes. My jellybean." He made a noise in the back of his throat. My tears ran freely; there was no way I could stop them.

"Mr. High." We both looked up to see a nurse approaching. "You can see your daughter now." Grayson and Dylan came up behind us. The nurse took them in and added, "Only two at a time please."

I smiled and nodded. "Dad, you and Dylan go in."

"But—"

"No, you and Dylan. I'll go in after with Grayson."

He glanced to Dylan and then nodded. They walked off together in silence. Grayson's hands came down on my shoulders, and as soon as they were through the doors, I turned in Grayson's arms, buried my head in his chest, and burst into tears. His arms tightened around me. He said nothing but let me cry.

Eventually, I calmed enough to string a sentence together. "She's going to be okay," I said. "Seeing Dad like that… I couldn't hold it back any longer."

"You shouldn't have wanted to."

"I felt I had to, for Dad's sake." Clearing my throat, I added, "Thank you for being here."

"I wouldn't be anywhere else, Kenzie."

"I appreciate it." I nodded.

"Why aren't you looking at me?" he murmured against my temple.

"I'm all snotty and gross."

I liked that I could feel his chuckle as well as hearing it. "I've seen you on cough medicine. Nothing else could faze me."

Lifting my head, I laughed. "True."

"Ah, no, baby. Hide your head, you're hideous."

I gasped, my eyes widening. He laughed, then cupped my cheeks and kissed me. "I'm joking."

My reply was a punch to the stomach. Then I curled back into him, only I did it smiling.

Little did he know I would be more of a mess again when I stepped into Lori's room. I also know he probably hadn't witnessed two women crying together. If he could put up with that, then he was a keeper.

It was later, after we'd walked back to the car, I found out Grayson Jackson was a man where nothing truly did faze him when it came to me.

I wasn't sure how much more love I could have for him, but it seemed to have grown that night.

WE'D BEEN IN town for a couple of days. It was lucky Dad had two spare rooms because Grayson and I were in one and Dylan was in another. Lori was at home also. She had a broken leg, cracked ribs, and a few more bumps and cuts. Other than that, she was on the mend and would make a full recovery. Grayson had called someone at work to let them know he and his assistant had been called out of town on a job. He refused to leave my side, and I was grateful for it.

Grayson Jackson meant everything to me.

I was in the living room with Lori playing cards and talking, which was after I kicked Dylan outside to help Grayson and Dad cook on the barbecue.

"He wants me to come back with you all."

Looking from my cards to my sister, I asked in a shocked whisper, "What?"

She nodded. "He told me before you came in."

"Told you?" I smiled.

She giggled. "Yes."

"What did you say?"

"I had to think about things."

"He cares for you a lot. He was a mess when he came to get us. He's always so carefree and fun loving, but that night he wasn't. He looked lost."

She blushed. "It's been hard being apart, but it's also been good. We've got to know one another."

"He's proven to me, at least, he means to take care of you. He hasn't looked at another woman since laying eyes on you." I grinned. "I've asked around as I was willing to cut off his balls."

"It's scary."

"Why?"

"He's… Dylan Jackson."

I shrugged. "So? His old days are past him."

"I know." She nodded. "But what happens if things change between us?"

Sighing, I said, "If you're worried about him changing you, taking control like Robert did for me, then don't. He wouldn't do that, like I know Grayson wouldn't with me. You've taught me that." I poked her in the knee.

Voices outside grew louder. Our eyes widened, and then we heard the back door opening and footsteps stomping toward our way.

Dad came in first, his face fuming with anger. Then Dylan, who looked just as pissed, and finally Grayson who was… grinning.

Dad stopped at the end of the couch with Dylan beside him, his arms crossed over his chest. Dad then said, "Puddin', did you hear this bullshit? This schmuck wants to take Jellybean back with him."

"Ah—"

"She's coming back, Mr. High."

"Bullshit," Dad roared, right in Dylan's face.

Dylan puffed out his chest and yelled back, "I will not have the woman I want to spend the rest of my life with away from me for one day longer. God knows what the fuck can happen, and what happened two days ago proves it. She will be coming back. We'll get her enrolled locally, even if I goddamn pay for it." He threw his arms out. "Hell, you can move also if that's what holds her back. You can stay on the guest floor in Grayson's building." I hoped he ran it by his brother first. I caught Grayson's eye roll, which told me Dylan hadn't. Though Grayson didn't seem too miffed by it. "Shit, even my woman can stay there until she moves the hell in with me when you've got used to the idea of me dating your daughter."

The room fell silent.

I glanced to Lori to see her eyes swimming with tears, but the blush also told me Dylan had just won her heart. He'd just won mine too. He loved her. He pretty much just told our Dad he was hers, and if Dad were silly enough to stay in the middle of them, then I would have words with him myself.

"Okay then," Dad said.

Dylan's head jerked back at his sudden change.

"Well, good." Dylan nodded. "And until you both move, I'm staying here."

"In the spare room." Dad glared.

"Fine." Dylan jerked his chin up.

"What about work?" I asked him.

"I've got it all sorted to have some time off," he said, but it wasn't to me. His eyes landed on my sister, and they stayed there. I stood, walked around him, and grabbed my dad's arm, tugging him out of the living room, with Grayson following.

"How's dinner coming along?" I asked in the kitchen.

He snorted. "Yeah, fine." He looked to Grayson. "Your brother's a pain in my ass, but I think he'll be good for her."

Grayson nodded. "He will be."

"Still, he ain't goddamn paying for her degree. I'm doing that shit, and if he wants to fight me about it, I'll take him on."

"If it gets Lori there, I don't think he'll fight you over it," Grayson told him.

"Damn," Dad muttered before he walked out the back again. I started laughing when hands came around my waist. Turning, I wrapped my arms around Grayson's neck and met his gaze.

Smiling, I asked, "Are you okay with all this?"

"If it gets Dylan to stop harping on at me about it, then yes. If it makes you happy, double yes."

"It means my dad will be around a lot."

He cringed, then winked. "He's not bad if he likes a person."

"True. Though I think deep down he likes Dylan. He just loves giving him shit. Plus, Lori is the youngest. He's not happy with her growing up."

"He'll be better when he gets grandkids."

Tensing, I blinked slowly. "I guess." Grayson mentioning children did something funny to my belly. Especially when I imagined myself large with his baby inside of me. The making the baby part was also going to be fun. In fact, my clit pulsed. It had been a while since Grayson and I had been with each other because it would be just weird if we did anything in my childhood home with my father down the hall. Grayson had agreed with a wince.

His lips twitched as if he knew where my thoughts had gone. "You ready to get back, baby?"

"I'm more than ready," I whispered against his lips. We were leaving the next day to get back to work before things went under, and since I knew Lori would have two doting men in the house to take care of her, I was ready to get home.

"Will you two quit sucking face and get out here to help me," Dad called from the door.

Grayson and I broke apart and looked to each other, and then we burst out laughing.

Chapter
TWENTY-SEVEN

WE HAD BEEN home a week and thankfully things were back to normal after such a big scare. I was getting dressed in my room while Grayson got changed in his, well, his room which was still on my side of the apartment.

"We're going to have to change things around," came Grayson's voice from the doorway. I had been doing up my heels when I heard him. After nearly jumping out of my skin, I stood and glanced over my shoulder.

"What do you mean?"

He stalked toward me. His hands landed on my waist where he tugged me so our bodies crashed together. "I like watching you."

My head jerked back, my eyes widening. "Okay."

"By having my things in another room, I miss out on see-ing you get dressed, watching you put on those sexy-as-fuck shoes. Once my side is done, you can either move into my room with me, or I'll move my things in here."

"As in… live together."

He snorted. "We already are."

That was true. I told him as much and smiled.

"You don't have any complaints about it?"

Biting my bottom lip, I thought about it, and really, I came up with nothing to stop the move. Like we said, we were already sleeping in the same bed each night. We woke up together, ate together, and spent the most amount of time possible with one another.

"No," I stated.

I was sure Grayson felt the same way I did. Not only did we love each other, but after the fear of losing Lori, I didn't want to miss out on anything. Grayson was what I wanted for my future. Time was precious and risking it over silly things wasn't in the cards.

"Good." He grunted right before he kissed me. His forehead then touched mine, and I saw his smile, before he said, "I'd also like to state weekends should be spent naked."

I threw my head back and laughed. His lips touched my neck while he chuckled against them.

"Come on, boss. We can talk about it over dinner. You promised me a meal, and we'll be late for our reservation."

He rolled his eyes with a smirk and then took my hand, leading me out of the apartment.

THERE WAS ONLY one problem dating Grayson Jackson, and that was he got a lot of attention from women. Actually, even a few men checked him out. I wasn't usually a jealous type. I understood why they looked. My man was hot. But I couldn't help feeling sometimes like I wanted to fork a few women in the eyes. Especially after they looked at me walking hand in hand with him with snide expressions, their upper lips high, their brows drawn down. I knew what they were thinking. What would a man like him be doing with a woman like me?

The old me, the one who had been with Robert, would have been embarrassed for Grayson. I would have doubted my appearance and wondered if I were good enough for the man standing at my side. The woman I was before Robert was the same person walking hand in hand with Grayson, and I ended up ignoring them and pushed from my mind if they were judging me. I didn't care. No, that wasn't right. The reality was being judged sucked ass. It hurt, even though I really wished it didn't. But Grayson always let me know how important I was to him. I meant something to *him*. So his confidence in me, helped my own confidence.

There was also the fact Grayson thought I was shit hot. It helped immensely.

So even though the waitress, who led us to our table, checked out Grayson, I ignored it and kept my hand in his, smiling up at him when he looked behind at me. Officially, this was our first dinner date. We'd been out to lunch before, been to the zoo, movies, and theater. But never had we dressed up to go out to dinner with just the two of us.

When he'd suggested it that morning in the shower, I actually blushed and shyly told him how much I would love it.

Grayson pulled out my chair. I quickly sat, and he walked around the other side to his seat. We were in the far back of the French restaurant, the lighting low, romantic, and the soft violin music playing in the background was sweet. My stomach rolled in nerves and excitement all at once. I liked being out with Grayson. I loved and felt proud to be at his side.

We placed our orders for drinks, and the waitress slipped off to fill them. I picked up the menu and opened it.

"My parents were never around when Dylan and I grew up," Grayson said suddenly.

I placed my menu back down and looked across the table to him.

He smiled sadly. "We had a nanny. She was what our mother should have been like. Warm, sweet, loving. As we grew older, we thought all mothers were like ours. Until we'd stay at friends' houses and realized they weren't. So many times I grew jealous of my friends because they had a doting mother and we didn't. Still," he chuckled, "we knew in the end we were better off without her attention. She was all about herself, much like our father. They hated each other, but still stayed together, both having partners on the side. We were never beaten or anything like that. We were just invisible to them, unless at a function or otherwise." He sighed. "What I'm trying to say, I never want that sort of relationship with my children and wife. I'll be around. I'll show all our children how much they mean to me and make sure they know they can come to me for anything at any time."

All.

Our.

Children.

He'd said it, and just hearing it stopped my heart, breath, and body for all but a second.

Reaching my hand across, I clasped his and said, "You will never be like them. I can see the concern in your eyes, but you're warm, sweet, and so very loving like your nanny brought you up to be."

"Sweet?" He quirked a brow at me.

Laughing, I nodded. "Yes. When you're with certain people."

"Certain people I care very much for."

My body tensed with nervous anticipation.

He chuckled, pulled my hand up, and kissed the back of it. Then he placed our hands back on the table. "Later, when we're alone in *our* bedroom, I'm going to worship your body, and while I'm inside of you,"—my pussy spasmed, my nipples hardening, and I found it hard to breathe from thinking about Grayson sliding inside of me—"I'm going to show you just how much I care for you."

Blushing, I lowered my eyes, licked my dry lips, and stuttered, "T-that, um, sounds, ah, l-like a nice time."

He threw his head back and laughed. Shaking his head, he smiled across at me. "You always surprise me. Make me laugh suddenly, smile, and give me the urge to want to fuck you whenever you do something cute and funny. Which is every day."

Grinning, I told him with a flick of a hand in the air, "I guess I'm a lucky woman."

"You are, but I'm the fucking lucky man to have you walk into my business wanting a job. I've never met a woman like you, Makenzie Mayfair. No one has ever argued with me about paying for anything, yet you do."

Shrugging, I said, "I don't like to be dependent on any-one. I make money… which may come from you, but I think I do an okay job to earn that money." He nodded. "So, of course, I'm going to want to pay for things when we're out. If I ever learned anything from Robert"—Grayson glared. I smiled at him—"it's that being with someone is a partnership. No one should be more than the other. Though you do make my eyes roll in the back of my head when you do that thing with your mouth—"

"Drinks," the waitress announced.

Tugging my hand from his, I covered my face with both hands and groaned. Grayson again threw his head back and roared with laughter. When I looked up, I saw the waitress was blushing just as much as I was. She quickly placed the drinks down and mumbled, "I'll be back soon for your order."

I couldn't blame her for running away. "I bet she wishes she was in my seat now."

He snorted. "There would be no chance of that. She sees the pricey suit, the—"

"Hot body," I quickly added.

He smiled and shook his head. "She sees the money. Where you never have. You've seen me."

"I have." I nodded. "Plus the hot body."

He hummed. "I'll have to make sure to keep up my workout."

"No. I have a feeling no matter how you looked, I would still… adore you. Though working out together could be fun. I saw a machine on the gym floor I'd like to try out. You could be lying down while I ride you and—"

"Ready to order?" the waitress all but shouted.

Groaning, I palmed my face and said to her, "I'm just not having any luck around you."

At least Grayson thought it was funny.

After a fast scan of the menu, I picked. "I'll have the chicken cordon bleu, please."

"And you, sir?" she asked, running her eyes over Grayson.

Only he was looking at me and grinning smugly, for some reason. "I think I'll have something quick to eat so we can head home and work out together." I choked on my sip of wine. "So I'll have the salmon, thank you."

We handed over our menus, and she quickly scuttled off.

"I think I need to start keeping my mouth closed in public."

"Never," Grayson stated. "It's charming, just like you are, and I would never want you to hide who you are, no matter who we are around."

I slid my eyes quickly down to the table as they misted with tears. That man. My man. The things he said, not just that night but every day, hit me right in the heart with a sledgehammer. In a good, warm, fuzzy way.

For some reason, I glanced toward the door, which was when I spotted her.

Harper.

My eyes widened, and I gasped. If Harper saw us, she would soon jump to conclusions. Didn't matter they were the right ones. I hadn't even thought about how we looked when we'd entered holding hands, but right then I wasn't ready for people to know, and I didn't know if Grayson was either for our relationship to be out to all the public, as in people at the office. I was sure Harper would say something.

"What?" Grayson demanded.

I couldn't answer as I was sliding from my chair to disappear under the table.

"Kenzie," Grayson clipped low. "What on earth are you doing?"

"Shhh, if she sees us like this, she'll know. If she sees me, she'll see it in my eyes what you mean to me, and then she'll tell everyone."

Crouching under the table, I saw Grayson adjust in his seat to look around. I knew when he saw her because he scoffed.

"Baby," Grayson started in a soft tone, "get back up here. I don't give a fuck who sees us and when. She can tell the goddamn newspapers, and I wouldn't give a shit."

"Sir," a new voice said from beside the table. "This place is not that type of establishment."

"What are you talking about?" Grayson demanded, his tone rough, annoyed.

"Your lady friend under the table. I would prefer you to continue that elsewhere," he sniped in a snotty tone.

"I'm not doing what you think we're doing," I called from under the table.

"Well, perhaps you will get up then."

Grumbling to myself, I ducked back under the table cloth to stand beside the table. While the waiter glared at me, I narrowed my gaze back and adjusted my dress.

"Makenzie?"

My body stiffened.

It couldn't be.

What were the chances?

Slowly, I turned to the right and found my ex standing there. Had Harper and Robert conspired together to have both our exes there that night?

"Robert, what are you doing here?" I noticed out the corner of my eyes the waiter take a step back and disappear. He must be over his little misunderstanding and left us to our new visitor. Really, I would have taken a scolding and the chance of being kicked out over seeing and talking with Robert.

He smiled. "Having dinner of course. You look wonderful," he commented, stepping forward as his hand came to my elbow. I heard a chair scratch back on the floor. Then as he leaned in to kiss my cheek, while I stood there dumbly in shock, I heard a throat clear right beside us.

Robert shifted back a step before his lips touched my cheek, which I was grateful for. Already I felt like washing my elbow in bleach.

"Oh, you're the boss, right?"

"Yes." Grayson sneered. "Grayson Jackson."

"Right. Robert Mayfair. The last time I saw you, you were trying to butt into mine and my wife's business."

"Ex-wife," I butted in quickly since Grayson's jaw clenched and his nostrils flared so widely I was worried he would blow in a wrath of fury. So I added, "You signed the papers, Robert. You can no longer call me your wife."

"Of course." Robert smiled.

"Grayson," was called just behind him. We all turned to look at Harper standing there. "What a pleasure to see you." Then her eyes landed on me. "Business meeting is it?"

"No," Grayson bit out. He reached out blindly, while his eyes were on Harper, and once he snagged my arm, he pulled me toward him. As soon as I was at his side, he let go of my wrist and wound his arm around my waist.

Tentatively, I placed my arm around his waist also, which I was rewarded with Grayson glancing down at me and smiling.

His expression hardened when he looked back up to Robert and then Harper.

Robert scoffed. "So you had slept with the boss to get the—"

Grayson tensed. "You say one more word about her, and I will fucking end you." He looked to Harper. "Are you goddamn serious? Going out with him?"

My eyes widened.

Robert and Harper?

She stepped up to my ex and curled her hands around his upper arm, smiling.

I lifted my hand to pinch my lips together. A giggle wanted to burst free. However, it was as if it didn't want to be silenced, so I snorted, then coughed, then started giggling behind my hand.

Robert and Harper.

God, I couldn't have picked better for the two.

Her smile faltered when she looked at me. Did she think I would be jealous? Her eye twitched as I kept laughing while Grayson grinned down at me.

Placing my hand on my chest, I puffed out my breath. "Whoa, sorry. I couldn't stop."

"What's the matter with you?" Robert asked. "This is hardly the place to act like that."

I was certainly receiving a lot of looks from laughing aloud. But I didn't care, and Robert couldn't make me care since he had nothing to do with my life any longer.

"Funny, that's what the waiter said when he caught me giving Grayson a blow job under the table."

Robert's eyes widened while Harper's narrowed, and I felt Grayson chuckle beside me.

"Well, I never—"

"Anyway," I interrupted. "We both hope you have a wonderful night."

Grayson snorted and added, "We don't."

I smacked his stomach. "We do because we're happy, and we're going to have an amazing night as soon as we get out of this place." Tugging on Grayson's jacket, I caught his eyes and suggested, "Let's leave here and go get takeout. We can take it home and eat while we're naked." I was emboldened, pride at my courage and sass flickering to life in my stomach.

His grin was slow, but big and wicked. "Sounds fucking perfect."

Turning my back to them, I picked up my bag just as the waitress stepped up to the table with our plates.

"Sorry." I smiled. "But we're going." I reached into my bag for my purse, but Grayson's arm came around my waist as his other placed money on the table.

"I was about to pay," I moaned, annoyed.

"I know," he mumbled against my neck, then kissed there. "However, you were taking too long to find it in your bottomless pit of a bag. I'd like to move the night forward into the naked time."

Rolling my eyes, I smiled and shifted to peck his lips. "I'll forgive you then for calling my bag a bottomless pit and for paying, but next time it's my turn."

He snorted. "We'll fight about it then."

"Deal."

Grayson then took my hand and we walked from the restaurant, leaving our shocked exes standing where they were, with our heads high and never looking back to our past. The people in it weren't worth it. Nothing was, but the man who was beside me and my crazy family.

TRUE TO HIS word, after Grayson and I grabbed some burgers and took them home, we were soon in the bedroom.

"Slowly," he ordered in a growl behind me. Glancing over my shoulder, I smirked and slowed my action when pulling down my panties. He had already ripped my dress and bra from me as we backed our way into the room kissing. "Fuck yes," he bit out.

As I was bent over, stepping out of my underwear, I paused when I felt his hands glide over my ass.

"Love your ass. Christ, love your body. Can't get enough of you." He gave my ass a light tap before he ordered, "Stand up. Leave your heels on."

My clit pulsed, my body shivering as I stood. He stepped up behind me, both hands reaching around to my breasts. Only one stayed there though. He gently massaged it while his other hand ran up my chest to circle my neck. His grip tightened only a little, and I breathed hard and fast while wetness pooled below. He rubbed his hardness against my butt.

"I wanted to make love to you, but all I'll be able to manage is to fuck you." His grip around my neck loosened. With his fingers on my chin, he tilted my head up and sideways so he could have my eyes. "Do you want to be fucked, baby?"

"Yes," I moaned.

God, yes. Throw the slow lovemaking out the window and fuck me hard.

"Turn around and lie on the edge of the bed." His hands dropped from my body. My breaths were hard to find as I turned to find him undressing. I caught his smirk as my eyes ran over him for the third time. After shrugging off his shirt, Grayson leaned in to kiss me. I wrapped my arms around his neck to take the kiss further, but Grayson pulled back and shook his head. "Lie on the bed, Kenzie."

Licking my lips, I nodded and lay back so my butt just touched the edge and my legs hung over, feet still planted on the floor.

Grayson slipped out of his pants, socks, and boxers. He stepped forward, his hand landing on my knees. I quivered with excitement and desire as he glided his fingers up my legs, over my stomach to my breasts. He stepped forward, his legs going on each side of mine so he could lean down and claim my mouth while his hands played with my nipples, tugging, twisting, and pinching just the way I liked it.

His cock jutted out, nudging me. I reached up and took hold of it. Immediately, he bucked his hips forward and hissed through his clenched teeth onto my lips.

I only managed to get my hand sliding up and down his length a few times before he broke the kiss and stepped back.

"Need to be inside you." His eyes were low and hard. Clenching his jaw, his nostrils flared. Primal lust rode my man hard. He wanted me. I loved that he wanted me, that I could drive him insane, like he did me.

When his knees touched mine, he smiled down at me before he slid one knee between my legs. I opened them willingly. He cupped my mound, placing one finger just at the entrance of my center. "Want to eat you, but the need to fuck you outweighs it." I nodded, words escaping me. His finger entered me, and I gasped, arching my back off the bed. I felt his touch, his hand moving up, running over my stomach and chest again and again. Opening my eyes, I caught his. He said, "When I come, I'm doing it here," my chest, "And here," my stomach. "I'm marking this body as mine."

Oh God.

That was the hottest thing I had ever heard.

When I nodded, he grinned. His finger moved out of me. His hand on my stomach left, and he gripped me under my knees, lifting my legs high and wide. His hands moved to my ankles as he stepped forward and lined himself up with me.

Grayson turned his head and kissed my ankle. "Fucking love your shoes."

I couldn't help but giggle; only I quickly stopped when he slid his cock all the way in with one smooth thrust, causing both of us to groan.

His grip tightened around my ankles when he pulled all the way out and pushed back in slowly. I panted as my walls started to quiver.

"I'm close," I told him.

"Not yet," he clipped, pulling out faster and then back in.

"Grayson," I breathed.

"No," he ordered.

My stomach tightened, the sensation started running to my pussy.

"God, yes," I cried as Grayson fucked me harder and faster. Glancing up at him, I saw his gaze was dipped. He was watching himself enter me over and over.

"Grayson," I called. His eyes met mine.

"Fucking beautiful and mine."

"Yes." I nodded.

"Christ. Come for me, baby."

"Yes," I yelled, my walls tightening around him. He dropped my legs to lean over me, still pumping me hard and fast and wonderful. "God, yes." I moaned, reaching up to cup his neck. "Love you," I cried, still coming all over him.

He grunted, then groaned. "Love you, baby. Fucking love you."

"Yes." I smiled.

"Shit, fuck, I'm coming," he pulled out, fisted his cock and I looked down between us to see his load shoot out the tip over my stomach and chest.

As soon as he stopped, he dipped two fingers inside of me once, his fingers sliding out and up, touching my stomach and trailed through our essence. His warm, heated eyes met mine. "This is us," he said low, almost a growl.

"It is."

"Meant for me."

"And you for me."

"Fuck yes."

He dipped down and touched his lips to mine. Against them, he said, "And I meant what I said, Makenzie. Love you."

Wrapping my arms around his neck, I pulled him close, his body lined to mine. "Good, because I meant it too," I said and kissed him once again. When he pulled away, our heavy breaths mingling with one another, I added, "Can I take my shoes off now?"

I knew I would get a reaction, and it was one I loved the most. Grayson threw his head back and laughed.

He rubbed his nose against my neck and cheek. "Only you," he whispered.

I knew what he meant. Only I could make him laugh at a moment like that, and I was glad for it.

Being me, my old self was amazing.

Chapter
TWENTY-EIGHT

LORI AND DAD finally moved our way around a week ago, two months after her accident. She was completely healed and starting at her new college the following week. Grayson suggested they could stay on the guest floor. I'd asked why when we had plenty of room with us. He smirked and told me, "Baby, I like the fact we can walk around naked or have each other when we like in any room we want." Which we had. Well, just about every room. We even christened Grayson's old room now the renovations were done. It still looked similar to my side, but his living room had been extended. So there were only two bedrooms on his side. Actually, I couldn't keep calling it his side. Especially when he warned me not to call it that again when the whole floor was our joint space.

Dylan visited Lori nearly every day. She had told me about how much he'd doted on her and helped Dad pack everything up. He'd organized for the movers, her college, and even a job for Dad in the mailing center within Grayson's business. Even Dad had warmed to him and only called him schmuck a few times.

It was just the previous day when Lori and I went for a pampering to get waxed and our hair and nails done. I may have screamed down the shop, but we had fun in the end. It was when we drove back that she'd confided in me about how worried she was about when she and Dylan moved to the next stage in their relationship. He'd been very patient with her, yet he didn't know how much experience Lori had. Which was a lot less than me. In fact, it was none.

I told her it could be scary, because the first time always was, but to make sure it was something she really wanted. I didn't want her to rush into it because Dylan was begging for it. She said he wasn't. If anything, he wanted her to wait, but she wanted to move things along. As she restlessly rubbed her hands down her thighs in the car, she'd said, "He gets me so twisted up inside from just a kiss. I want more."

"I can understand that." I'd smiled my reply. "But if Dylan does anything to upset you, you have to call me right away, and I'll come around and deal with him."

"I'm going to stay at his house tonight."

I'd gripped the steering wheel tightly in my hands. She was my baby sister after all. "Are you sure?"

She'd blushed. "Yes. It's been two months, and he's proved his character to me in everything he does. I know if we did do something tonight, it would mean more to both of us than anything he has had in the past."

"You're right. He's been wonderful with you, and I know he'll keep being the same man he's proven to be. Still, I'll have my gun ready in case." She giggled. "Now, what did Dad say about it?"

She'd sighed. "You mean after he screamed and ranted for over an hour? He told me I was an adult, and I could do what I liked. Then he threw a packet of condoms at me and walked out of the room grumbling under his breath."

Laughter had burst from me. "I'm surprised he didn't complain how you were turning him gray and how he wasn't made for shit like this." Even though he was already starting to gray.

"Oh, he did, but that was earlier on."

"Don't worry. I'm sure once you and Dylan get things moving along, Dylan will want you to move in with him. He's already around all the time."

She'd giggled. "True, but I won't be ready for that for a long time. I'll just have sleepovers at his place. Which, by the way, is amazing. Have you seen it?"

"Actually, no I haven't."

She'd snorted. "I suppose you have been busy with a certain boss of yours." She'd then smiled over at me. I'd returned it before moving my eyes back to the road. "I'm so happy for you, Kenzie. I haven't seen you this happy in such a long time."

Nodding, I'd said, "We may have our days where we want to kill each other, but the good days outweigh the bad tenfold. I know how lucky I am to have found Grayson."

"Yes, and so is he. He's totally smitten with you."

"Like his brother with my sister." We'd laughed. "We could never have planned it even if we'd tried. Snagging two amazing brothers."

"I know. But I'm glad for it."

Reaching for her hand, I'd given it a squeeze. "So am I."

Thinking of the drive had me picking up my cell to double-check for messages. Lori hadn't called, and all I could do was hope Dylan took care of her.

Shaking my head, I went back to writing my e-mail, just as Grayson called me into his office. Getting up, I opened the door. He looked up from the computer and asked, "Baby, can you grab me a coffee?"

"Of course, have you had anything to eat yet?"

He smiled, eyes warming. "Not yet."

"I stored some breakfast bars in the cupboard, and I'm sure I saw some muffins in there Darby baked and brought in. I'll grab you one as well."

"Thanks." He winked.

Closing his door, I made my way down the hall into the break room.

After making him his disgusting black coffee, I grabbed a plate for his chocolate muffin, since I knew he had a sweet tooth and loved chocolate. I also placed two breakfast bars on the plate as well.

Walking back to my desk with my eyes downcast, on the coffee to make sure I didn't spill it, I heard my name being called. Glancing up, I stopped. Randal stood at my desk.

I hesitantly looked to Grayson's office; his door was still closed.

"Hi, Randal. What are you doing here?" I smiled. He was still a friend after all, even if I knew Grayson didn't care for him.

"I popped in to see—"

"Puddin'," Dad called as he walked up to my desk. "You heard from Jellybean?"

"No, Dad. Not yet."

He harrumphed and looked to Randal. "Who're you?"

"Randal Muller." He held his hand out to Dad.

Dad looked at his hand, his eyes narrowing and crossed his arms over his chest.

Don't, Dad. Please do not say one word.

"Dickhead Randal."

"Dad!" I cried. "Sorry, Randal, I guess he hasn't had his medication."

Dad scoffed. Ignoring me, he asked Randal, "Does Grayson know you're here?"

"I did not," came from beside us. Jumping, I turned my head to see Grayson just inside his doorway.

Laughing nervously, I explained, "Randal just popped in to say hi."

"Really?" His brow quirked.

Nodding, I placed his coffee and snack on my desk and stepped around Randal and Dad to get to Grayson's side.

Was it extra quiet on the floor?

It was. I glanced around to see people everywhere looking our way.

"I was about to let Randal know I was busy and catch up with him another time, but then Dad arrived."

He glared down at me. "Were you?"

I bit my bottom lip and whispered, "Was I what?"

"Going to catch up with him another time?"

Laughing nervously again, I said, "Well, not in the way you think, but as friends, yes."

"I can see I've come at the wrong time," Randal said.

"Maybe don't come at all," Dad mumbled, still loud enough for all to hear. Grayson's lips twitched.

"No," Grayson started, eyeing Randal. "It's fine. Come by whenever you like."

Randal's head jerked back. "Ah, thanks, I think. Makenzie, always a pleasure seeing you." He smiled. I nodded. "Grayson and…"

"Makenzie's dad, Trent."

"Right. Nice to meet you."

"Is it? Is it really?" Dad asked.

Closing my eyes, I dropped my head and shook it.

Randal chuckled and started to move off. "I'll catch you another time, Makenzie."

"Actually," Grayson started. Looking up, I saw his jaw clenching, his nostrils flaring, and he uncrossed his arms, taking a step forward. "I forgot to let you know one thing."

Randal turned toward us. "What's that?"

However, Grayson didn't reply.

He didn't say a word.

Instead, he looked down at me, smiled, and next I was up against his front, his mouth descending and his lips touched mine. It didn't end there though. His tongue poked out to say hi, and I responded with my own welcome. Which I did whenever Grayson kissed me. Losing knowledge of where I was, I brought my hands up and wound them around his neck, while Grayson's hand on my waist tightened.

Dad's chuckle brought me back to myself, and I broke the kiss. My cheeks were already flamed with heat when I glared up at my man and then slowly turned to find so many more eyes on us.

Grayson also shifted, so his front was to my back. His hands landed on my shoulders, and I just knew he was smirking over my head at Randal.

"Good play and about time." Randal smiled.

Grayson stiffened.

Randal laughed and rolled his eyes. "This was an honest visit to a friend. I actually wanted to have lunch with her to let her know I had met someone."

Randal's words didn't sink in because my heart was beating double time. Word would soon spread. Angelia, Darby, hell everyone I had lunch with would wonder why I hadn't said anything. I knew I had a lot of explaining to do. It would be up to them if they listened to my reasoning on why we didn't want anyone to know.

"Wait," I said. "You've met someone? That's great, Randal. I hope to meet her one day." I elbowed Grayson in the ribs and stated, "See, you didn't need to piss on me in front of everyone because Randal stopped by."

Grayson snorted. "True. Still, I enjoyed doing it, and it was about time everyone knew what was going on between us. Besides, you don't think I notice the men around here looking at you. It was fucking driving me insane. Now they know I'll kill them if they keep it up."

Shaking my head, I told him, "Don't be ridiculous. No one was watching me like you think."

Grayson glanced to Dad and then Randal. They all burst out laughing.

"What?"

"Puddin', my girls are stunners. Men are gonna notice it, and you've always been blind to it."

"Dad, you don't know what you're—"

"Makenzie, it's true. Men take notice when you walk into a room. Which was why Robert was an idiot for the way he was with you," Randal added.

"Anyway, this awkward conversation can be saved for another day, say never." Ignoring all the muttered conversations around us, I reached up and took Grayson's hand at my shoulder, pulling it down as I stepped to his side. "Randal, you'll have to come over for dinner one night and bring your girlfriend."

"I'd love to, now I know Grayson won't kill me." He moved forward, kissed my cheek and stepped back, smiling. "I'll call you."

"That would be great."

As he walked off, Grayson whispered into my ear, "I'm surprised you're not freaking out now that everyone knows."

Snorting, I told him, "Oh, I am, just on the inside." Which was true.

"Speaking of killing someone, your brother is on that list," Dad said.

Sighing, I looked at him. "Dad, you really have to let Lori live her life. She's twenty-one, not sixteen."

His clenched his jaw. "I know."

Smiling, I placed my hand on his arm and said, "I know you know and I know it's hard for you to do it, but she's not stupid, and neither is Dylan. They care for each other completely. Now go home or better yet, go for a walk and when Lori gets back, leave her and Dylan be. They're happy. I'm happy, and I want you to be happy. You know Grayson's housekeeper is—"

"Do not even go there," he clipped.

"You're not too old for—"

"Makenzie, one more word," he warned.

"She's really pretty." Not that I actually knew because she was like Santa Claus to a child.

"That's it. I'm not talking to you about this sort of shit. I'm outta here."

"Now you know how Lori would feel," I called to his back as he walked off.

"You're good." Grayson chuckled into my neck. "I've got to get back to work. Thanks for the snacks and coffee."

Spinning, I pinched his side. "You are not leaving me out here with everyone talking and looking."

He kissed my nose. "I am because I know you can handle it."

"Can I? You'll probably find me later in the women's bathroom because I've locked myself in from all the questions."

He rolled his eyes. "No one will question you, except maybe the people you have lunch with."

"How do you know?"

"They won't want to get on my bad side."

Grinning, I said, "This is true."

GRAYSON HAD BEEN right. No one dared question me over our make-out session. However, when I arrived at the table for lunch, I was bombarded with questions. Still, they were different to what I had been expecting.

"We knew it would happen, but when exactly did it?" Angelia asked.

"How did you know?" I queried.

Hudson snorted. "The man isn't stupid. He saw his catch, and he wanted to reel you in as soon as possible. But when did it finally happen?"

"Was it the kiss at the awards?" Dara asked.

"No." I shook my head. "Still, what made you think something would happen?"

Darby leaned sideways into Angelia and giggled. "He's been jealous of your… suitors since the start, and even your ex."

My brows rose. "What?"

They all looked at each other. "Have you seriously not seen it?" Ryan asked. "He's pissed all over you from the beginning. Shit, he even came down to my floor one day and in his subtle way found out if I was dating and mentioned you had just broken up with your husband. It was his way of telling me to stay the fuck away or he'll kill me. To start off with, I didn't think it was so he could keep you to himself."

"Not until I overheard him talking to Ethan and giving him a similar lecturing," Abby added.

"I-I mean, I know he, um, cares for me, but not right from the start."

Again they all looked at each other. "Maybe because she was new she didn't see the change in him?" Angelia suggested.

They nodded. "True," Dara said.

"What do you mean by change?" I laughed. "He's still about ready to kill anyone who annoys him."

They laughed.

"Again, that is true, but he's less intense and actually smiles," Abby explained.

"And he says hi to people who say something to him first."

My head jerked back. "Does he?" I hadn't noticed. Though when I was around Grayson, I did tend to become a little distracted by him.

"Honey," Angelia started, "you have been the best thing since Nutella donuts. It's another reason why people won't care about you and Grayson because you have tamed the beast. He's happy, and it shows around here a lot."

"Now, when did it all actually start?" Hudson asked.

With a light, warm heart and a smile, I told them how it all began. Their acceptance and understanding pleased me, and even if they mainly liked the idea of Grayson and me because he was more tolerable at work, I enjoyed knowing Grayson and I didn't have to hide any longer. As soon as I told them when Grayson and I started dating, Dara cheered. It seemed Dara was still the champion to beat when it came to table bets. She'd been closest to when Grayson and I started dating. The first bet, when I would get fired, was canceled since I was still in my assistant position.

My phone in my bag started ringing. I quickly pulled it free and saw Lori's name on the screen.

"Your man?" Ryan smirked.

Smiling, I said, "No, my sister. I have to take this. Be back soon." I stood from the table and pressed Accept Call as I walked away. "Lori?"

"Hi," she greeted back, and I relaxed, my shoulders dipping forward when I heard her cheerful tone. It was then she told me how her night went, and I listened to it all with a smile on my face and tears in my eyes. Lori, my baby sister, was growing up. I missed out on a lot when I was with Robert and I would regret it always. However, I was happy I found my backbone and made a move to be with my family once again. I was also ecstatic I was there for her now to share her new, scary but wonderful moments with her.

I also owed Dylan a big box of chocolates for making my sister giddy with glee.

Chapter
TWENTY-NINE

EIGHT MONTHS LATER

LOOKING DOWN TO my hand again, I smiled, but my body also shivered with nerves. I held in a plastic lunch bag the pee stick I'd used one month ago, which confirmed I was pregnant and had been for a month.

I hadn't told Grayson yet because… well, I was scared. I knew he wanted children. I just wasn't sure if he'd want them so soon, so I thought I would wait until I was over the fearful part before I told him. Thank God, I didn't get morning sickness or anything so he didn't start questioning, and there was a week there where he had to fly out of town to deal with a client when I pretended I had my period.

My shoulders slumped. I did feel terrible for not telling him. But I didn't want to get his hopes up in case anything happened.

Actually, I had been a chickenshit keeping it from him.

Especially since it wasn't that long ago that when we talked about children, he'd asked me how many I wanted. I'd told him it depended on the amount of pain I would go through. He'd chuckled and smiled at me. There was a certain glint in his eyes that nearly made me blurt out my news. However, I didn't. He was busy with work, and I didn't want to stress him until I was in the all clear.

At least he would be there for the important appointments. I was sure I was still in shock myself because we had been safe. There was only that one time when I got sick and had to have cough medicine again. At first, I had refused, even after a rough coughing fit. Dad, Dylan, and Grayson had to hold me down to take it, and then after, Dylan and Dad quickly disappeared leaving Grayson to deal with me on his own.

Which was good in the end. It seemed with the right partner and under the influence of cough medicine, we spent the night in bed. I had even managed to convince Grayson to go skinny-dipping in the pool on the gym floor. He only nearly drowned me once when the cleaner walked in, and Grayson, while I gave him head as he sat on the side of the pool, shoved my head under the water and kicked the cleaner out.

Not that it bothered me at the time. I'd popped back up, coughed the water out, and got back to business while Grayson threw his head back and laughed.

It was the next morning, I had forgotten to take the pill.

One mistake and I was knocked up.

Still, just the thought of a mini-Grayson and me growing in my belly placed a smile on my face and warmth in my heart.

It was time to tell the father he would soon be… well, a father.

My bedroom door opened. I gripped the pee stick in my hand, hiding it as Dylan and Lori entered.

"There's a thing called knocking," I said with an eye roll for added effect.

Of course they ignored it. My sister and Dylan had been inseparable since Lori had moved. Seriously, I couldn't have picked anyone more perfect for her. Dylan was always there to help her study, cook, or help her relax. He even took her to college and back to our apartment building whenever he got the chance. Unless she was staying at his house. He also met her at college for lunch, when she was between classes. Though I think in a sense he was like his brother, and went to piss on his territory. Not that Lori minded.

"I just asked Lori to move in with me, and she accepted."

Grinning, I cheered and stood, still with the stick in my hand, to hug them both. The news wasn't a surprise. Dylan had been hinting at it for some time, and Lori had confided in me she wanted to.

"That's great news," I said.

"So," Lori started, "we're going out to dinner to celebrate. Let's go." She took my free hand and dragged me toward the door.

"Hold on. Usually I would love to, but Grayson and I have things to do tonight."

"Not anymore. Grayson said he was going to meet us there as soon as he's done checking over Ethan's stuff for his concert tomorrow," Lori explained. Unease turned my stomach.

Ethan had turned into a star overnight. His first release flew to the top of the charts. He then again hit the charts, when the song he did with Evelyn went live. Since then, he'd had many other charting songs. I was over-the-moon happy for him. The best part of it all was he was still who he had been before he'd shot to fame. In fact, he had settled down with Evelyn out in the country. We had them both, and Monty, for dinner many times. Like we did for Randal and his girlfriend, Monica.

"But—" I started.

"No buts about it. You have to celebrate with us. We'll be living in sin just like you and my brother," Dylan said with a chuckle from behind me as we stopped at the elevator.

"How'd Dad take it?" I asked.

Dylan snorted. "He loves me, so he was happy for us."

Lori giggled and moved to Dylan's side to wrap her hands around his arm, leaning in. "He'll be okay, eventually."

Dad had finally been warming to Dylan. I knew a move like this would set things back a little though. At least Grayson and I got a kick out of whatever Dad would call Dylan. However, it wouldn't take Dad long to accept the situation. Deep down he adored Dylan as he had proven himself by sticking by Lori and treating her like the angel she was.

The elevator doors opened, and we stepped in. My hand still clasping the pregnancy test.

"Wait," I cried as the doors started to close. "I need my bag." At least then I could put the damn stick away. I went to press Open, until Dylan grabbed my wrist.

"You won't need it. Our treat and we're driving anyway."

Damn it.

Sighing, I leaned back into the wall with my hands behind my back. My thoughts drifted to Grayson. I was excited like always to see him, but I somehow, somewhere had to hide what was in my hand. I didn't want him seeing it while Dylan and Lori were around. When he found out, it should be just the two of us.

"You aren't," Dylan said, his tone low and annoyed.

Blinking, I asked, "Aren't what?"

He rolled his eyes. "She thinks she'll be paying half when she moves in."

"Hmm," I mumbled.

"What does that hmm mean?" He narrowed his eyes at me.

Shrugging, I explained, "Grayson and I had the same argument months ago. I told him if he didn't let me pay my way since I was working, he wouldn't get any in the bedroom."

Dylan's eyes widened. He looked to Lori, "Do not—"

"That sounds like a great plan, sister." Lori grinned.

Dylan groaned. "Kenzie, you shit."

Giggling, I bumped his shoulder with mine. "What are BFFs for? Though," I started, and looked to my sister, "I'm not in college working for my degree."

It was Lori's time to glare at me.

"Ha!" Dylan burst out. "See, so I'll pay until you get a job in nursing."

Lori grumbled a "We'll see."

It was true though. Grayson and I had a similar argument. I had also mentioned about getting a different job. His reply was a gruff "No." I'd argued my point, that we could be seeing too much of each other. His brow rose, and he'd stated, "If you try and find another job, I'll come find you, and drag you back." He took me into his arms. "You make my day easier. If I didn't have you with me, I'd be a tyrant to work with. Do you want people to get fired?" He was playing dirty. I knew and so did he by the smug smile he had on his handsome face.

Rolling my eyes, I'd replied, "Fine. But I swear, if you don't let me pay half the bills, you won't be getting my booty for a very long time." He'd growled in the back of his throat and called me evil, but I'd won something out of it at least.

Dylan and Lori chatted to each other on the drive to the restaurant. Even though I had just eaten, I could have something small. I was happy for them. They wanted to celebrate. I'd share the moment with them and then I would take Grayson home and tell him he was going to be a dad.

I laid a hand on my stomach and looked down. I wondered how everyone would be once they found out. I knew Dad would be happy. In the last month, he'd been going on about how good it would be to have a grandchild crawling around. Lori and Dylan would be just as happy. I knew they'd make a wonderful aunt and uncle. Even Vice would be a great uncle. Actually, I couldn't find anyone who would be against my pregnancy. Everyone at work was used to the fact I was with the boss. They found it amusing when I would argue back with him, not caring what he would say because I knew he wouldn't ever put me down in any way.

Grayson and I were in the heavenly stage of our relationship, with halos and all, so why was I still nervous about telling him?

I wasn't sure.

At least by the end of the night, it would be over, and I could finally relax. If there were a small chance he didn't want the baby…. Sighing, I laughed at myself. I was being stupid, overthinking things. Grayson would want our baby.

The car stopped, and I looked up to see us parked in front of the restaurant where it had all started.

Where I finally decided to leave Robert and where I met Dylan.

"What are we doing here?" I asked.

Dylan glanced to Lori and then back to me. "Hope you don't mind, but we love the steak here."

"Oh," was all I managed. Shrugging it off, the valet opened the door, and I got out. "Thank you." I smiled. The younger man blushed.

Lori linked her arm in mine—at least it was my free of pee stick one—as we waited for Dylan. "You've been quiet tonight," she commented.

"Sorry. I really am super happy for you both. I just have something on my mind."

"Do you want to talk about it?"

"Tomorrow. Let's enjoy your celebration dinner, and soon we'll be celebrating your graduation. How do you think you're doing?"

"Good. At least the professors tell me so."

I bumped her hip with mine. "You know I'm proud of you."

Smiling, she nodded. "I know, but I appreciate you telling me."

"Ready to eat?" Dylan asked, coming up beside us.

"Yes," Lori replied.

"Of course." I nodded.

Dylan stepped ahead as we walked toward the door and opened it for us. I was too busy thinking of when Grayson was going to arrive to look around and take things in. It had been so hard for the last month to keep my mouth shut. I prayed I could last a couple more hours, even with the pee stick burning in my hand. Maybe I should just throw it out. However, I soon rejected that thought because I was sentimental. It was the first stick I peed on out of the other twenty I'd tested. It meant more to me than the others. I was going to end up grossing my child out and placing it in its baby book to show him or her when they were older.

A quick movement beside me caught my eyes. Looking there, I spotted Dad. Smiling, I greeted him, "Dad, you're here to celebrate as well. That's nice of you."

He looked to Lori, Dylan, and then around. "Sure," he mumbled and rubbed the back of his neck.

Narrowing my eyes, I studied him. He looked flushed; he wouldn't meet my gaze. My father was hiding something from me.

Placing my hands on my hips, I leaned in and asked, "What did you do?"

"Trent, how about we go get a drink?" Dylan offered.

"Yeah." Dad laughed. "Sounds like a great idea."

Lori dropped her arms when I stepped forward and grabbed Dad's wrist. "Dad, if you've done something to mess with their night—"

He laughed again.

Oh God.

What had he done?

I shifted this way and that to look around the room to see if I could find if Dad had booby-trapped anything.

"Puddin'," Dad started, "you look like you need a drink." He tugged his arm free and then took hold of my hand.

That was when I started to notice the people sitting around the tables. "Oh, there's Ethan and Evelyn. I wonder what they're doing here. Wait, there's Randal, Monica, and…" Turning around, I glanced at everyone I knew. "Why are Dara, Ryan, Hudson… Hell, why is everyone I know here? Dad, did you set them up to prank Dylan and Lori on their special night?"

He sighed. His hand hit his forehead as he shook his head back and forth and mumbled, "You've got your mother's brains."

My head jerked back. What did he mean? Was I missing something?

"Kenzie," Grayson called.

A smile was already on my lips when I turned to find Grayson standing behind me. It only faltered, and my brows rose when I watched him dip down to one knee.

I just about ate my heart when he asked, "Hands please." He held his up and waited for mine.

The only problem was I had one pee stick to get rid of. Flattening the test against my leg, I slid it down and heard it hit the floor. Grayson did also, but once I took his hands, he looked back up at me smiling.

"It may have been presumptuous of me, but I asked everyone here tonight." I tilted my head to the side. He chuckled.

Wait one second.

He was on his knee.

In front of me.

Jesus. I was so slow on the uptake.

Did it mean… could it be possible he really wanted to tie himself to me forever? *Legally?* Was he sane?

I mean, I knew we would be tied together when the baby was born, but he had a choice if I were to have his last name or not.

Shaking my thoughts from my mind, I offered him a shaky smile.

"This is where it all started. Where you made your first change in life. What you didn't know at the time was that you were not only making changes in your life, but mine also. Here you left your dickhead ex"—people laughed—"here you met my idiot brother"—more laughter while Dylan rolled his eyes, and I looked on with tears in mine—"and it was here you began your life again. The day you walked into my life, you took my breath away. Since that day you have taught me many things, but most of all that love was real. I love you more than anything, so it was only a matter of time until I made it certain you were mine in all ways. Makenzie Mayfair, will you do me the honor of becoming my wife?"

"Yes," I yelled almost instantly, which caused another round of laughter. "Yes," I whispered as tears ran down my cheeks. "Yes." I nodded.

As people clapped and cheered around us, I looked at Grayson to see his smile was bright. His eyes shone with tenderness as he pulled a ring from his pocket and slid it on my finger. In one swift second, he was standing and taking me into his arms. His mouth descended on mine and claimed me. He lifted me and swung me around. I pulled back, wrapped my arms around his neck, and laughed.

Meeting his gaze, he said, "Thank you."

Puzzled, I said, "I should be thanking you for taking me on and keeping me."

He grinned and shook his head. "No, thank you for bringing me out of my hole and showing me there's more to life than work. Love you, baby."

"Honey, you have made me—"

"What's this?" I heard Dylan ask, and I froze.

"What?" Grayson asked me, planting me on my feet.

Slowly, I turned to see Dylan pick an item off the floor and hold it up.

No, no, no.

"Dylan," I cried and went to snatch it away, but he stepped back and held my test up high.

"It looks like…." He stiffened and glanced to me. "Is it yours?"

"What is it?" Grayson asked.

"I was going to tell you tonight."

"What you got?" Dad asked Dylan.

"Oh my God." Lori gasped, her hand covering her mouth.

"Wait," Dylan started and then turned a little green in the face. "Did you pee on this?"

He threw it at me. Only I didn't get to catch it. Grayson's hand came out and snatched it up. He flipped it over, and I watched as his whole body tensed.

He raised his wide eyes up from the stick to meet mine. "Is… what… does this mean?"

Biting my bottom lip, I nodded.

"It's yours?" he asked.

I nodded again and then stepped closer to him to whisper, "I was going to tell you tonight."

"How long?"

I sniffed, then laughed nervously. "I'm past the scary time. Two months now."

People started to whisper around us. Dad boomed, "What's goin' on?"

"Why did you wait?"

Shrugging, I said, "I honestly don't know. I've only known for a month. I guess in case anything happened, I didn't want to get your hopes up."

"You're pregnant." He blinked slowly.

"Yes."

"With a baby."

Smiling, I said, "Well, I hope so."

"The night of the cough medicine?"

"Yes."

He cupped my cheek with his free hand. "Never keep it from me again, please. Through it all, the bad, scary, and good, I want to be there for you."

My bottom lip trembled. I nodded and cried, "I won't ever keep anything from you again. I promise."

"I know you won't, or I'll tan your ass."

"Well, now you're just asking for me to lie." I grinned.

Grayson chuckled. He tucked the test into his pocket and placed his hands on my hips. His forehead dipped down to touch mine. "Now the night is even better."

"It is? I didn't spoil it?"

"You could never." He kissed me lightly, then looked up and around. Smiling, he yelled, "We're having a baby."

"Holy fuck, yes!" Dad shouted.

Epilogue

Seven Months Later

I LAY ON the bed with my legs spread wide and someone in between them.

Only it wasn't Grayson, and I wasn't feeling very pleasured by what that person was doing.

"Can you hurry?" I asked the doctor, who wasn't our usual doctor. She was apparently busy on a flipping vacation.

So we just happened to get a male doctor, who was the only one free when we strolled—actually Grayson strolled, while I waddled—into the hospital.

"Sorry." He smiled as he stood and ripped off the gloves. Grayson grunted and glared at the doctor as he came to help me sit up on the bed. "You're only four centimeters dilated, and your water hasn't broken yet. You still have some time to wait."

My eyes widened. I gulped and said, "But, it's already so painful."

He chuckled, and I wanted to kick him. "I can offer you an epidural. Though your records show you want a drug-free birth," he commented, looking down at my chart.

"No, thank you. Nothing." I shook my head. Only I second-guessed my choice when another contraction hit me. I gripped Grayson's arm and breathed through it while he rubbed my back.

"You're doing great," Grayson whispered into my ear.

Slowly, I turned my head and looked up at him with a glare. "It's your sperm that got me into this mess. You should be going through the pain, not me."

He smiled down at me. "I wish I could be, baby."

I couldn't really complain; he had been amazing since I woke in the middle of the night in agony. He was calm and collected and got me dressed and ready for the short drive to the hospital. However, he couldn't hide the fear and worry in his eyes from me. Seeing it in there helped my nerves a little.

We had decided to get married after we had the baby, both of us wanting our child to be a part of the special day. I never thought I would see Grayson so doting, but he had been with me. He was there for every appointment, running me baths, massaging my feet, even cooking.

Grayson Jackson was going to be an amazing father.

"I need to stand up."

Grayson placed a hand around my back and took hold of my hand with his other. Gently, he scooted me off the bed, and I stood beside it.

The doors to the room opened and in walked Lori, Dylan, and Dad.

The doctor said, "You can't all be in here."

"You can't tell me to leave my daughter when—"

I moaned. Another contraction hit and then I felt warmth between my legs. I looked down to see water hitting the floor and running down my legs.

"I'll be in the waiting area," a pale Dad said with a cringe.

I saw Dylan blanch also, then gag. "I'll keep him company." They both quickly disappeared.

Lori laughed, shaking her head at them, and then came over to my other side. "How are you doing?"

"It might be best not to ask if you want children yourself," Grayson offered.

I snorted. "Actually, he's right."

"You both know I'm going to be a nurse. I will know pain and a lot about it."

"This…" I panted as another contraction started. "…is… different."

Why do women willingly go through it? It was hell on earth.

Breathing through my nose, I said, "You had better love this child, Grayson, because it's the only one you're getting."

"Have I told you lately how much I love you?"

"Shut the fuck up," I snapped, though I caught his eyes and smiled. He chuckled.

"Let's get our lady naked."

"Fuck off," Grayson bit out.

I quickly grabbed Grayson's hand in case he thought to kill the doctor, shook my head, and said, "I'm staying in my nightgown."

Grayson grumbled a few swear words under his breath. He didn't want our doctor to be so young. Grayson whispered to me earlier he was worried the pubescent teen wouldn't know what he was doing. However, all the other doctors were delivering other babies, so we were stuck with him.

I wasn't sure if Grayson was annoyed because the guy got to see my vagina or because he was worried I'd somehow fall for the doctor and run off with him. Which was ridiculous as no man could ever compare to who I had at my side.

Another contraction and every reassuring word from my sister and my fiancé drove me madder and madder. If I had the strength, I would have hit them both.

Okay, so unbelievable agony and I didn't mix; it seemed to turn me into a raging bitch.

Still, no one could blame me, right? My insides were preparing me to give birth to a watermelon, and I had to squirt it out of my poor tiny hole.

I'm so sorry, vagina, please forgive me, and when the time comes, I'll have Grayson make it up to you.

"Baby, why are you patting your pussy?" Grayson asked.

"I'm apologizing to it, Grayson. Someone has to."

I ignored Grayson's chuckle as Lori cleared her throat.

"I have to say, this is a nice room," Lori said, trying to take my mind off things. She left my side to look out the window at the view.

"You're one lucky woman to have a husband like yours, Mrs. Mayfair," the doctor commented while he busied himself with whatever he had to do.

Glancing at my soon-to-be husband as I rested my hands on the bed and leaned over it, I asked, "What did you do?"

He shrugged. "I wanted you to be comfortable."

"What did you do?" I snapped.

He sighed and shot the doctor a glare. Only our doctor was Mr. Happy and just smiled back. "I arranged for a masseuse to come in to help you relax."

"Grayson," I groaned. "Relax? I couldn't relax even if I was high on marijuana right now."

He moved in closer, his lips at my ear, and his hand to my back circling it. "You deserve the best when you're delivering such a precious child into the world."

I sniffed, my hormones getting the best of me. "If I wasn't in so much pain, I would go down on you for it."

"La-la-la," my sister sang from the other side of the room, while the doctor chuckled.

There was a knock at the door. The doctor walked over to answer it. As soon as he had it opened, he stepped to the side, and another man, this one in his twenties, walked in.

"Fuck no," Grayson barked. "You, out, I'll still pay, but there isn't any way you're touching my woman. You're supposed to be a girl."

I started giggling when the man explained, "Missy was in an accident while trying to perform a kama sut—"

"Out," Grayson yelled.

The man quickly backpedaled and left. Lori and I shared a look, while the doctor actually chuckled, receiving a glare from my jealous man.

Another wave of pain hit me, and I clutched the bedsheet on the double bed tightly and moaned.

"This… is… not… fun." I glared down at the bed.

"You're doing great," the doctor offered. Both Grayson and I scowled up at him. He made a zipping motion against his lips.

"Are you sure she isn't dilated more?" Lori asked as she took a look at my chart.

"I just checked before you got here. Only four centimeters. Why don't we see if you can get a nap in before the real fun starts?" he suggested.

I scoffed. "Why don't I shove a—" Grayson covered my mouth.

"Give us a fucking minute alone," Grayson demanded. The doctor gave him an understanding look. Our tones didn't bother him at all. Then again, it probably happened all the time. Seemed us women were crazy during the birth business.

"I'll go grab a coffee."

I hoped he burned his tongue on it.

As soon as he was out the door, I asked, "Is it wrong I'm visualizing slitting his throat right about now?"

Grayson flinched. Lori giggled and shook her head.

"I did some time in the delivery unit for my degree and some of the stories the nurses told me… let's just say they've never had so many death threats before."

"I don't like that you're calm," I stated, glaring at her.

"What would you like me to do?"

"I don't know," I yelled through another contraction.

"They're getting closer," Grayson said. "Doesn't that mean the baby's coming soon?"

"It could—"

"Could?" I cried. "Could? I want it out and now!" My bottom lip trembled. I wasn't sure I was cut out for this. "I think you got a bad model in me, honey. I'm not good with any of this."

"Baby, you're perfect. We'll get through it. I promise." His tone was gentle but held an edge to it. I was scaring him, but I couldn't help it because the pain was scaring me.

"I-I feel like I need to push," I told them.

"Where in the fuck is that doctor?" Grayson clipped.

Lori raced out of the room. I could hear her yelling, and the door was opened again. Lori returned with the doctor behind her.

"Okay, it's coming along quicker than I thought it would. Usually the first one is always longer. No wonder you're in so much pain."

Fucking, motherfucking pubescent doctor, who probably still had wet dreams.

"Where's a real doctor? Don't we need an adult doctor to deliver?"

"Oh no, I'm fully qualified."

"How many fucking doctors do you have? Shouldn't there be a billion? If we want an adult doctor, we get a goddamn older doctor," Grayson yelled.

"Honey," I called, panting, "shut up about doctors. I'm about to squeeze our child out."

"Shit, fuck, sorry. Sorry, baby."

"Mrs. Mayfair. You need to lie down?"

Shaking my head, I said, "No, I don't think I can."

"You have—" He cut off when I screamed.

"Can I push? I want to push?"

"Yes, if you feel it, you push when you want. It means you're ready, but…."

The doctor moved behind me as I rested my top half on the bed, and I felt my nightgown being lifted up over my butt. "I think you're ready to lie down."

"I don't want to." I shook my head. My body wasn't ready to move; it meant spending more energy I didn't have on doing something I didn't feel I had to. "I'm not moving—"

"The procedure—"

I sensed Grayson tense beside me. "If she doesn't want to move, she doesn't fucking have to."

The doctor mumbled something under his breath, but he said no more and I was grateful. Lori got on the bed in front of me. She had a damp facecloth and wiped my forehead. More pain and an urge to push, I sucked in a deep breath and pushed with all I had.

"Good, baby. You can do this."

"Just rest through the contractions as much as you can," the doctor urged.

"I'm so proud of you," Lori whispered. "Look at us. Two hot brothers. I've moved in with mine, you're engaged and having a baby. Who would have thought how happy two Jackson men could make us?"

I let out a laugh and nodded. "Oh God," I cried and bore down again, shuffling my feet wider. The doctor was down on his knees behind me, and all I could do was hope with all the pushing I didn't poop on his head.

Sucking in a breath, I scrunched up my face and pushed through the pain.

"Yes, baby," Grayson said, his hand still on my back rubbing.

"Grayson, honey. Place your balls in my hand."

"Kenzie." Grayson chuckled.

"No. Dangle those beauties out in my hand so I can squeeze the fuck out of themmm!" I screamed.

"I see the head, push," the doctor urged behind me.

Another breath, another wave of pain, and another clench down to get our baby out.

"One more," the doctor called.

"Come on, baby, you can do this." Grayson kissed my neck.

"I fucking better," I mumbled.

I dug my forehead into the bed, fisted the sheets tighter while both Lori and Grayson called out their encouragements. The whole time I wanted to throw their words down their throats. Still, I bore down and pushed.

A sudden feeling of loss swept over me as my baby broke out of its jail and wailed into the world. Turning my head, I panted.

"Shit. Shit, fuck me, shit. Makenzie, baby, you did an amazing job." I blinked up at him and smiled. My man had tears in his eyes. He kissed my cheek, my shoulder, and back.

"It's a boy," the doctor cried. "Dad, come and cut the cord."

Grayson disappeared. I felt tugging, but I wasn't bothering about anything except for the cry of our baby boy. It meant he was out. He was safe, and he was ours to cherish.

"Oh my God." Lori sniffed as she lay down on the bed, her head next to mine, her eyes on my tired ones. "You did it."

"I did."

She gasped. "I have to tell Dylan and Dad." She got up and raced out of the room.

After I had delivered the disgusting, but necessary afterbirth, Grayson helped me stand and guided me onto the bed, where I lay back and held our bundle of joy, Noah Jackson.

Leaning my head down, I smelled our boy and sighed, tears prickling my eyes. We had made Noah together.

Glancing up to Grayson, who was already smiling down at us, I said, "We made him."

"We did." Grayson sat on the edge of the bed. Leaning in, he first kissed my lips and then kissed Noah's forehead. "I've never been happier, except for the day you walked into my life. Thank you." He kissed me again.

"Thank you for taking on me and my crazy butt."

He chuckled. "No one could compare to you. Love you, baby."

"Love you, Grayson Jackson."

The doors opened, and Lori came in, but missing was Dylan and Dad. She smiled as she walked toward us. She stopped beside me, staring down at Noah. "He's perfect."

"He is, just like his mom," Grayson said.

"Where's Dad and Dylan?" I asked, handing Noah over to his father. At first, Grayson looked unsure. I reassured him with a hand to his back. He relaxed and beamed down at our son.

Lori giggled and produced her cell. She pressed some buttons and showed us a picture. Dylan and Dad were sound asleep curled up with each other.

Grayson and I both laughed. "You have to show them when I'm around."

"Oh, I will. Now hand over my nephew." Lori took Noah from Grayson and murmured a few words down at him as she walked over to the window.

Grayson's fingers touched my chin. He brought my head around, our eyes meeting.

"We'll marry as soon as he's able to walk down the aisle in front of you." I nodded, once again tearing. "That's if I haven't knocked you up again by then." Tears dried up, and I glared at him. "Too soon?" He chuckled.

"Yes. Way too soon."

Two Years Later

GRAYSON GOT WHAT he wanted. Noah didn't exactly walk down the aisle in front of me. Instead, he ran right into his father's arms. I'd grinned up at Grayson from my dad's side, who was crying. Grayson had winked, and his eyes had then drifted to my stomach. He did, in fact, knock me up, and of course, he was smugly proud of it. Only there was no way I would be delivering drug-free… at least I hoped.

Six months after our beautiful wedding day, Mikala Jackson was born into the world *drug-free.*

Through it all, one thing was clear. I'd risked so much on changing my life. And not a day went by that I wasn't grateful I'd been brave enough to make it happen.

Because when those risks worked out, hell, it was something beyond special.

Acknowledgements

Lindsey Lawson, thank you for being there from the start and encouraging me along the way.

James Bogers for your lyrics. I wouldn't have been able to come up with anything like you did. The songs are amazing.

Becky Johnson, thank you for being so freaking amazing. You always have my back and I appreciate it. I'd be lost without you.

Justine Littleton, thanks for your help!

Wander Aguiar and Andrey Bahia, working with you both for the cover has been a delight.

Hawks MC: Ballarat Charter

Holding Out (FREE) Zara and Talon

Climbing Out: Griz and Deanna

Finding Out (novella) Killer and Ivy

Black Out: Blue and Clarinda

No Way Out: Stoke and Malinda

Coming Out (novella) Mattie and Julia

Hawks MC: Caroline Springs Charter

The Secret's Out: Pick, Billy and Josie

Hiding Out: Dodge and Willow

Down and Out: Dive and Mena

Living Without: Vicious and Nary

Walkout (novella) Dallas and Melissa

Hear Me Out: Beast and Knife

Breakout (novella) Handle and Della

Fallout: Fang and Poppy

Standalones related to the Hawks MC

Out of the Blue (Lan, Easton, and Parker's story)

Romantic comedies

Making Changes

Making Sense

Fumbled Love

Trinity Love Series

Left to Chance

Love of Liberty (novella)

Paranormal

Death (with Justine Littleton)

In The Dark

CONNECT WITH LILA ROSE

Webpage: www.lilarosebooks.com

Facebook: http://bit.ly/2du0taO

Instagram: www.instagram.com/lilarose78/

Goodreads:

www.goodreads.com/author/show/7236200.Lila_Rose

www.ingramcontent.com/pod-product-compliance
Lightning Source LLC
Chambersburg PA
CBHW071744110726
47908CB00006B/1691